BLOOD RELICS

A James Acton Thriller

By
J. Robert Kennedy

James Acton Thrillers
The Protocol
Brass Monkey
Broken Dove
The Templar's Relic
Flags of Sin
The Arab Fall
The Circle of Eight
The Venice Code
Pompeii's Ghosts
Amazon Burning
The Riddle
Blood Relics

Special Agent Dylan Kane Thrillers
Rogue Operator
Containment Failure
Cold Warriors
Death to America

Delta Force Unleashed Thrillers
Payback

Detective Shakespeare Mysteries
Depraved Difference
Tick Tock
The Redeemer

Zander Varga, Vampire Detective
The Turned

BLOOD RELICS

A James Acton Thriller

J. ROBERT KENNEDY

ISBN-10: 1508400091

ISBN-13: 978-1508400097

First Edition

10 9 8 7 6 5 4 3 2 1

In memory of Frédéric Boisseau, Franck Brinsolaro, Jean Cabut, Elsa Cayat, Stéphane Charbonnier, Philippe Honoré, Bernard Maris, Ahmed Merabet, Mustapha Ourrad, Michel Renaud, Bernard Verlhac and Georges Wolinski.

BLOOD RELICS

A James Acton Thriller

"But one of the soldiers with a spear pierced his side, and forthwith came there out blood and water."

John 19:34, King James Bible

"When your time comes to die, be not like those whose hearts are filled with fear of death, so that when their time comes they weep and pray for a little more time to live their lives over again in a different way. Sing your death song, and die like a hero going home."

Tecumseh

"Pale Death beats equally at the poor man's gate and at the palaces of kings."

Horace

PREFACE

The pace of scientific progress is breathtaking at times, the gap between discovery and market incredibly tight now. What is discovered today can be in consumer hands within twenty-four months, if not sooner. In the past, scientific discoveries often took many years, sometimes decades to make it into the public's hands. This gave scientists, politicians, ethicists and the general public time to evaluate whether some of those advancements should actually be permitted to happen.

Today that buffer once provided by time is gone.

Now the question is whether or not that is a good thing.

Scientists are now considering trying to bring back the wooly mammoth, confident they have the technology to actually accomplish this. But should this be allowed? If we can bring back extinct species, should we? If we can bring back the wooly mammoth, what about others more recent like the dodo? And if we bring back the mammoth, then decide it was wrong, do we have the right to then kill it?

And what if the technology is taken to the next step? With a single blood cell we can create a clone of an animal and in theory, a person. With the pace of progress racing forward at breakneck speed, some of these experiments are discovered by the public *after* the successful results are already completed, meaning Pandora's Box could be unleashed on humanity before it even knows it exists.

And what if we take it beyond animals and to human beings?

Or one human being.

Born two thousand years ago.

AUTHOR'S NOTE

A portion of this book deals with the crucifixion of Christ, the rest dealing with the characters' beliefs around this event. Whether you believe or not is immaterial to the enjoyment of the book as it serves as a backdrop to other events. Though loosely based on the Gospels, artistic license has of course been taken for these scenes and no offence is meant.

Notre-Dame Cathedral, Paris, France
Present Day

"Oh my God, Laura!"

Professor James Acton dove across the room, sliding on the marble floor as bullets flew overhead, glass and shards of ancient stone raining down upon him as he desperately tried to reach his wife. Screams of agony from one of the cathedral's defenders momentarily drowned out his wife's own cries as he scurried on his stomach trying to cover the few short feet to her prone form, his hands, cut and bleeding from the shattered display cases, leaving a crimson trail.

He winced as something sharp sliced into his knee.

"Hold on!"

He could see the agony on the face of his wife, Professor Laura Palmer, as she gripped her stomach, a rapidly expanding red stain oozing out from between her fingers, her blouse already soaked with blood.

Bullets tore open the floor in front of him causing him to scamper backward, taking cover behind a large display case. He looked for his friend, Interpol Agent Hugh Reading and spotted him behind a pillar on the opposite side of the room from him.

And closer to Laura.

"Can you reach her?"

Reading poked his head out and immediately a bullet ricocheted off the stone pillar. He jumped back, shaking his head. "I'm pinned down."

Acton tried once again to reach his wife, and again was sent diving for cover. He looked behind him at the French police, their gunfire dwindling, their numbers severely thinned by the explosion, caused he guessed by a grenade of some type. Their attackers, so effective over the past few days, had always arrived well equipped and well organized.

And always unexpectedly.

But today they had been expected.

Or at least anticipated.

The gunfire from the defenders diminished yet again as someone cried out. He watched as one lone man, covered by a pillar, returned fire, followed by the distinctive click of an empty magazine.

The gun clattered to the ground and the opposing fire immediately stopped.

He dove.

Boots pounding on the marble were ignored as he finally reached his wife, cradling her in his arms as he moved her hands to see the wound. "It's okay, I'm here," he said, his beloved looking up at him, her intense pain overwhelming, her face weary.

And pale.

She's lost so much blood.

Suddenly Reading was at his side, his cellphone pressed to his ear. Acton lifted his wife's blouse, blood oozing from the wound, unsure of what to do other than press on it.

Then an idea struck him.

A final, desperate, crazed idea that he couldn't believe he was even contemplating.

He jumped up as their attackers rushed past, ignoring the unarmed trio. Reaching into a shattered display case, he grabbed a clay jar and returning to his wife, reached inside, scooping its dried contents with his fingers. As he began to remove his hand he felt something press against the back of his head.

"I'll kindly ask that you not do that."

He opened his hand, its contents falling back into the jar, then slowly placed the ancient piece of pottery on the floor beside him, raising his hands, Reading already doing the same.

"You have to let me save my wife."

Another man rushed up beside them, decked out in gear any Special Forces soldier would feel at home in. "All clear, sir."

The gun was removed from the back of Acton's head. "Secure these two."

Acton was hauled to his feet, his hands quickly zip-tied behind his back. He watched as the same was done to Reading while another man began to examine Laura.

"We need to get her to a hospital, now!" cried Acton. A gag was shoved in his mouth then one end of a roll of duct tape slapped against his chest. Within moments he found himself taped tightly to a pillar, Reading struggling nearby in the same predicament.

"Status?" asked the man apparently in charge, his accent distinctly German. Decked out head to toe in black, his only discernable features a tanned, chiseled chin with a thick moustache above his grimacing mouth.

"She'll die without immediate help."

A whip of the leader's hand had his men jumping to action. "Take her with us."

"No!" screamed Acton against his gag as he wriggled his shoulders and waist in a futile attempt to get loose. Laura cried out weakly as she was lifted by two of the men and carried from the room.

"Status on the relics?"

"All have been retrieved," said another man as he held up the jar.

"Then we're done here."

The room quickly emptied of their attackers as sirens sounded in the distance. Acton slumped against his bindings as he gave up his struggle to free himself, all hope lost.

His wife was gone, taken from him with a stomach wound that looked fatal, and he was powerless to help her, to stop these men who hadn't yet hesitated to kill in their mad quest.

He sobbed into his gag as he realized he would probably never see her alive again, never hold her in his arms, feel her breath on his face, caress her cheek as they made love, or start the family they had been talking about having.

She would die alone.

And he swore he'd kill every last one of those responsible.

Jerusalem, Judea
April 7th, 30 AD
The Third Hour

"What's happening?"

Longinus cocked an ear, trying to pick out from the amassed crowd any tidbit that might reveal what the commotion he was hearing was all about. His eyes, failing him for years now, revealed only dark shadows in front of him, details of his surroundings long since lost to the ravages of what the garrison doctor had called cataracts.

Incurable.

"You'll never see properly again, and in time, you won't be able to see at all. At least anything we would call seeing."

"How long?"

The doctor had shrugged. "A year. Years. There's no way of knowing, it's different for everyone. If you're lucky you'll finish your term of service and get your pension before it gets too bad."

Well, he hadn't. With only a few months left before he was due to return home, he was now pretty much useless as a soldier. But his friends were helping him as best they could, he well liked in his contubernium.

And his best friend, Albus, was almost never far from his side.

Including today.

"Looks like another crucifixion."

"Again?" Longinus frowned, shaking his head. One of the few blessings of being blind was not having to see another person nailed to a cross, left out in the sun to die for all to see, their crime sometimes written on a piece of paper, sometimes wood, tacked to the cross as a warning to anyone else who might dare to break the law. "I wonder what this one has done."

"Who knows nowadays? The Prefect might just have been in a bad mood." There was a grunt of surprise from his friend. "There's two others with this one." Albus gasped. "By the gods! You should see the first one, he's in rough shape. His back is so bloodied it's soaked completely through his robe. And"—there was a pause, Albus' gentle hold on his arm slipping for a moment—"there's something on his head. It looks like thorns! A circle of thorns!"

"What? Like a crown?" Longinus had never heard of anything like that being done before, and he had seen countless crucifixions in his time, and now, with his poor eyesight, it was one of his more common duties to join the guard at the crucifixion site and wait for the death of the convicted.

"They can't run away from you up there!" his commander had cried, roaring with laughter. Longinus had laughed with him, used to the constant jabs at his expense, those low in the ranks, condemned to the menial tasks of a soldier, always on the lookout for an opportunity to revel in the misery of their peers.

But he was thankful. His commander could have dismissed him, but instead had found a purpose for him.

Just three more months!

Then he'd be heading home to his family.

It had been so long since he had heard from them, and even longer since he'd seen them. The pessimist in him wondered if they were even alive, and on the bad nights, when doubt and loneliness welled up with the self-pity he sometimes gave into over his condition, he couldn't seem to bring up an image of them, a frustratingly crushing experience that would send him rushing into the darkness that was his existence, to drown his sorrows in drink until he forgot why he had been sad in the first place.

It's been so long!

He felt tears flood his eyes as a pang of sorrow stabbed at his chest.

"Longinus! Albus!"

Longinus immediately recognized the voice of their commander. He was close. He felt Albus' grip tighten slightly, gently guiding him so that he'd be facing the man, then they both snapped to attention. Decanus Vitus knew full-well of his condition, but those more senior didn't. If it became too obvious to those around them that one of Rome's finest wasn't up to par—such as by standing at attention facing the wrong direction—Vitus would be forced to do his duty and dismiss him.

Thus violating his contract, thus forfeiting his pension.

If only I had lost my sight in battle!

But no, he was cursed to have lost it naturally, from old age and weak stock apparently.

"I want you two to accompany this procession to Golgatha, help with the crucifixions, then stand guard until the last of them passes."

"Yes, sir!" they both replied.

Vitus lowered his voice and Longinus could see his shadow lean in closer. "You should hear this one's story. Ridiculous! Clearly mad." The hot morning sun quickly returned to its assault on his face as Vitus stepped back. "I'll see you back at the barracks. Report to me as soon as they're all dead."

"Yes, sir!"

Longinus heard the commander walk away, Albus taking him by the arm and leading them toward the ruckus. "Stand aside!" shouted Albus, the crowd of the subjugated immediately parting to let them pass, and once they had done so, returning to their shouts. Most were hurling insults or taunting the condemned men, something he had heard every single time he had drawn this duty over the years.

In his experience most of those lining the streets never knew the convicted, never knew their crimes, instead merely thrilled in taking a break from their daily struggles to enjoy seeing someone whose day was guaranteed to end worse than their own.

The distinctive sound of the wooden crosses, dragging on the hard packed dirt and stone filled his ears, the jerking motions as they advanced with each halting step bringing their bearers inexorably closer to their own doom, seemed particularly slow today.

"The first one, he's weak," explained Albus, answering his unspoken query. "There's so much blood, they must have really beaten him."

"Please, my Lord, let me help you!"

"Stand back," shouted Albus at the woman who had spoken. "Do not interfere with the procession!"

"But let me at least wipe his brow, he's so exhausted!"

There was a pause then acquiescence from his friend. "Very well."

The dragging of the cross stopped for a brief moment and he could hear the woman whispering words of comfort to the man, words he couldn't hear above the shouts of the crowd, a crowd he noticed seemed to have a larger number of people than usual unhappy with what was happening. Women were wailing in sorrow, men were shouting in anger not at the men bearing their crosses, but at the soldiers enforcing Prefect Pilate's orders.

The splintering of wood dragging on the unforgiving ground resumed, a hint of renewed energy then a gasp from the crowd. A loud crash and a man's weakened grunt of shock suggested to him that the man had fallen, his heavy load tumbling to the ground.

"You there, come here!"

Longinus turned toward Albus' voice as a shadow approached.

"What is your name?"

"Simon."

"You look like a traveler."

"I've just arrived from Cyrene."

"You look strong. Take his cross or we'll be here all day."

"But I have business to attend to!"

Longinus heard a hand-width of sword drawn from its scabbard. "Your business can wait."

"Very well," replied the man, no fear in his voice.

Longinus listened as the man lifted the cross from the ground, the scrape strong, swift, but instead of it continuing up the road, it stopped.

"What's happening?" he whispered to Albus, not wanting anyone to know he couldn't see.

"He's helping the man to his feet. A few women are cleaning him up. I think they're friends, perhaps family."

Longinus nodded as the scraping continued, still a staccato rhythm as the cross dragged with each of the man's steps.

A woman wailed, joined by several others.

Suddenly the procession stopped again.

"Daughters of Jerusalem, do not weep for me, weep for yourselves and for your children…"

"Who's speaking?" asked Longinus.

"The condemned man," hissed Albus in his ear. The crowd immediately fell silent, as if this man's words meant something more than the usual pleas of innocence so often cried by the condemned.

His voice was weak but confident, as if the man had not yet lost his will to live, his mind and soul still resilient, merely his body failing him.

"…for the time will come when you will say, blessed are the childless women, the wombs that never bore and the breasts that never nursed! Then they will say to the mountains, 'Fall on us!' and to the hills, 'Cover us!' for if people do these things when the tree is green, what will happen when it is dry?"

"Move along!" shouted Albus, ending the man's speech, the sound of Simon carrying the cross resuming, the crowds swarming along with the condemned men surging forward, faster than before as the strong, fresh traveler seemed intent on making quick work of his task so he could return to his original plans.

The sun was hot and unforgiving already though it was still morning. The uphill climb out of the city, to the hillside known as Golgatha, was grueling even for Simon, a man whose voice had suggested he was large. Albus' gentle grip on Longinus' arm never wavered, and neither did the wails of the women following the procession, the bulk of the crowds abandoning their pursuit once the city gates were cleared, though a strong contingent of those delighting in the misery of these three men followed, their hatred seemingly focused solely on this poor soul who had been severely beaten.

"We're here," whispered Albus. "You stand guard here," he said in a louder voice, pushing on Longinus' arm, spinning him to face the crowds. Longinus could see the mix of dark and light in front of him. He jabbed the base of his spear into the dirt, taking a wide stance and extending his right arm with the spear to his side, his other arm held out to block the crowd.

"No one passes," he said in a commanding voice, immediately halting the advance of the shadows cast before him. The crowd stopped and he put his hand on his hip, listening, even the coldest of those gathered shunned into silence at the gruesome task now being carried out.

The distinct sound of the three crosses tossed off the shoulders of their bearers, the wood clattering on the solid rock, was followed by pleas from two voices he didn't recognize, clearly the men that had accompanied the other weakened man, the man whose words still confused Longinus.

"If people do these things when the tree is green, what will happen when it is dry?"

What did it mean? What tree?

"Drink!"

"What is it?" asked the weakened voice.

"Wine with gall. It will help with the pain," replied Albus, his voice beseeching the man to take the liquid offered to all the condemned.

"No."

Longinus' eyebrows rose slightly. He couldn't recall the last time, if ever, one of the condemned had refused the acidic wine mixed with wormwood, the combination dulling the senses for what was to come.

Who is *this man?*

A hammer hit an iron spike, someone cried out in agony, the gasp of the crowd suggesting the man who had shown so much courage and strength up to this point.

But he can't escape the pain.

He tried to tune out the taps of the hammer, instead returning to his thoughts on the man's words. *Perhaps the tree was a metaphor?* That made sense, but Longinus wasn't much for metaphors, in fact he wasn't much for any of the flowery language those who would call themselves philosophers and scholars espoused whenever he heard them. Speak plain, speak straight, then there's no misunderstandings.

Perhaps the green tree means when times are good?

That made sense. Perhaps he meant if things like this were done in good times, then what horrors might be seen when times were bad?

Another spike, another cry. He forced himself to not wince with each tap of the hammer, each one eliciting a shriek from one of the gathered women. He wondered who they were, what connection they had to this man, for it was sympathy that he was hearing for this one man, not the other two. In fact, all the support, and all the hatred, seemed exclusive to this one soul, and he again wondered what he must have done to elicit such diametrically opposed reactions from those gathered.

The tapping of the hammer echoed across the rocky hilltop, different this time, and he recognized the sound made when something was tacked onto the cross.

Probably his sentence.

The sound of the first cross being lifted, its base slipping into the hole dug long ago, the thud followed by a cry from the poor soul condemned to die in such a horrendous fashion, signaling at least the beginning of the end of these doomed men's time on Earth.

The other two men were next, the impact of their crosses slamming into their holes reverberating through the stone Longinus stood on.

It was a feeling he had never noticed before, he never before particularly caring about any of those who had been condemned.

But something was different here today.

Something *felt* different.

As if some great injustice were being committed, something that they would later come to regret if they continued.

He shivered.

Feet scraping on the rock behind him had him turning slightly.

"How are you, my friend?"

It was Albus. He nodded. "Fine. Who is he? The one they're all crying over?"

"I've never heard of him, but according to the sign Pilate wanted nailed to his cross, he certainly thought a lot of himself. No wonder they sentenced him to death, and no wonder so many of these people are pissed off."

"Why, what does it say?"

"It says 'This is Jesus, the King of the Jews'."

BLOOD RELICS

Cathedral of San Salvador, Oviedo, Spain
Present Day, Two days before the Paris assault

Father Rodriquez leaned over and poked the fire, getting a little more life out of it before stoking it one final time, his eyes heavy. It had been a long day, the world inside the walls surrounding him not immune to the struggles of these times his beloved country found itself in. An economy nearly bankrupted by the Great Recession and a foolish dalliance in expensive green energy had resulted in a youth unemployment rate of nearly fifty percent.

Which meant a restless youth.

His days were filled with endless parades of mothers leading young sons—literally by the ear sometimes—to see him, to give them a talking to in a too often futile effort to keep these bored and frustrated young men on the straight and narrow.

And too often his nights were filled chasing away those same men looking to blow off steam with a little vandalism.

He hooked the poker on its stand then picked up the book he had been reading from his lap, one of his perennial favorites, Robinson Crusoe. Reaching over to the small side table without looking, his hand instinctively found the glass of red wine he had been nursing. He began to read one of his favorite parts of the book then closed his eyes, taking a sip of the wine as he savored the effect the tannins had on his tongue. His mind wandered, picturing himself on some deserted island in the middle of nowhere, building a home to not only protect himself from the elements, but from cannibals as well, disguising his new home from outside eyes.

He opened his own, looking about the sparse rectory. The life of a priest was a lonely one. Gone were the days where parishes were so well attended that several priests were sometimes required. There was no more camaraderie among those of the cloth. It was a lonely existence, but it was the one he had chosen so long ago.

Fifty years next month.

He looked at the crucifix his proud mother had given him the day he had graduated from the seminary.

Oh Mama, I look forward to seeing you and Papa again.

They had both died in the past few years, his mother's a difficult death, Alzheimer's taking her mind long before her body. But they were at peace now, together he knew in the Kingdom of God.

He winced, a stabbing pain in his knee reminding him of just how many years he had put onto his own bones. He would be retiring soon, something he felt would probably kill him long before any disease might. He couldn't imagine the boredom. Though he complained silently of the stream of people entering the church day after day looking for him to solve their problems rather than they themselves doing the obvious, he would miss them.

The people of this community were his friends.

His family.

Though it wouldn't hurt some of them to invite me to dinner from time to time.

Too often he spent his evenings alone, heating a can of soup on his small stove, his old radio providing his only company.

No one wants to dine with an old man who reminds them of their sins.

He laughed, shaking his head and taking another sip of wine, its numbing qualities slowly taking hold, the pain in his knee subsiding if only slightly.

Looking back at the page, he began to read about the elaborate fence Crusoe was building when he heard a loud bang from outside.

Those cursed teenagers!

He placed his glass of wine and book on the table, struggling to his feet. Slipping into his slippers and tightening the belt on his robe, he grabbed a flashlight and opened the door, walking down the short hallway to the church itself. This was the second time this week, fifth time this month, that someone had attempted to get in. He knew it was teenagers tormenting him, their laughter and snickers from the alleyways echoing across the cobblestone streets when he'd poke his head out the door.

But he had to investigate. He couldn't ignore the possibility that there might be an actual thief.

For he had been entrusted with one of Christianity's most precious relics.

A Blood Relic.

The very cloth used to wrap the head of Jesus Christ when he was lowered from the cross.

The Shroud of Oviedo.

It was priceless, irreplaceable.

Stored in the original part of the church since the ninth century, it now stood behind the mighty stone walls of the now much larger cathedral, and iron bars that were rarely opened to the public.

But walls could be breached, locks picked, and display cases opened.

"Who goes there?" he cried into the dark, his flashlight playing across the darkened pews, the only light from prayer candles still flickering nearby and the occasional shaft of moonlight from overhead.

There was no reply of course, but he heard the creaking of the gate as it swung open, sending his heart racing as he rushed forward, faith and duty rather than intelligent forethought sending him hobbling toward the danger, his only weapons God and a flashlight.

"This is a house of God!" he cried into the darkness as he rounded the corner that led to the original structure, the Chapel of St. Michael.

The beam of a flashlight suddenly blinded him. He raised his hand to shield his eyes as he heard glass smashing inside the now unlocked chamber.

"No! Please! You can't do this! These relics are precious, priceless!" He raised his flashlight, shining it not at the man now trying to blind him, but inside the chamber.

And to his dismay he saw someone lifting the Shroud from its protective case.

"That contains the blood of Christ himself! You cannot take it, you mustn't take it!"

"Don't worry, Father. We'll take good care of it."

The man spoke passable Spanish but with a slight accent that made him think he might be German.

These weren't teenagers out to have some fun at his expense.

"Who are you?"

"Nobody you need concern yourself with."

Fear and rage gripped him and he charged toward the man, a foolish act he knew, but the only one he could think to do.

A muzzle flashed in front of him and he felt a searing pain in his chest as he dropped to his knees, his advance stopped. Tipping over to his side, his flashlight rolled away from his outstretched hand, its beam revealing two men gently placing the shroud in some sort of case, a curious fog or haze roiling from the top of it. One of the men closed it, the case snapping shut with a hiss, giving him some small comfort that their intentions appeared not to be vandalism, but theft.

And as he felt the life blood flow from him, he began to pray to his Lord and Savior for forgiveness in failing to protect the holy relic that contained His healing blood.

Footsteps approached him, somebody kneeling at his side, shining a flashlight in his face then down at his chest where he had been shot. He could see the man's silhouette as he rose, a cellphone to his ear.

"Yes, we've retrieved the relic. Unfortunately the priest interfered." There was a pause, the sound of someone yelling on the other end. "I'm sorry, but he charged me…no, I don't think he can be saved…very well, father."

The phone snapped shut and the man placed a hand on Father Rodriguez's shoulder. "I'm sorry, Father. You were never meant to be harmed."

"Wh-why?"

"Why are we taking the Shroud? Because some men are not so prepared to die as you are, Father."

He felt a pat on his shoulder then the fading sounds of boots on the stone floor, a floor that felt colder by the second as he grew weaker and weaker.

Then a smile spread across his face as he closed his eyes.

I'll see you soon, Mama and Papa.

Golgatha, Judea
April 7th, 30 AD
The sixth hour

"Father, forgive them, for they do not know what they are doing."

Longinus' jaw almost dropped as he realized who this man was, this man whose voice resonated with a timbre that at once suggested wisdom and love with inner strength and courage despite the surety he was soon to die.

Father.

This was the man he had heard about, the rabbi who claimed to be the son of the Jewish God. He himself didn't believe in their god, the entire notion of only a single deity ridiculous. Any reasonably educated person knew there were gods for every aspect of human life, from war to love, that could be called upon in time of need, each focused on their one duty to the exclusion of all others.

How could a single God have the time to deal with *all* of man's problems?

But this man here, this man who made the ridiculous claim he was the son of a god, was clearly mad. To not only claim he was the son of a god, and therefore by extension a god himself, was insane. But to do so *here* of all places, on this day of all days had to be the very definition of lunacy. Today was Passover, from his limited understanding of Judaism the biggest religious holiday of the year. To come to Jerusalem during the Passover with apparently hundreds if not thousands of followers was insane, especially allowing himself to be greeted like a king upon arrival with people throwing their garments on the ground for him to walk on.

It was suicide!

And he had arrived on a donkey.

The very idea of a king riding a donkey!

He chuckled as behind him he heard the guards arguing over the garments the prisoners had worn, all divvied up in short order, the final item, the "king's" undergarment, drawing particular interest.

"Let's not tear it," he heard one say.

"Let's decide by lot who will get it." It was Albus who suggested this, the sounds of the impartial method of decision making soon heard, Albus crying out with joy, apparently the winner.

A shadow approached and he held out his arm. It stopped, but what sounded like an elderly man began yelling. "You who are going to destroy the temple and build it in three days, save yourself! Come down from the cross, if you are the Son of God!"

There was laughter among the crowd, another joining in on the taunting. "He saved others, but he can't save himself! He's the king of Israel! Let him come down now from the cross, and we will believe in him."

More laughter.

"He trusts in God. Let God rescue him now if he wants him, for he said, 'I am the Son of God.'"

The taunts continued, the hatred in the voices unsettling. Longinus had heard taunts before, usually from the victims, usually from a murder victim's family, taunting the condemned, taking pleasure in reminding them of the exquisite hell that awaited them.

But this man had harmed no one.

Though according to what he had overheard, he might have caused great harm. Apparently Prefect Pilate was prepared to shutdown Passover for fears of an uprising, a Jewish rebellion. Hundreds if not thousands could have died had it been allowed to happen. Pilate had told the Jewish leaders to handle it themselves.

Apparently this was how they had chosen to do that.

Kill a single man, an insane, blasphemous man, to save thousands of others.

He had to admit it had a perverse logic to it.

"He saved others; let him save himself if he is God's Messiah, the Chosen One!"

He had heard enough.

"Silence!"

A hush descended upon the crowd, only to be replaced by his own fellow soldiers behind him. "If you are the king of the Jews, save yourself."

This seemed to embolden one of the others crucified along with the so-called king. "Aren't you the Messiah? Save yourself and us!"

His counterpart replied with equal vigor. "Don't you fear God since you are under the same sentence?"

Longinus turned slightly, listening to the second prisoner with curiosity. It wouldn't be the first time that a criminal had begged forgiveness once facing imminent death, but they rarely defended each other.

"We are punished justly, for we are getting what our deeds deserve. But this man has done nothing wrong." There was a pause, the voice changing slightly as the man seemed to turn his head. "Jesus, remember me when you come into your kingdom."

The raspy, weak voice replied, and Longinus' felt a shiver travel his entire body. "Truly I tell you, today you will be with me in paradise."

The surety with which the man said these words was inspiring, as if he actually believed the madness he was preaching. Cries from several women in the crowd was proof that many here believed his words too.

And he could understand that.

In the few hours he had been exposed to the man he hadn't said a negative word, hadn't begged for his life, instead having begged for forgiveness for those who were doing him ill, and delivering words of comfort to others.

He was truly an inspiring man.

I can see why people would follow him, despite his madness.

"I'm his mother, may we pass?"

Longinus nearly jumped, not having seen even the shadow of the woman who now stood before him. The pain in her voice was clear, the anguish palpable, and he felt his own chest tighten as he imagined how his mother would feel should it be he nailed to a cross, waiting to die.

He nodded.

Several sets of footsteps trudged on the arid ground, those who passed whimpering or sobbing, clearly believers in this man's message. He looked up at the sky and could spot the bright orb of the sun overhead, and judging by the growl in his stomach, he suspected it was around noon.

He won't last much longer, not if he was beaten as badly as Albus said.

"Woman, here is your son," said the voice, weaker still. "Here is your mother."

It was times like these he wished he could see for he had no idea what the words meant. Who was he talking to? Was it his mother? Was it his brother? It couldn't be, for surely a mother would know her own son.

This man speaks in riddles!

He sighed.

Maybe he's going mad with the heat?

The sun was beating down on them now, Golgatha outside the city on a hilltop, there no chance of shade here, the stone and dried dirt they stood upon getting so hot it almost baked the sandal clad feet of those who felt compelled to accompany the condemned.

Which meant the crowds had thinned even more, and he suspected by the time the end arrived, it would be thinner still.

The insults were few now, those whose hearts were filled with hatred seemingly not willing to endure the heat in the name of their convictions.

Footsteps approached from behind, a hand gently gripping his shoulder. "There's no need to stand guard anymore, come sit with us." Longinus nodded, turning and walking forward, his steps slow, deliberate, as he followed the shadow of Albus, nervous he might trip on the uneven ground. The shadow stopped and Albus grabbed his hand. "Let me help you, old man!" he said with a laugh, a good cover as Longinus sat where he stood, Albus guiding him to the ground before sitting beside him.

Something was placed in his hand.

"Drink."

Longinus took a long drag of the harsh liquid, the wine having long turned to vinegar, losing any of its pleasurable qualities once intended by the vintner.

A gust of wind swept over them providing a welcome respite from the heat if but for a moment.

"Look!" cried someone to his left. A shadow crossed his path, a large shadow, and it took him a moment to realize it wasn't a shadow at all. He looked up and felt his heart slam in his chest.

The sun was gone.

Corpo della Gendarmeria Office
Palazzo del Governatorato, Vatican City
Present Day, Two days before the Paris assault

Vatican Inspector General Mario Giasson hung up the phone, shaking his head. Someone had stolen a priceless Blood Relic in Spain, murdering a priest in the process. He had always wanted more security put in place for these relics, in fact, he had always been a proponent of bringing all these relics, so important to Christian belief, behind the massive walls surrounding them.

But his concerns had always been dismissed, and he understood the reasoning. These relics were sometimes critical draws to the churches that held them, precious to their parishioners, usually safely held for centuries. Over the decades security measures had been put in place from locks, gates and protective cases, sometimes even alarm systems, but rarely were guards present.

It was simply too expensive.

We rely too heavily on the goodness of man.

It was an evil world, something that seemed reinforced with his daily reading of the news, and this phone call had merely cemented his view a little more. An aged priest, near retirement, killed protecting a relic he had no business protecting, a relic only precious to those who believed, and should they truly be believers, a relic they wouldn't dream of stealing.

He knew that thinking was naïve. All believers aren't good people, of that there was no doubt. The classic example were the deeply religious Mafioso that so populated the country surrounding this tiny city state. How men could commit murder with one hand and hold rosary beads with the other, was beyond him.

I hope there's a special corner of hell reserved for them.

An alarm sounded and he jumped to his feet, rushing out into the security office, those manning the computers and security monitors shouting out questions and answers, the main feeds on the wall of monitors beginning to switch to the area in question.

"Report!"

The nightshift supervisor, Alfredo Ianuzzi, turned in his desk. "Silent alarm from Saint Peter's Basilica, Saint Longinus display, sir."

"Saint Longinus? What's kept there?"

"There they are!" shouted one of his men, Francesco Greco, pointing at the screen. Giasson watched as three men, all in black, submachine guns in hand, raced through the deserted nave of St. Peter's Basilica, it having been closed for the night hours ago.

"Notify the Swiss Guard. I want this place locked down!"

More alarms sounded, a coded alert sent out over the PA system. On the screens guards raced toward the Basilica and St. Peter's Square. Giasson grabbed a radio from the charging station and rushed out the door. Sprinting toward the square, he held the radio up to his mouth, pressing the Talk button. "Report!"

"They've just cleared the Portico," replied Ianuzzi. "Our guards are moving to intercept."

"Do we know what they stole?"

"Not yet."

Giasson burst through a set of doors, startling several priests deep in conversation. He tried to remember what relics might be worth stealing in the Saint Longinus display, but was drawing a blank.

Then a thought hit him, almost bringing him to a halt.

He forced himself forward, despite his lungs burning from his unusually long sprint. He raised the radio again, gasping out his question. "Are there any Blood Relics stored there?"

He surged through the outer doors and into St. Peter's Square, dozens of the Swiss Guard racing toward the obelisk that towered over the center of the massive gathering place.

"Sir, the Holy Lance is kept there!"

My God!

Two Blood Relics stolen within hours of each other was too much of a coincidence. Which meant these people were either the thieves and murderers from Spain, or were connected with them somehow.

But they wouldn't be getting away today.

Gunfire sprayed the ground in front of him and he skid to a halt, ducking.

"Look!"

He heard someone shouting closer to the main gates, their voice carrying over the cobblestone. Looking, he gasped. A set of intensely bright lights were rapidly approaching the gates, a thumping sound getting louder and louder as what could only be a helicopter raced toward the tiny nation, it surrounded on all sides by a densely packed Rome.

The helicopter cleared the gates with what looked like only feet to spare, the guards all turning their attention to the new arrival as its nose pulled up, killing its forward momentum. As it slowly turned the lights blinding him changed direction and he was able to see the side doors were open, people inside throwing down ropes.

"Stop them!" he shouted as he resumed his charge. But it was too late. The three men hooked onto the ropes and the chopper rose, banking back toward the main gates as the thieves were pulled from the ground, slowly reeled in as his men were left staring at the rapidly receding helicopter, unable to open fire lest their bullets find innocent flesh on their descent.

Giasson shook his head in awe as he watched the helicopter bank around the corner, still barely above street height, the three men swinging wide, almost hitting the buildings as they continued to be pulled inside.

He raised his radio. "Get me the Roma Polizia." He paused for a moment, then nodded, a decision made.

"And put in a call to Agent Hugh Reading of Interpol."

BLOOD RELICS

It was dark now, almost as dark as night, at least it might as well have been for Longinus. Everything was a dark, gray mass to his failing eyes. Nighttime had once been his enemy, he making it a point to try and be inside by nightfall, in his bed laughing with his comrades, or sleeping. But as he adapted, he realized that nighttime provided him the cover he needed at times for his ailment. Walking with a hand held out tentatively, running along the wall as a guide was the norm, everyone doing it, nobody judging you or asking you questions, and he had found when it was dark, when the noise of the day had given way to slumber, his other senses were heightened.

It was as if he could sense where things were.

And with the wind whipping around them, almost unabated for the past three hours since the darkness had fallen upon the land, Albus describing thick, black, billowing clouds overhead, he had found himself simply closing his eyes, listening to the sounds around him. Albus was at his right, the other soldiers, four in number, farther still to his right.

All were scared.

Mourners were gathered at the foot of the cross occupied by the man named Jesus, their whimpering and sobbing still heard, as if carried by the wind directly to his ears. The pleas and whining of the two criminals had given way to silence, though they were still alive.

And Jesus had said almost nothing since the sky had darkened.

"My God, my God, why have you forsaken me?

27

Longinus turned to the voice, surprisingly strong, the heartbreak and anguish so genuine, he knew this man's time had come, the body's last gasp at life often providing a final surge of energy to the condemned.

One of the mourners sobbed. "He's calling God!"

He's not long for this earth.

"I thirst."

The voice was weak again. Longinus held out his spear in the direction of the others. "Soak a sponge in wine." He could hear the sounds of wine sloshing nearby then something pushing on his spear as it was stuck to the end. He wasn't sure why he had felt compelled to offer up this gesture, but there was something about this man that he felt connected to. What it was he had no idea, but the sense he had, as inexplicable as it was, was that this man, despite his madness, was a good man.

And why he should suffer from thirst, on top of all the other cruelties he had endured, was beyond him. He could see no harm in whether a man's thirst was temporarily quenched as it did little to extend his suffering on the cross, it would simply make it more comfortable, albeit slightly. And with this man having refused the wine and gall, he must be in sheer agony.

He felt Albus' hand on his shoulder, nothing being said, but Longinus knew his friend was silently thinking, "Are you insane?" But with a swiftness that surprised him, he stepped forward, swinging the spear high above his head and coming to rest in a spot he simply *felt* was the right spot.

He heard the man sucking on the sponge, stopping after a few seconds.

He lowered the spear, a sensation of wellbeing almost overwhelming him in the knowledge he had done something good for a good man.

Albus squeezed his shoulder, removing the sponge from the end of the spear.

One of the soldiers nearby spat. "Now leave him alone. Let's see if God comes to save him."

Longinus waited, standing, listening to the last gasps of a dying man as his friends and family wept at his feet. He found himself praying to this God, to this single deity he had never believed in, and still didn't, but if he were a god, like his own, perhaps he might listen to the prayers of this non-believer as he silently begged for a final end to this man's suffering.

A cry suddenly erupted from overhead, the final words moaned out to the heavens above. "Father, into your hands I commit my spirit."

A crack of thunder tore apart the sky above them and the earth shook. Those around him screamed in fear as Longinus dropped to a knee, extending a hand to steady himself, vibrations travelling up his arm and into his very soul. Flashes of lightning cut through the darkness that was his world, the thunder so immediate he feared they might all be struck by this god's wrath, for that was what it had to be.

A wrath of some titan enraged by the death of one of his believers.

And as the sound of rocks splitting around them, of thunder overhead, and an earth that refused to be still at their feet continued, a sense of foreboding gripped him as somebody shouted out nearby.

"Surely, this man was the Son of God!"

Hugh Reading Residence, London, England
Present Day, Two days before the Paris assault

Interpol Agent Hugh Reading snorted then froze, wondering what had woken him. His phone vibrated on his bedside table. He grabbed it, looking at the time.

Bloody hell!

It was one in the morning, an ungodly hour for anyone to call, especially something showing as a blocked number.

He swept his thumb over the touchscreen and held the phone up to his head.

"Hello?"

He cursed as he heard his Darth Vader voice, forgetting he was hooked up to his damned CPAP machine. Reaching over he pressed the button to turn it off then tore the mask off his head, tossing it beside him as he sat up, shoving his tongue around his mouth, unsticking his lips from his gums.

Forgot to add water to the bloody thing.

He was still learning how to use the machine, but he had to admit it was changing his life. He'd been dragging his ass for months, and until he had been prescribed it after a sleep apnea diagnosis, he hadn't realized how much so. In fact, he felt twenty years younger, and judging by the fact he'd apparently been a snorer for years—even his ex-wife confirming it to their son when he had shown him the contraption on a recent visit—he might have been less than his best for years.

What had really concerned him was the fact sleep apnea could cause heart damage, something he had never known. He had of course heard of sleep apnea and knew it meant that you stopped breathing during the night and that in turn would cause you to wake up slightly, but he had always assumed that just meant you were tired.

But heart damage?

He was lucky, it apparently caught in time, and though he had had serious reservations about ever being able to sleep with a mask over his face, he had found it remarkably easy, the greatest incentive being the fact he had more energy now than in years, and with his body not trying to protect itself from the lack of oxygenated blood, he was actually sleeping through most of the night rather than up several times for a squirt.

It was a life changer.

He held the phone up to his ear.

"If this is a crank call, I'll make it my life's mission to seek you out and destroy you."

"Agent Reading?"

He sat up straight.

"Yes?"

"This is Mario Giasson, I'm sorry to wake you, mon ami."

Reading smiled. "Mario! I know you do things a little different at the Vatican but you do sleep, don't you?"

Giasson laughed. "Trust me, my friend, I am well aware of the time and I wouldn't have called if I didn't need your help."

Reading frowned, leaning over and flicking on his bedside lamp then picking up his pad and pen he kept handy for just such an occasion. "What's happened?"

"Are you aware of what a Blood Relic is?"

"Not a clue. I think you meant to dial Jim and Laura, they're the experts in bloody relics."

Giasson chuckled, continuing. "No, I've got the right man. Blood Relics are objects that are believed to have the blood of Christ on them."

"Oh." Reading wasn't very religious so didn't give such things much thought, but his experiences over the past few years with the Actons had taught him that far too often those who *did* believe were more than willing to kill for those beliefs.

"I know, I know," said Giasson, "you don't believe in such things, but somebody out there clearly does."

"Why?"

"Last night a priest in Spain was murdered, the only thing taken a shroud that is believed to have been used to wrap the head of Christ after he was taken down from the cross. And tonight, before my very eyes, the Holy Lance, also known as the Spear of Destiny, was stolen from the Vatican by four men who were quite literally pulled out of here by a helicopter."

"Any casualties?"

"Thankfully no. Just my pride."

"Well, that grows back. God knows I've had mine wounded enough." He paused, jotting down notes. "So two Blood Relics in the same night. Sounds like too much of a coincidence."

"Exactly. I was hoping you could get involved since this crosses borders."

"I will if I can. I'll have to see if I can get the case allocated to me."

He could almost hear the smile through the phone. "I've already taken care of that, mon ami. You were assigned a few minutes ago."

Reading shook his head, the power of political connections never ceasing to amaze him. "Then I suppose I'll be seeing you in the morning."

"I look forward to it."

"I think however I'm going to need some help."

"I thought you might. Please inform the professors that the Vatican looks forward to hosting them once again."

"I'm sure they'll be thrilled."

Golgatha, Judea
April 7th, 30 AD
The Ninth Hour

"We need to get out of here while we can!" shouted Albus, the howling wind beginning to settle, the ground beginning to still. Longinus shoved himself to his feet with the help of his spear, looking up at the sky as the clouds began to part, the sun making its presence felt once more.

And then it was still, as if nothing had happened, as if all their sins had been forgiven.

The wails of this man's followers continued, their grief rolling over the hilltop unabated as they mourned their loved one's passing. He felt Albus' hand grip his shoulder. "What just happened?" His voice was low, terrified.

Longinus shook his head, looking up at the shadow of the man so hated and yet so loved. "I fear to imagine."

"This is taking too long," said one of the other soldiers, crossing in front of Longinus. "Our orders are to make certain this is over before Passover begins."

"Break their knees!" ordered another.

Longinus grimaced. It was one way to certainly hasten death. By breaking the knees the men couldn't use their feet to hold their body weight, which meant they'd be forced to literally hang from their hands, soon taking away their ability to breathe as the muscles lost strength.

"Please no!" cried the prisoner to the left, almost immediately followed by the gut-wrenching sound of bones crushing beneath the large mallet kept here for just these occasions. Whimpers of pain could be heard as footfalls approached the body of Jesus.

"He's dead already," said the man.

"We have to be sure. Break them anyway."

Longinus felt an overwhelming sense that this was wrong, that this final indignity shouldn't happen. "No!" he shouted, stepping forward, once again inexplicably certain of what he was doing and where he was going. He held out his hand, blocking the shadow from approaching the cross.

The man backed off.

Longinus raised his spear and thrust upward, the feeling of flesh being pierced, the blade going deep yet not hitting bone, telling him he had once again hit his mark.

Then something unexpected happened.

Something wet hit his face, splashing in his eyes and he cried out in pain, releasing his grip on the spear, it clattering to the rock beside him as his hands rubbed at his eyes, trying to rid it of whatever was burning at them. He dropped to his knees, Albus rushing to his side, exclaiming, "It's water! It's water and blood!"

And as the pain began to settle, the words sinking in, he opened his eyes and gasped as he looked up at the body.

A body he could see in all its tortured glory, as clear as the day he was born.

And he began to sob as he watched the water and blood flow from the wound, something he had never seen in all his years.

"Surely this was a righteous man!"

Professor James Acton raised his wine glass and smiled at those gathered around him at the dinner table. These were his friends, his loved ones, the people he cared most about in the world, the only people missing his parents who lived far enough away that last minute dinner invites weren't usually accepted, and his friend Interpol Agent Hugh Reading who, living in England, definitely wouldn't be accepting an afternoon invite.

"To good food and good company."

"Hear! Hear!" replied his best friend, Professor Gregory Milton. They had known each other since their college days, Milton a graduate student who had taken a young Acton under his wing over twenty years ago in New York City. They had been nearly inseparable since. Acton watched as his friend took a sip from his glass then returned it to the table, adjusting himself in his chair, something for a while Acton thought would never be possible again. Milton had been shot in the back a few years ago while trying to help Acton escape some people hell-bent on killing him. He had been paralyzed from the waist down, but fortunately the paralysis turned out to be temporary and he was slowly recovering. It was hard, torturous work, but he knew his friend well, and he knew he had made a commitment he would never break—to dance at his young daughter's wedding, whenever that might be.

Since she wasn't even ten yet, he had plenty of time.

Those who had shot his friend were people he surprisingly now called his friends, or at least good acquaintances—he certainly no longer feared them. Delta Force's Bravo Team had been told he and his students were a domestic terrorist group and were given orders to eliminate them. It had been the most terrifying experience of his life, but it had brought him to London, England where he had met Professor Laura Palmer and the police officer pursuing him, Hugh Reading.

His wife, Professor Laura Palmer, sat at the other end of the table, smiling at him. She was the most gorgeous woman he could imagine, someone he found to be more beautiful with each passing day, his love for her growing with every moment they spent together. They had met by accident and had been a couple ever since. Though his work and hers often had them on opposite sides of the globe, her recent decision to take a job at the Smithsonian rather than her college in London meant they were now spending much more time together, finally settling in a single house rather than splitting their time between her London apartment and the home he had bought over a decade ago.

"Laura, you've outdone yourself tonight," said Sandra, Milton's wife. "This beef wellington is to die for."

Laura smiled, nodding toward her husband. "Though I'd love to take credit, all I did was prepare the salad and set the table. James is the chef in this house."

"If I let Greg be the chef we'd be eating nothing but grilled cheese sandwiches and Kraft Dinner."

Acton's eyes flared slightly as he signaled appreciation for two of his college staples with a moan and pat of his stomach. "Nothin' wrong with those."

"Exactly," agreed Milton, turning to his wife. "I survived on my cooking just fine before I met you."

Sandra dropped her chin slightly, giving him the stink-eye. "Are you saying you could live without me?"

Acton laughed as his friend tried to backpedal before the hole got too deep.

"No! Of course not, that's not what I meant." He paused, then placed a hand on her leg. "You know I can't live without you."

"Damned right."

Everyone at the table laughed, including a polite giggle from the entourage's newest member, graduate student Mai Lien Trinh. She had been forced to leave her native Vietnam during the incident in Hanoi that he and his wife had found themselves entangled in, and Milton had agreed to allow Acton to hire her as an assistant while she completed her studies. She had lived with them until just recently, finally saving enough money to get herself a decent apartment just off campus, but since her arrival he and Laura had almost come to think of her as an adopted daughter, she painfully shy and completely unfamiliar with Western ways.

It was almost like raising a child in a compressed period of time.

Though there was no teaching the American sense of humor.

Sandra turned to Mai. "So, Mai, Laura tells me you've got your own apartment now?"

Mai nodded, her eyes directed at her plate. "I moved in last week."

"Settling in?" asked Milton.

She nodded, pushing her fork through the carrot puree. "My neighbor is noisy though. He plays his stereo too loud."

"You can ask him to turn it down," suggested Sandra.

Mai rapidly shook her head. "I couldn't do that."

"Then tell the super." Laura leaned closer to Mai. "You have a right to peace and quiet in your own home."

Mai shrugged. "Maybe."

Laura sat back up. "If you want I'll send James over to give him a good kicking."

Milton jabbed the air with his fork. "Now *that's* a good idea."

Acton wiped his mouth with his napkin, tossing it on the table. "What apartment is he in? I'll go kick his ass right now!" Mai's jaw dropped and her eyes shot wide open as she stared at him, the horror clear.

Maybe we've gone too far this time.

He began to laugh, sitting back down and reaching over to pat her on the shoulder. "We're just joking, Mai, don't worry. *But*, if you want me there when you talk to him, I'm more than willing. It might make it easier for you."

She seemed to settle down slightly, her tensed muscles from the threatened ass-kicking relaxing as her flushed cheeks slowly returned to their normal light brown. "Maybe."

It seemed her favorite word. He knew she missed her home terribly, especially her brother, but unfortunately her life there was over, at least for the immediate future.

She would need to adapt.

Fortunately she was turning out to be quite the computer whiz and had enrolled in several classes, most of her free time spent consuming every bit of information she could on a variety of subjects. Acton had a funny feeling the new opportunities provided in an open society were going to lead to her changing her major from archeology to something entirely different.

His phone vibrated in his pocket.

"Excuse me," he said, retrieving the phone, his eyebrows popping. "It's Hugh."

Laura looked at her watch. "It's one in the morning there," she whispered.

Acton swiped his thumb. "Trouble sleeping? Need us to sing you a lullaby?"

Reading's deep laugh came through the earpiece and Acton could almost picture the man smiling, though he already detected a note of grumpiness. "With this new CPAP machine I'm sleeping like a baby."

"Good to hear. My dad has one of those, too. He's an old bastard like you though, so that's to be expected."

"Respect your elders."

Acton tossed his head back, laughing. "Listen, we're in the middle of dinner. Greg and Sandra are here with Mai and Laura. Can I put you on speaker?"

"Nothing I hate more than speaker except for maybe call waiting."

"Oh wait, I've got another call."

"Ha ha. Put me on speaker, you bastard."

Acton tapped the icon and placed the phone on the table. "You're on speaker."

"Hello?"

Everyone replied at once, even Mai murmuring a hello, she yet to meet Reading in person.

Reading cursed. "Yeah, this is going to work."

"Why are you calling at such a late hour?" asked Laura. "Is everything okay?"

"I'm fine, if that's what you mean," replied Reading, the tiny speaker doing little justice to his voice. "But there's a problem at the Vatican. They need my help, and I need yours."

Acton looked at his wife, a sense of foreboding shivering up his spine at the thought of returning to where so much pain had been experienced. "What's the problem?" His trepidation was clear in his voice.

"Apparently a priest was killed in Spain tonight, some cloth stolen, and a team of four stole some artifact from the Vatican, escaped by helicopter."

"Jesus," muttered Acton, the imagery his mind concocted impressively terrifying.

"Funny you should mention him."

Acton's eyes narrowed. "Why?"

"According to Mario both artifacts that were stolen were something called 'Blood Relics'."

Acton sat up straight, his eyes opening slightly wider as he looked at Laura. "Did you say 'Blood Relics'?"

"Yes. Mean something to you?"

"Of course. They're any object thought to have come in contact with the blood of Christ."

"You mean when he was crucified?"

"Exactly."

Laura rose and rounded the table, taking a knee beside Acton. "What was stolen?" she asked.

"Some cloth in Spain—"

"Probably the Sudarium of Oviedo," interrupted Acton as he pushed out from the table slightly allowing Laura to sit on his knee.

"It was a shroud used to wrap his head after he was brought down from the cross," explained Laura as she sat. "What else?"

"Some spear from the Vatican. The Holy Lance or something like that. Is that the spear that bloke in Passion of the Christ used to stab him in the side?"

Acton nodded, putting a steadying hand around Laura. "Yes, it's also known as the Spear of Destiny. It's odd though, that particular spear has never been authenticated."

"You mean it's a fake?"

"No," replied Laura, "just that it's never been authenticated. The Church doesn't deny it's the real thing, they just don't claim that it *is* the real thing, either."

"And this cloth?"

"*That* they claim is real," said Acton. "Though who knows, it's never really been tested. Most of these artifacts aren't tested because no one wants to have their claim to fame disproven."

Reading yawned. "Sorry, my beauty sleep was interrupted."

"And you can ill afford that," laughed Acton.

"Piss off. Well, proven or not, somebody out there is willing to kill for these things."

"Any clues?"

"Not yet. I'm catching an early morning flight to Rome. Any chance you two can join me? I think these guys are just getting started, and rather than try to guess my way through an investigation, I'd rather have two talking encyclopedias with me."

Acton looked at Laura, his eyes asking the question. She nodded. He grinned. "We'll join you as soon as we can."

"I'll have our jet readied and we'll be airborne as soon as possible," said Laura.

Our jet.

Acton had to admit he never got tired of hearing that. When he had begun to fall for Laura he had no idea she was rich, and it wasn't until she had been kidnapped that he had any inkling just how rich she was. And it wasn't until they were married and she had given him access to everything that he realized how incredibly rich she was. She wasn't a billionaire, but she was closer to it than from it. She was truly a one-percenter, and now by extension so was he, though the humble home they lived in certainly hid their wealth well.

Both of them were content to lead simple lives, with the money she inherited from her hi-tech entrepreneurial brother upon his accidental death at one of her dig sites they funded their own projects and traveled in comfort. But one of their greatest pleasures was helping less fortunate students with anonymous donations that would allow them to come on digs that they otherwise would have been forced to just hear about through their classmates' social media accounts.

That was what he loved most about the money. Helping the kids.

A close second though was traveling in style wherever and whenever they wanted, Laura part of some jet sharing company.

"Rest assured I'll be flying economy," grunted Reading.

Laura winked at Acton. "Why don't you wait for us and we'll swing by and pick you up."

There was a pause and Acton stifled his laugh as he pictured their friend debating on what to say.

"I'll see you in bloody Rome."

The call ended and Acton laughed, gently smacking Laura's bum as she rose.

"I'm just going to make a quick call to arrange the flight then I'll be back. Finish your dinner before it gets cold."

She left the room and Acton cut off a piece of his wellington, savoring the taste. He swallowed. "You know, I'm a damned good cook if I do say so myself."

"No argument here, but you should taste my KD. I put extra butter with whipping cream, makes all the difference."

"Sounds artery clogging."

"Hey, after you get shot in the back and almost die, you tend to look at things differently."

"What, like life is precious and you shouldn't be risking it?"

Milton gave Acton an are-you-kidding-me look. "Coming from you, that's pretty rich."

Acton shrugged. "Hey, it's not like I go *looking* for trouble."

"Nooo, you're just shit-magnet and attract it like flies."

"Gregory!"

"Sorry, hon." He turned back to Acton. "A *crap*-magnet."

"That's much better, dear."

Milton turned his head slightly away from his wife and gave Acton a toothy grin.

"Greg, I can see you in the hutch mirror."

"Shit."

"Keep digging."

Milton shook his head, his eyes bulging at Acton. "Save me," he hissed.

Laura entered the room, giving him the out he was searching for, Acton content to let him dig to Middle Earth.

"So, any luck?"

Laura nodded as she took her seat, placing her napkin on her lap. "All arranged. We leave at midnight, so that gives us time to finish our dinner and should put us in Rome for tomorrow afternoon with the time difference."

"Good," said Sandra, picking up her fork. "I'd hate to see all Jim's hard work go to waste."

Acton swallowed another bite. "Me neither. This stuff is almost as good as sex."

"James!"

Acton held up his hands in mock apology. "Hey, I said *almost*. Sex with you is definitely better."

He caught Mai's flushing cheeks out of the corner of his eye.

"Sorry, Mai. Eventually you'll get used to my sense of humor."

Milton grunted. "And when you do, you'll know you've truly become a heathen."

"Hey, I resent that," said Acton, jabbing the air with a speared piece of beef. "Who's jetting off into the great unknown to try and save the Blood Relics of the Son of God? Not just any heathen would do that."

He popped the meat in his mouth, chewing slowly.

Milton took the conversation to a more serious tone. "Why do you think they're stealing these things?"

Acton shrugged. "I'm guessing it has to do with the healing properties they're rumored to have."

This seemed to pique Mai's interest. "Healing properties?"

Acton nodded, swallowing. "Yes. The belief is that the blood of Jesus can heal. The most famous example is the Roman soldier"—he snapped his fingers as he tried to remember—"what's his name—"

"Longinus. *Saint* Longinus now." *Laura for the save!*

"Right, Longinus. His actual name was Cassius—"

"*That* you remember?" interrupted Milton.

"But for simplicity sake, most texts refer to him as Longinus, his baptized name." He shoveled some carrots into his mouth then took a sip of wine. "The story is that he stabbed Jesus in his side to make sure he was dead, and when he did so, blood and water poured out, some of it getting into his eyes. Did I mention he was blind?"

Mai shook her head.

"Yeah, according to the accounts he was either blind, or suffering some sort of affliction of the eyes. Some stories say he was blind in one eye, others say both, others say he just had an infection. Whatever the truth is, he was apparently cured right then and there, and from that point on became a believer."

"And the spear? You said it might not be the real one at the Vatican?"

Acton shrugged. "No one really knows. There're several places that claim to have the spear. Besides the one just stolen, there's one in Vienna and one in Armenia."

"And Antioch," added Laura.

"Why don't they test them to see if they're even from the same era?"

"Well, there's a few reasons, not the least of which is people don't really want to know. As long as it hasn't been proven fake, then they can claim it's real."

Laura gave him a chance to eat a few more bites. "The most famous example is the Shroud of Turin. Small pieces were given to scientists to carbon date and it was dated to at least a thousand years after Christ's death."

"But a lot of people dispute those results. Some say that parts of the cloth many not be original, instead patches added after the fact to repair damage over the centuries, others claim that carbon from a fire in medieval times actually contaminated the samples. And that's the problem. A negative when testing something like this doesn't really prove anything, but people think just because there was a scientific test that it's conclusive."

Mai's meal was forgotten. And so were her nerves. "But why would anyone sew in another piece of cloth when they knew how important it was?"

"Well, take King Tut's mask. You know, the famous blue and gold king cobra?"

"Yes, I've seen pictures."

"Well, just last year workers at the Egyptian Museum in Cairo broke off the beard and rather than tell anyone, they just glued it back on. That glue is now causing damage to the mask."

"Unbelievable!"

"We see it all the time, unfortunately." Laura put her fork down, her meal finished. "Many times we find artifacts or structures that we now consider priceless, but during the centuries or millennia were just things handed down over time. Imagine you have an antique table handed down through the generations. If something were to happen to it, you would fix it. In some cases, you might need to even replace a piece, let's say one of the legs. Because it's precious to you, you would insist the work is done properly so you could never tell that the leg had been replaced. Sometimes this even involves artificially aging the wood or stone. Now imagine five hundred years from now somebody finds that table and wants to carbon date it. If they take a portion from the replaced leg, they'll find out it was only five hundred years old instead of the actual seven hundred years. This is why the dating might be a science, but the selection of what to date can sometimes be an art."

"They actually broke the beard off of King Tut?" asked Sandra. "That's incredible! How'd they find out?"

Acton pushed his plate away, finished. "Somebody noticed a ring of glue oozing out in a photograph."

"So back to the original question of why," interjected Milton. "Do you think someone could really be after these things for their healing properties?"

Acton pursed his lips, leaning back in his chair, swirling his wine. He sighed. "I can't think of any other reason. There's so many other priceless artifacts kept with the two that were stolen, you'd have to think they'd have taken them as well if money were the motive."

"My God!" said Sandra. "Do you think it could actually work?" Her hand darted to her husband's arm. "Do you think they might try to clone *him*?"

Acton's chest tightened slightly as a shot of nervous adrenaline shot through his system at the thought. "I-I don't know." He looked at his wife, memories of The Vault, a hidden chamber under The Vatican known to almost no one, momentarily overwhelming him. "Are we getting ourselves into something that we shouldn't be? Something bigger than us?"

Laura seemed to pale slightly.

"Maybe you two shouldn't get involved."

Acton looked at his friend and shook his head. "No, Hugh's expecting us. And if this is some type of cloning effort, it needs to be stopped."

"But why?"

Everyone turned to Mai who withered from the attention.

"What do you mean?" asked Laura, gently.

"Well, isn't your entire religion focused on the second coming of Christ? Maybe this is how it was meant to happen?"

Acton paused for a moment as he contemplated her words. They were a simple truth spoken by a Buddhist with no vested interest in something she didn't believe in, which made her words all the more poignant. Could that be what this was all about? Some religious zealot trying to get a sample of DNA that they would then use to create a new baby Jesus?

It was a fantastically terrifying idea, something he hoped no one would actually be foolish enough to try and do. All you would be doing was creating the body, and though he wasn't terribly religious by any stretch of the imagination, even his own basic understanding told him it was the Holy Spirit that was actually the Son of God, not the flesh and blood that had walked the Earth.

He looked at Laura.

"I think we focus on the job."

She nodded. "Agreed. We help Hugh stop the murderers and thieves and use their motives against them. We'll leave the ethical and metaphysical debate to others."

Acton sucked in a deep breath, grimacing.

That could be easier said than done.

Golgatha, Judea
April 7th, 30 AD
Approaching the Twelfth Hour

"Are you okay?"

He felt Albus' hand on his shoulder, shaking him as tears filled his eyes at the sight of the man hanging above him, dead, water and blood still flowing out of the hole he had made only moments before, it now a trickle but still inexplicable. Turning toward his friend, he looked at him and smiled.

"I can see."

Albus' jaw dropped, a jaw he hadn't seen clearly in years, the expression on his face one of pure shock. Shock he could discern with ease once again. The idea of seeing again was something that had never occurred to him. His thoughts on it had always been one of hoping that the shadows he could make out would continue to at least be discernable, it giving him at least some warning of something coming at him.

But to see again?

Never in a lifetime could he have imagined something so wonderful.

His friend let go of his shoulder, dropping to his knees in front of him, looking at him skeptically. He held up two fingers. "How many fingers am I holding up?"

"Two. And your hair is much grayer than I remember."

A smile broke out on Albus' face as he grasped him by both shoulders, shaking him in excitement. "You *can* see! It's a miracle!"

They both looked up at the man, slumped on the cross high on the hilltop, the two other men on either side in their last gasps of life, their knees broken, their chests heaving as their lungs, straining to provide precious air, slowly failed as their bodies finally gave in to the inevitable.

But he didn't care.

They were criminals.

But not *this* man. He pushed himself to his feet, feeling remarkably well, though he was sure it was the rush of the moment, the excitement fueling his weary bones. Twenty-five years in the Roman Army didn't leave the body in good shape, his body still beaten but his soul replenished, he now feeling a vigor he hadn't since he was a boy.

Life was worth living again.

He stepped toward the cross, raising a hand and touching the foot of the man he had listened to for almost six hours, a man who was clearly everything he had said he was.

He turned as the mourners approached and smiled.

"He truly is the son of God."

"He's my son."

The broken lady collapsed to her knees, several of the women, and the man who he assumed was the one Jesus had spoken of as her son earlier, rushed to her side.

"I was blind and now can see."

"Even in death he saves," said a younger woman, taking his hand and squeezing. "Now you see don't you? Now you see he was an innocent man, a man who hurt no one, and in his final moments granted comfort to those around him, and sight to one who would see him dead."

Longinus felt a vicelike grip take hold of his chest, the excuse of only following orders seeming a weak one, but it was all he had.

He decided to leave it unspoken, the woman not appearing to hold him any ill will.

"Is it true?" Longinus turned to see the other soldiers he had been waiting with surrounding him. "You can see us?"

He nodded, smiling. "As good as the day I was born."

"Unbelievable!"

"It *is* unbelievable. Either you were lying before, or you're lying now."

Longinus frowned at Severus, a hateful man if there ever was one. He had known him for over a decade and he was liked by few, hated by many.

"You sneer at me while accusing me of being a liar?"

Severus' eyes flared for a moment, as if shocked his facial expression had been seen.

"I can see now, plainly." He looked at the four men, Albus standing at his side, ready to remove Severus' head for having falsely accusing his friend. "You, Severus, have a patch over your eye, Tiberius a cut on your knee and Marcus, you remain as ugly as I remember you. No, uglier."

Marcus roared with laughter, grabbing him and hugging him, his hands thumping on Longinus' back. "You *can* see! It's amazing!" He felt the hands of the others slapping him with joy as he let go of Marcus, looking at Severus.

Severus' head was slowly shaking. "I don't believe, but I must. You've been blind for years. No one would fake that for so long and stay in the army. You'd slip up at least once, someone would catch you, but…"

Longinus put a hand on Severus' shoulder. "It *is* a miracle." He turned and pointed at Jesus. "Performed by him."

Severus dropped to his knees, clasping his hands against his chest. "What have we done?" he cried. "If he can do this, if he can give a man back his sight, then he must be what they say he is! His god will surely destroy us now! We're condemned to burn in Hades for eternity!"

"No, you are mistaken."

It was the mother who spoke, putting a comforting hand on Severus. "Our God is a god of love and compassion, my son taught us that."

"Join us, let us teach you his ways," said the younger woman.

Longinus' head bobbed slowly as he realized his life had new meaning and a new purpose. He had been given a second chance, a chance to live again a whole man, unencumbered by an illness beyond his control, with all his faculties and abilities restored.

And they would be needed.

For he was now determined to spread the word that this man truly had been what he had said he was.

The son of God.

And no one could sway him from that opinion.

"We must remove the bodies," said Severus. "Our orders are to have this cleared away before Passover begins which is soon." He pointed at the two criminals, none of whom had family or friends present. "They'll be dead soon." He nodded toward Jesus. "Let's get him down first."

"I'll do it," said the man identified as the son.

Longinus took him by the arm. "What is your name?"

"John."

"You knew this man well?"

"He was my teacher. My rabbi. My friend."

Longinus looked up at this teacher, seeing the crown of thorns for the first time, rivulets of blood now dried on the poor soul's face from where the skin had been torn by the barbarians that had committed this tragic joke. He wanted to be enraged by this, to lash out at those responsible, his own fellow soldiers, but he couldn't, he couldn't summon the anger.

Instead he felt an overwhelming sense of contentment that seemed determined to compete with the sorrow he was feeling.

He dropped to his knees, beating his chest as he stared up at the body of this great man.

"I pledge my life to your good name."

And as he prayed to this new god, Albus and the others joined him, their swords and spears discarded as they united with him in prayer, it evident they were as affected as him by these turn of events. The shaking of the earth and skies had made it clear that this man was indeed powerful, but the miracle performed just with the touch of his blood was undeniable.

He was a force for good.

The blood!

He looked down at the large pool of blood at the base of the cross, it captured in a natural indentation of the stone, and wondered if it should be collected.

How many could be cured by this?

As if reading his mind, the loved ones of Jesus began to collect this precious fluid, transferring it into several jars, mopping up what remained with cloths.

Imagine the good that could come of this!

BLOOD RELICS

Imperial Treasury, Hofburg Palace, Vienna, Austria
Present Day, One day before the Paris assault

Dietrich Kruger strode toward the front entrance of the massive Hofburg Palace, its stark white façade now a gentle gold, the strategically placed lighting emphasizing its spectacular architectural elements. A steady flow of tourists walked past him, their visit finished, only a few late arrivals climbing the stairs to the entrance with him.

He winced, a stabbing pain shooting up his leg forcing him to stop in his tracks. He massaged the pain out with a few quick squeezes, forcing himself forward.

It's only going to get worse.

When he had felt the pain the first time it had terrified him, his father and grandfather before him suffering from the same affliction he now faced. In fact, if his grandfather were to be believed, his family had been suffering this affliction for at least six generations, it killing them all before their time, and striking them down in the prime of their lives, relegated to the sidelines of life as their bodies slowly withered.

It was the Kruger family curse.

He had known his fate his entire life, his family never hiding the truth from him. It had allowed him to live life to the fullest in his first thirty years on this Earth with the knowledge the last thirty, or much less, would most likely be lived in unproductive misery.

But six generations of hopelessness had changed as technology rapidly advanced. His father was convinced that eventually a cure might be found, though too late for him. But it wasn't a scientific cure he had become hell bent on acquiring.

It was the miraculous.

His family had long known of the Blood Relics, but there was nothing they could do about them, there no way to get their hands on them, nor to conceivably get any blood from them.

But modern technology had changed all that.

It was now possible to retrieve DNA from samples many thousands of years old, and his father was now convinced that if they could acquire the true blood of Christ, they'd be able to replicate it in a lab, enough that it might be used as a cure for their affliction.

He had to admit he had been skeptical at first, and still was to a point, but the fervent ardor exhibited by his father whenever they discussed it was infectious, and when his father had taken a turn for the worse, he had rushed into action, using some of the many millions built up over generations to put together a team of mercenaries that would acquire every last Blood Relic known to man should it become necessary.

No matter who stood in their way.

As he cleared through security, his father's words echoed in his mind.

We mustn't become sinners in our quest for salvation.

Dietrich had never been much of a religious man though he did believe in God and an afterlife—he had to, living his entire life knowing he was going to die lonely and in pain. It gave him hope that the miserable existence he had during life was but a mere fraction of his overall existence, that there was some reward for all his suffering, his family's suffering, when it was all finally over.

Another shooting pain caused him to gasp.

"Are you okay?"

He looked at the young ticket agent as he handed over his 11.50 in euros. "Fine, just an old football injury."

She smiled, looking at his chiseled features then down at his left hand as he accepted the ticket. He swore he saw a note of disappointment at the sight of his wedding ring. He smiled at her then turned left, walking with purpose toward the reason he was here. Silently praying, he used his peripheral vision to take in the guards patrolling as unobtrusively as they could, most of the tourists probably paying them little mind, but to him, they were of primary concern.

He didn't want a repeat of what happened in Spain.

His father had been outraged, and he himself devastated. He had never thought he'd kill someone, but the priest had charged at him and he had panicked. The Vatican operation had gone quite smoothly and according to plan, nobody killed, nobody even injured.

But you weren't there.

Tonight he hoped would be uneventful. His father had given orders that if it looked like someone might get hurt, they should abort, but with his father's rapid degeneration over the past twenty-four hours he had decided those orders might very well need to be ignored.

He wasn't going to let his father die just to protect strangers who by the very nature of their work knew they might be hurt or killed in the line of duty.

Though he had no plans to go out of his way to kill them.

He spotted one of his men out of the corner of his eye, three of them already inside to assist in the mission, several outside to provide cover should things go awry. The man walked past, bumping into him.

"Excuse me," the man muttered, continuing on, leaving behind the distinctly heavy weight of something in his pocket. He slipped his hand inside and felt the cool metal of a handgun, a handgun smuggled in a week ago by his men under the guise of a maintenance crew.

He suddenly felt much more confident.

He rounded the corner and entered a smaller room, hardwood floors contrasting with burgundy walls, half a dozen lit display cases ringing the room. Even the bejeweled crown to his left, priceless by any measure, couldn't distract him, his eyes immediately drawn to the display case one of his men had surveilled a week ago in preparation for the mission.

His pulse quickened.

The center of the case contained a large gold and jewel encrusted cross, standing erect, to its right a smaller less ornate cross lying flat on red velvet. He ignored them. To the left was what he was after, the metal tip of a Roman spear, about a third of it wrapped in gold at the center by someone lost to history, the simple Roman soldier purported to have wielded it far too poor for such ornate trappings.

But this was the second such spear he had been tasked to retrieve. And it wouldn't be the last. His mission was to retrieve *anything* that might have the blood of Christ on it, even if its pedigree was suspect.

They could take no chances.

"Excuse me, can you show me where the bathrooms are?"

He looked slightly to his right and saw one of his men talking to the only museum staff member in the room. The woman nodded, following him out the door, the room now empty, the tourists gone.

He pulled a diamond tipped glass cutter from his pocket, pushing the suction cup in place, quickly circling the arm containing the incredibly sharp tip several times, the glass quickly cut through.

He pulled the glass free then reached inside, picking up the artifact almost reverently.

An alarm sounded immediately as a pressure sensor was tripped, ending his momentary lapse. He yanked his hand and the relic free of the glass, walking swiftly toward the door, one of his men walking by just as he arrived. He dropped the spearhead inside a bag the man held open just as a security guard arrived.

Dietrich pointed in the opposite direction as his man quickly walked away. "I saw a man run that way," he said, the guard and several new arrivals immediately rushing in the direction he had indicated. Heading for the entrance, he caught sight of his man approaching the doors just as they were sealed shut by security.

No matter.

He pulled the Beretta from an inside pocket, placing it against the head of a young female tourist. "Open the doors now or she dies!"

Screams erupted as the few remaining tourists bolted in every direction, security running toward the scene, those with guns drawing them.

He didn't care.

Wrapping an arm around the woman and dragging her toward the doors, he repeated his demand.

No one complied.

He nodded toward one of his men who pulled a weapon, grabbing a female tour guide cowering in the corner.

"Nobody has to die here today! But if you don't open the doors in thirty seconds, she dies!" He pressed the gun against his hostage's temple harder. "If anyone gets any closer, she dies." The guards inching forward froze, but the doors remained locked. He raised his gun and fired into the ceiling, plaster raining down on them, a fine mist of dust slowly wafting its way to the marble floor. "Now!"

"Open the doors!" shouted someone and he heard a buzzing sound behind them, the red lights over the doors turning green. One of his men pushed on the door and it opened. He slowly backed toward it, the gun back against the woman's head. He cleared the doors as the guards slowly moved forward, their weapons still pointing at him. Firing two shots at the ground, he let go of the woman, rushing down the stairs and jumping into the waiting car with the others, the tires already squealing as the driver floored it, sending them careening toward the exit and the traffic maze that was Vienna.

Taking a sharp right they blasted past several police cars obviously responding to the emergency call at the museum. Dietrich turned in his seat and cursed as they locked up their brakes, pulling one-eighties as they began their pursuit. His driver took another hard right into an alley and came to a screeching halt, all of them jumping out as one of their outside men beckoned them, a manhole cover lifted from the street. Dietrich climbed into the hole, quickly sliding down the metal ladder as the others followed, the cover replaced overhead as he hit the bottom with a splash.

Sprinting forward, he rounded a bend in the storm drain and smiled.

Six dirt bikes were waiting as promised.

He jumped on the lead bike, kick starting the engine and activating the specially programmed GPS. He gunned the motor, the front tire lifting slightly as he sped away from the access point, the other engines roaring to life behind him.

As he climbed the curved walls while taking a bend to the left, he smiled knowing one more relic had been retrieved, and nobody had been hurt.

I'll save you yet, father.

The Temple Mount, Jerusalem, Judea
April 10th, 30 AD

"His body was clearly stolen."

Longinus looked at the rabbi, the man's withering stare intimidating, one of the negatives of having his eyesight returned being the effect of such things—especially now accustomed to merely hearing someone's displeasure rather than seeing it as well.

Sweat dripped down his back, his segmented armor hot as he, Albus, Severus and a young soldier named Tiberius, all guarding the tomb of Jesus earlier, stood at attention in front of their commander and several Jewish leaders.

"Surely you must realize that this insane notion being spread by his followers of resurrection is blasphemous lunacy!"

Nobody said anything, lowly soldiers never speaking unless asked a direct question.

And this didn't count.

"None of you have anything to say for yourselves? A tomb you are sent to guard is opened and the body stolen under your very noses?"

Again no one said anything, for they all knew the truth.

The earth had shaken once again and the stone had rolled away, a spirit of some sort appearing, proclaiming the resurrection. It had been terrifying, and even he had run away with the others in fear. One of them had reported the events and they had all been summoned, questioned for hours once the tomb had been confirmed empty.

The rabbi snapped his fingers and out of the shadows several men appeared carrying cloth covered trays, each containing what appeared to be generously filled purses. The rabbi picked up one of the purses, the tinkle of coins inside music to many a poor soldier's ears. He stepped in front of young Tiberius, taking his hand and dropping the heavy sum in his palm, closing the man's fingers over the cloth.

He took another purse, then another, moving down the line, all the while explaining the price of this reward. "You are to say, 'His disciples came by night and stole him away while we were asleep.' And if this should come to the governor's ears, we will win him over and keep you out of trouble."

The rabbi stepped in front of Longinus, turning to take the final purse from the final tray. He reached for his hand but Longinus, the spear he had pierced the body of Jesus with gripped tightly in one hand, clasped his free one behind his back, shaking his head.

"I will not lie."

The rabbi's eyebrows rose slightly, his friends shifting slightly, clearly uncomfortable.

"You want more?"

Longinus shook his head, firmly. "There isn't enough silver or gold in the Empire to make me lie about the miracle I witnessed today. I was blind and now can see. That cannot be denied. You murdered the son of God, the messiah you have all been waiting for, and now you want to cover up your mistake." Longinus squared his shoulders. "I will have no part in it."

The rabbi returned the purse to the tray.

"Very well." He leaned in, lowering his voice. "But the truth often comes with a heavy price."

Professor James Acton beamed a smile at his good friend Interpol Agent Hugh Reading as he descended the steps of the Gulf V private jet chartered by his wife. Reading was standing beside the Vatican Inspector General, Mario Giasson, a man he had come to know quite well when the Vatican had been overrun by Muslim protesters. He had little contact with the man outside of the Vatican events, though he knew he was a family man and reliable under fire.

Reading on the other hand he knew quite well.

They gave each other a thumping hug.

"How ya doin'?"

Reading exchanged a hug and cheek kisses with Laura as Acton shook Giasson's hand.

"A little tired, but I'm out of the office so that's always good."

Acton knew his friend had mixed feelings about his new job. After the events that led to their meeting, he had become too public to stay at New Scotland Yard as a detective so he had taken a job at Interpol instead, giving up murder investigations for international police investigations.

Which involved too much "bloody" paperwork for his liking.

But thanks to a few incidents over the past several years, Reading had definitely seen his share of action. Acton and his wife seemed to have a knack for getting into trouble, and Reading too often found himself either along for the ride, or riding in to the rescue.

It was nice for a change to be coming to help him, though Acton had a nasty feeling gunfire was in his future.

Laura climbed into the limo first, the men following. "So what's the latest?" asked Laura as they settled in.

Reading frowned. "They raided a museum in Vienna just a few minutes ago."

"Let me guess, the Holy Lance kept in the Imperial Treasury?"

Giasson nodded. "We've put out a warning to all of the museums and churches that have Blood Relics, but unfortunately the focus is on terrorism right now and religious icons aren't a high priority for the police, especially considering the circumstances."

Laura leaned into Acton's shoulder as they took a turn. "What do you mean?"

"Well, the theft at the Vatican involved four men on the ground and at least three in the helicopter."

"Which means they're well equipped with a lot of money behind them," added Reading.

"And the theft in Austria apparently involved at least four inside plus a getaway car and dirt bikes placed ahead of time in the sewer system. They just found those before we left to pick you up."

"So no sign of them." Acton chewed his cheek. "Surely there's security footage from Hapsburg?"

Reading nodded. "It's being pulled now."

Laura brought them back to the original question. "You were saying that the police weren't being overly cooperative?"

"It's not necessarily that they're not being cooperative, it's that they just can't afford the resources. If we're talking a team of half a dozen well-armed men, putting one or two officers at a church is almost useless. Reckless even. Really you need to station at least half a dozen at each of these locations, otherwise they're little better than lookouts. Or targets."

"So you don't think it would deter them?"

Giasson shook his head. "We have over one hundred armed men at the Vatican and that didn't deter them."

Acton crossed his leg, Laura putting her hand on his knee. "So we don't know who they are or what their motivation is."

"I have a feeling your theory is right," replied Reading.

"That someone is trying to get their hands on the blood of Christ for its healing properties?"

Reading nodded. "Basically we've got a religious nutter out there willing to kill because of a fairytale."

Giasson cleared his throat. "That *fairytale* as you call it is believed by over two billion people."

Reading blushed, Acton smiling as his friend went into backpedal mode. "I didn't mean the whole Jesus thing, I just meant the blood curing the guy's blindness. That's not actually in the bible, is it?"

"No," agreed Giasson. "In the Gospel According to John there is reference to a soldier piercing the side of Jesus, but there's no mention of him by name, or of his sight being restored."

Acton leaned forward. "But in later accounts, he *is* included. If you read the Biblical Apocrypha you'll find mention of him by name, and in other texts that were rejected as not canon the miracle is referred to. The problem with that era is if a text contradicted the Gospels in any way, it was rejected, even if the other ninety percent agreed. This excluded many accounts of the events surrounding Jesus that might very well be true."

"Assuming any of it's true," said Reading, immediately holding out his hand to stop Giasson. "I know, I know, billions believe. I'm not saying I don't believe, but wouldn't it be nice to have proof?"

"Proof of the miracle or even the resurrection is impossible," replied Giasson. "Even if you had a dozen firsthand accounts, they'd all be dismissed as simply stories."

"True," agreed Acton. "I think however there is plenty of evidence to prove, or at least strongly support, His actual existence. You can ignore the Bible if you want, but it is actually considered an historical text, most of the New Testament written within a century of Jesus' death. And there are dozens upon dozens of other texts that weren't included in the New Testament like I mentioned. But if you want to dismiss it as a creative writing project, then simply read the Roman historians of the era. Everyone from Flavius Josephus to Pliny the Younger refer to Him and to His followers."

"It all had to come from somewhere," said Giasson. "Whether you believe He was the Son of God or not is a matter of faith. To deny His existence entirely I think is simply wishful thinking on the part of those who are so anti-religious they blame it for all that ails them and the world."

Reading raised his hands in defeat. "I'm sorry, you're right. I've never been much of a churchgoer or a believer. When you've been in war like I have, when you've seen what one man can do to another, you can be forgiven for wondering how any god could allow it to happen."

"Perhaps the best thing any god could do would be to let men fail individually so that man can learn collectively from their mistakes."

Acton squeezed his wife's hand, her words as usual inspiring. "This entire discussion is irrelevant. We've got someone who obviously believes in the healing properties stealing these artifacts and killing if necessary—"

"Though I hardly see how killing an elderly priest was necessary," interjected Laura.

"Agreed. Even if you identify who they might be from the security footage that doesn't mean you'll catch them. Not only do we need to stop them from steeling additional relics, we need to recover what was stolen."

"I have a feeling the security footage won't lead anywhere," said Reading. "They didn't seem to be too concerned about having their faces on camera."

"Does that suggest anything to you?" asked Giasson.

"That either they're so well known that it doesn't matter—they haven't been caught yet, so why would that change? Or they're completely new and only intend to be active for a short period of time before disappearing underground."

"Or, they're so well protected, even if we caught them it wouldn't matter."

Reading grunted at Acton's suggestion. "It wouldn't be the first time. And if it weren't for the murder, the entire thing could get swept under the rug if it were some billionaire's son getting his kicks. But as it is…"

"Well, I think our course of action is clear," said Acton as they pulled through the gates of The Vatican.

"What's that?" asked Giasson.

Laura smiled. "We go to the one place irresistible to any Blood Relic hunter."

Reading's eyebrows slowly climbed his forehead. "Where's that?"

Acton and Laura answered in unison.

"Paris."

Roman Barracks, Jerusalem, Judea
April 10th, 30 AD

"Longinus!"

Longinus turned to see his commander, Vitus, enter the barracks. He looked concerned, almost scared. "What is it?"

Vitus stepped inside, looking around to see who might be listening. Albus rose from his bunk, as did the others who had been witness to the resurrection, they having spent most of their off-duty hours together, talking of the miracles they had witnessed.

"They've ordered your death!" hissed Vitus.

"Who?" asked Albus, standing beside Longinus, placing a protective hand on his friend's shoulder.

"The rabbis! I don't know what you did, but you have to get out of here, now!"

Longinus' eyes opened wide in surprise. "Desert?"

Albus gasped. "Desertion means the death penalty if he's ever caught!"

"He's dead if he stays here," replied Vitus. He looked over his shoulder, leaning into the tight group of soldiers. "If anyone asks, I sent you on a forced march outside the city walls. Punishment for insubordination. No one will miss you until tomorrow."

"I'm going with you," said Albus.

"And I!" echoed the others.

Vitus frowned, but nodded. "I understand. But you must go *now*." He held out his hand and Longinus grabbed his forearm, squeezing tightly. "Good luck, and may I never see any of you again."

"Thank you, my friend."

Vitus gave a final squeeze then let go, turning on his heel and leaving the barracks. Albus looked at his friend. "Where will we go?"

"I have an idea on that," replied Longinus as he began to put on his armor. "We know where his family is staying. I say we find them and seek their help. They did ask us to join them."

"That's right," said Severus. "And he had thousands of followers. Maybe some of them can help us."

"It's our only hope." Longinus helped Albus with his armor. "We'll join the followers of this teacher and learn his ways."

He grabbed his spear, eyeing the still bloodstained tip.

"Let's go before they come for us and it's too late."

They stepped out into the fading sunlight, quickly forming ranks and marching toward the gates. Taunts from the guards greeted them, Vitus obviously having informed them of their "punishment".

"Enjoy your march, ladies!"

"Don't stay out too late, boys!"

They ignored them, keeping character, just four men scared to do anything else that might piss off their commander, intent on completing their punishment and moving on with their tours of duty.

They cleared the garrison gates and turned left, toward the gates of the city itself, their double-time march harsh in the unforgiving armor, the sunbaked ground under their feet still giving up the heat gained during the day, relief not yet making itself felt. As they exited the city they turned toward Golgatha, knowing that behind its mound prying eyes would be few, hopefully none.

They also knew it was where some of the followers of Jesus had gathered to mourn his death.

Imagine their joy in hearing the news of his resurrection!

He looked at the tip of his spear, jutting out in front of him then at his side with each stride, the bloodstain still visible. It had clearly been this man's blood that had cured his blindness, and he couldn't help but wonder how powerful this wondrous gift might be. Could it heal all wounds? Could it prevent death, or reverse it completely?

Would a wound created by the tip of this spear simply heal itself?

It was an interesting question, one he pondered as their grueling march continued, the sun slowly setting in the west as a chill began to settle on the harsh desert landscape. The very idea of a weapon that couldn't kill was a fascinating concept, and almost maddening, the images of stabbing enemy after enemy, to have them only rise from the dead and continue attacking, disturbing.

He shivered.

And vowed from that moment on he would never harm another living soul.

Kruger Residence, Outside Paris, France
Present Day, One day before the Paris assault

"Father!"

Dietrich Kruger rushed to his father's bedside, his mouth agape with shock. His father hadn't looked well in years, so long in fact that Dietrich had to rely on old photographs to imagine what his father *should* look like, but today he looked as if he had aged another ten years since he had seen him last.

A thin, boney hand reached out for him. "Son."

Dietrich sat on his father's bedside, holding his hand. "How are you feeling?"

"Like shit, how do you think I feel?" A thin smile inched across the man's face.

"At least you haven't lost your sense of humor."

A coughed laugh erupted and Dietrich out of habit reached for the glass of water sitting on the bedside table. He waited for his father to take a drink through the articulated straw.

"Our latest mission was successful," said Dietrich, returning the glass to the table. "We retrieved the lance from Vienna."

"And you've given it to the lab?"

Dietrich nodded, using his finger to push a tuft of thinning gray hair out of his father's eyes. "Dr. Heinrich said he'll begin testing immediately, but I'm not confident with this one."

"Neither am I. And the shroud from Spain?"

"It tested negative. No blood at all."

"And the Vatican?"

71

"The results aren't back yet, but they never claimed it was genuine."

"I fear we have little choice."

Dietrich nodded, frowning at his father's words. "I think you're right." The mother lode, if it could be called that, was at the Notre-Dame Cathedral. It contained what was purported to be the actual Crown of Thorns worn by Jesus, a piece of the original crucifix, and one of the nails used on the cross itself. It was also rumored to have a jar containing a sponge used to quench Christ's thirst.

A knot formed in his stomach.

"You must be careful," said his father. "It will be well guarded."

"Casualties may be necessary."

His father shook his head. "No one should die for me. *No one.*" Dietrich felt his hand squeezed. "Have you prayed for forgiveness?"

Dietrich nodded, his eyes clouding slightly as his chest tightened. "Every moment since. I never meant to kill the old man. If only he hadn't tried to jump me…"

His father patted his hand. "I know you didn't mean to, but we must be careful. If something goes wrong, just get out of there. We'll find another way."

"But you can't die, Father. If there's a way to save you, then I have to do whatever it takes."

"I've known I would die from this disease my entire life. If I die, then perhaps it will be your generation, or that of your son, that will be the one to put an end to this curse."

"But father!"

"But nothing. My life is worth no more than any other, and I won't see people dying to save me." A wry grin broke out on his face, a little bit of strength having returned to his voice, a hint of color in his cheeks. "But a little grand theft is perfectly okay."

He winked and Dietrich laughed as his mother entered the room.

"So you're back," she said as she perched on the other side of the bed, giving her husband a kiss on the forehead. "I understand it was successful."

Dietrich nodded. "A little excitement, but nobody was hurt and we retrieved the relic."

"Good work." She patted her husband's shoulder. "We'll get you well soon enough."

His father reached over and clasped his hand over hers, the love in his eyes obvious. "Ever the optimist, this one."

Dietrich smiled at the two of them, his love for both of them almost overwhelming. For her to have stuck by his side through everything, for her to have even agreed to marry him when she had been told of the disease that would eventually cripple then kill him, was remarkable. In an age when people left each other over the ever popular irreconcilable differences, when infidelity was a matter of pride in some communities, to see two people, together for over thirty years still deeply in love was inspirational.

He only hoped he and his wife Andrea would be so in love when his own body was so ravaged. A shot of pain in his leg caused him to wince, then a wave of self-pity suddenly overwhelmed him, his stomach tying itself into knots as he turned away so his parents couldn't see his face.

"It's begun, hasn't it?"

He nodded, unable to face his father.

"I was your age when I felt the first hints of what was to come."

His mother's arms wrapped around him. "I'm so sorry, dear."

It only made it worse.

"I'm going to go see Andrea and Hans." He rose, his mother's arms falling away. "I'll see you before I leave for Paris."

"Has it come to that?" asked his mother.

"It's our best hope." He wiped his eyes then turned to his mother. "Perhaps our only hope."

His father shook his head. "No, there's one other. But I fear it may be lost to history."

North of Jerusalem, Judea
April 13th, 30 AD

The sounds of joy seemed distant to Longinus as he felt the cool water rush around him, the pressure of the deep breath he was holding forgotten in the ecstasy of the moment. His entire body was submerged now, his racing heart pounding in his ears as he felt the strong hands of the disciple named Peter supporting him.

Suddenly he was lifted from the water, the rush of sounds around him almost overwhelming as water and tears streamed down his face, those gathered around him clapping and cheering the shared excitement of the moment. Peter's words were lost on him as he blinked the water out of his eyes, suddenly bear-hugged by Albus, his feet lifted from the water as his friend leaned back. He had been last to be baptized, insisting his friends who had joined him go first so that they may rejoice in the overwhelming happiness he himself was already feeling. In his mind he was already baptized by the blood and water of Jesus himself, but when Peter and the others gathered had suggested it, all four of them had jumped at the opportunity, their desire to be closer to God and his Son irresistible.

He stepped to the shore, helped by the others, his robes heavy and dripping from the water, but he didn't care. This was a joyous occasion in which the troubles of the past few weeks were forgotten. They had hidden with some of the followers of Jesus, shedding their armor and donning the clothes of peasants, hiding in the homes and camps of followers while the family and disciples of Jesus left to visit with the resurrected rabbi.

He had longed to see the man, to thank him, but knew this privilege of reunification should be reserved for those closest to him.

The man had done enough.

He had saved him.

And now he was determined to spread his word.

Should he survive.

The rabbis of Jerusalem had issued an unofficial warrant for him, for they had no power over a Roman soldier. The whispered word was that they wanted his head delivered to them, on a platter.

He was sure they'd settle for his guaranteed silence on what he had testified to that day in the synagogue.

Word was spreading about the crucifixion of this innocent man and the miracle of his resurrection, but so too was the lie that his body had merely been stolen. Those who had witnessed the miracles were unwavering in their belief, and their steadfastness was inspiring others to the cause, today there a long line of people awaiting their own chance at baptism by one of the closest friends of the Messiah.

He took a seat on a large rock, lying back and letting the midday sun beat down on him, drying his skin and clothes as the celebrations continued around him. As he lay there, the wide smile slowly began to wane as the reality of his situation made its presence known once again.

He was in danger.

But that was of no concern to him. If he died today, he would die content, without fear for he now knew what awaited him. He had led a basically good life and any of his transgressions had been forgiven when Jesus had given up his spirit and performed this one last miracle, restoring the sight to an aging man.

"Something vexes you."

Longinus opened his eyes and shaded them from the sun with a hand. John—the *new* son of the Messiah's mother, Mary—stood in front of him. He frowned. "I'm a danger to you all."

"We're all a danger to each other, that is the very nature of our existence. The word of our Lord is perceived as dangerous to those who would rule over us, whether they be the rabbis who ignore the proof that he is the prophesized one, or the Romans who would merely oppress us to feed their evil empire. The life of a follower of the word of our teacher isn't an easy one, nor should it be chosen lightly." He paused. "I thought you of all people would know that. Do you regret what you have done here today?"

Longinus felt a flutter in his stomach at John's words. He pushed himself up to a seated position, shaking his head vehemently. "No! Not at all! I wouldn't change a single thing I've done since that day, but it is *I* that is specifically hunted by name." He stood, looking at the gathered throng, still rejoicing in the events unfolding. "Should they come for me and find you with me, you all may be arrested…or worse." He sighed, placing a hand on John's shoulder. "I fear I must leave you all."

Albus walked up to them, concern on his face. "What's wrong?"

It was John that replied. "He's leaving us."

Though Longinus hadn't quite said the words, it was clear John agreed with the sentiment and knew his mind was already made up. It was time to leave these good people so they might be safe. Their lives would be hard enough without him adding to their troubles.

"But why! You're one of us, *we're* now one of them! Why would you turn your back on them?"

Longinus placed his free hand on Albus' shoulder, smiling. "It is *because* I am one of them that I must leave. I believe so much in what they are trying to do, that I have to leave so they aren't stopped by those searching for me." He let go of both men and picked up his spear lying beside the stone that had been his resting place.

"You are mistaken in what you say," replied Albus, his hand covering Longinus' grip on the spear. "*We* must leave. The four of us are deserters and the entire Roman Army is looking for us." Albus waved for the other two to join them. "We will leave together and die together should it be necessary."

Longinus nodded, joy filling his heart that his friends would be with him on the long journey ahead.

For he could think of only one place to go.

Home.

Notre-Dame Cathedral, Paris, France
Present Day, Day of the Paris assault

"They don't seem to be taking the threat seriously."

Reading nodded as they strode down the center of the massive Notre-Dame Cathedral in Paris. Its first stone laid in 1163, it was built over centuries, handcrafted in stages resulting in a breathtaking combination of architecture and artistry that Acton found himself never tiring of. He had been here several times before, making it a point to try to see it every time he was in Paris, but Laura had seen it on many occasions, Paris just a few hours by train from London.

He had been fortunate enough to be shown the Treasury on his last visit and was eager to see it again, the relics contained within breathtaking in their beauty and opulence, not to mention their historical significance.

Which was why he was surprised to have only seen a single police officer outside and none inside.

"You'd think with all the terrorist activity here lately they'd take a threat like this more seriously," observed Laura.

Reading grunted. "If this were terrorism, I have no doubt they would. But this isn't and they've got their hands full."

Just as 9/11 had changed American views overnight, so had the terrorist attacks in Paris affected the psyche of the people of France. Heightened security had been very evident on the streets of Paris as they made their way here, but Parisians seemed to be trying to move on with their lives, thumbing their noses at those who would have them cower in fear.

Acton knew Reading was right, the theft of Blood Relics wasn't terrorism, but to him any threat against archeological sites or artifacts *was* an act of terrorism, an attack on history, on culture, on humanity's past. The fact an officer was outside at least suggested that the French weren't completely ignoring the threat, and the young man had indicated his boss was inside, meaning at least two officers were assigned.

His mind drifted to the solidarity rally he and Laura had attended in Trafalgar Square while packing up some of her personal effects from her apartment in London. They had watched on the BBC the events of that horrible day unfold live for the world to see, the heart wrenching terror in the eyes of Parisians as they heard the news, terrified with the knowledge that the terrorists were still on the loose, their massacre of twelve at the Charlie Hebdo offices only the beginning of their plan.

All over cartoons.

It was disgusting. Ridiculous. Almost comical if it weren't for the death toll. And an illustration of how Islam was fundamentally incompatible with Western democracies. He had listened to and read Imam after Imam condemn the attacks in one sentence, then proclaim that though they believed in free speech, they felt it should be illegal to satirize a religion.

And what was truly disturbing was a recent BBC poll showing almost 30% of British Muslims felt the Charlie Hebdo attacks were justified.

Why? Because one group was so insecure in their beliefs that they couldn't accept them being challenged?

How many died because of Piss Christ?

He felt his chest tighten in anger with the memories and pushed them aside as they headed to the right, toward the Treasury.

Behind them somebody screamed.

Dietrich Kruger answered his phone against his better judgment, the unmarked black van they were travelling in just about to pull up in front of the Notre-Dame Cathedral. But the call display showed his mother's number.

And she knows what I'm doing.

"Hello?"

Before she even spoke he knew what she was going to say.

"It's your father, he's taken a turn for the worse."

"What's wrong?"

"I don't know." He could hear the worry in his mother's voice and it tore at his heart. "The doctor says he doesn't have much time."

"But it's too soon!" Tears flooded his eyes and the men in the truck turned their attention to readying their equipment, it the only form of privacy they could offer.

"I know, I know, I don't know why. You should come home now to see him before it's too late."

He gripped the bench seat he was on, the metal edge biting at his hand. "I can't help him there, but perhaps something here can." He released his hold. "I'll be home soon."

He ended the call, turning off the phone as the van came to a halt. The rear doors were opened and he stepped outside, raising his weapon and shooting the startled police officer standing at the entrance.

Nobody stops us today.

"Let's go!" shouted Acton as he grabbed Laura by the waist, propelling her toward the Treasury, Reading acting as a human shield behind them. They burst through the doors, surprising those inside including four police officers who spun toward them.

Reading held up his ID. "Interpol! We've got armed hostiles behind us!"

Acton continued hustling Laura deeper into the Treasury, past the display cases and toward the still frozen in place police. Finally they reached as the screams of panicking tourists and worshippers outside the now open Treasury doors reached their ears.

But it was too late.

Gunfire erupted from behind them. He felt Reading shove his shoulder, sending him to the right but he lost his grip on Laura as her momentum carried her forward. He watched in horror as he slammed into the marble floor, Reading jumping toward a pillar, Laura completely exposed. She turned, on her knees, facing their assailants, then rose as their eyes met, jumping toward his position as he reached out with his hands.

A burst of gunfire tore into the floor, shards of ancient marble ripping through the air like tiny daggers, slicing through anything in its path, including his outstretched arms. Laura winced, collapsing to the floor, grabbing at her stomach, her face one of confused shock as her eyes opened wide and her jaw dropped. She looked at him, holding up her bloodstained hands.

"No!" he cried, scrambling toward her as she fell to her side, a rapidly expanding stain on her white blouse confirming this was no wound from a shard of marble.

His beloved wife had been shot.

Dietrich didn't care anymore, didn't care who died, didn't care about the sins he might be committing. His father was dying and there was no hope of saving him medically.

All he had left was his faith.

His father was convinced that the blood of Christ could heal, and with today's technology the scientists under their employ were certain they could create the needed blood—all they needed was a sample, something with the DNA.

Which meant a genuine Blood Relic.

The problem was finding one. There were so many conflicting claims, so many disproven claims, that he had growing doubts they could find anything that might actually have the needed DNA. He found it unlikely that the genuine thorns and cloths and crosses and nails would survive to this day, but they were desperate.

Which meant he had to get his hands on everything, no matter how dubious the claims.

A woman dropped in front of him, crying out in agony as she reached for her stomach, and he felt a momentary pang of guilt as someone clearly close to her shrieked in heartbreaking shock.

Yet he continued squeezing the trigger of his Beretta as they advanced, the surprised French police barely getting any aimed shots off, his men, all experts, eliminating them in less than a minute, the last one running out of ammo, dropping his weapon.

They stopped firing, an uneasy stillness falling over the room as his men rushed toward the police position. A man dove from the sidelines, grabbing the woman and cradling her in his arms, comforting her as he inspected her wounds. He suddenly jumped to his feet, grabbing a relic from one of the shattered displays, an ancient jar long gilded in gold by misguided worshipers centuries before.

A Blood Relic.

The man reached inside, grasping what was supposed to be the remnants of the sponge used to quench Christ's thirst in his final moments.

He placed his gun against the back of the man's head. "I'll kindly ask that you not do that."

The man carefully removed his hand from the jar, raising his arms over his head. "You have to let me save my wife."

One of his men rushed to his side. "All clear, sir."

"Secure these two." He motioned for one of his men, a trained medic, to examine the woman. "Status?"

"She'll die without immediate help."

He frowned. He had taken this too far in his rage and fear. It wasn't fair that his father, such a good man, was dying from something he had no power over. He had never done anything wrong, never contracted the disease through some error in judgment, never eaten poorly, smoked or drank to excess.

His only sin was being born.

And so was his. Dietrich looked at the woman at his feet, clearly dying. It was one thing to kill police, at least it was their job, and now that it was said and done, his stomach was threatening to empty its contents at his feet, the guilt over what he had done almost overwhelming.

And he came to a decision.

He flicked his wrist toward the door. "Take her with us." Two of his men picked her up, carrying her from the room as her two companions, now bound to nearby pillars, protested. "Status on the relics?"

"All have been retrieved."

"Then we're done here."

Acton sagged against his bindings as the last of the attackers left the Treasury. Several gunshots sounded outside then the distinctive sound of a helicopter landing then taking off signaled their successful escape as sirens wailed in the distance. Tears flowed down his face, his eyes burning with the image of his dying wife cradled in his arms, the fear in her eyes the horrible, final memory he was doomed to live with for the rest of his life.

A life not worth living without her.

A life without a purpose.

He looked across at Reading, still struggling against the tape binding him to the pillar, the rage in his friend's eyes inspiring, igniting a spark in his own self, a warm, comforting hatred building inside as the tears, still staining his cheeks, stopped, his eyes glaring in the direction Laura's murderers had fled.

And he swore he'd kill them all.

He pushed back at the waist and forward at the shoulders as hard as he could. Beads of sweat formed on his forehead as he growled against his gag. The tape stretched but continued to hold him. He shook from left to right, taking advantage of the bit of give he'd managed to stretch out of the strong cloth-backed adhesive.

Suddenly he heard a tear to his right.

He continued his struggle back and forth, throwing everything he had into his jerks to the left, and the ripping sound continued. A final jerk and he felt his shoulders loosen noticeably. A megaphone outside sounded, the police finally having arrived but clearly having no clue what was going on inside, instead surrounding the cathedral until they could determine what was happening.

Which meant delays they couldn't afford.

As he writhed in his bindings, slowly loosening himself, he felt a sense of hope begin to return with each bit of progress. Laura had been shot in the stomach, a horrific wound, but it was an assumption. She was shot in what *he* called the stomach, but he wasn't a doctor. It might have grazed her, slicing her open without actually penetrating, or something else not so benign, but treatable should she receive medical attention.

And that was what was confusing to him now that he had time to think about it.

Why would they take her?

They had just killed half a dozen police officers. Why take her unless they were going to give her the medical attention she needed?

But what made them think they could get her that attention any sooner than the authorities?

They knew that the police would surround the building first, wasting precious time!

His heart leapt at the thought.

They must have left her at the entrance so the police would see her right away!

There was still hope.

A final jerk and his entire upper body was suddenly free. He twisted to his side, his hands grabbing at the tape still binding his waist, tearing at it with his zip-tied hands, and in moments was completely free. Hitching his hands behind his buttocks, he dropped hard against them, snapping the bindings as Laura's private former SAS security team had taught him, then ripped off the piece of tape covering his mouth.

He winced as he spat the gag out, rushing toward Reading who had managed to only free himself slightly. Acton picked up a shard of glass from the floor then sliced through Reading's bindings, pulling his friend loose before snapping his hands free.

He didn't wait, instead tearing toward the entrance, images of Laura lying on the cold steps outside while police did nothing in fear it might be a trap, propelling him toward her.

"Slow down!" shouted Reading behind him, but he ignored the pleas. "You'll get yourself shot!" He didn't care. If his beloved wife was dead, he wanted to be dead too. But if there was any chance she was alive, lying on the steps waiting for help to arrive, seconds would count.

He reached the massive doors and skidded to a halt, pulling at the handle, a shaft of sunlight bursting through when a hand on his shoulder whipped him back.

"Listen you daft bastard, you'll get both of us killed."

Reading stepped past him, opening the door slowly, holding his ID out. "I'm Agent Hugh Reading of Interpol! We're unarmed! Do you understand!"

Someone on the megaphone began to speak English and the two of them slowly emerged to find dozens of police, weapons aimed at them as more continued to arrive. Acton quickly scanned the area for any signs of Laura but saw none, breathing a sigh of relief at the realization the authorities must have already taken her to a hospital.

He and Reading removed their jackets, turning around so the police could see they were unarmed, then dropped to their knees, clasping their hands behind their heads as a dozen officers descended upon them.

"My wife, where did you take my wife?"

His question was ignored as he was patted down and handcuffed.

"The attackers are gone," Reading was saying, explaining the situation to the understandably cautious police. "Your men are inside. At least one is still alive, but I think the others are dead."

"My wife! I need to know what happened to my wife!"

A man stepped toward them, apparently in charge, Reading's ID in his hand. He motioned for the handcuffs to be removed. "I'm sorry for this, Agent Reading, but we can no longer just take people's word that they are not involved."

Reading took his wallet and returned it to his pocket as Acton rubbed his wrists. "Completely understood. Listen—"

Acton cut his friend off. "I need to know what happened to my wife. They took her with them. Did you find her?"

The man's eyes narrowed. "I'm sorry, but I don't know what you're talking about."

Acton felt his chest tighten. "You mean there wasn't a woman here, outside, shot in the stomach?"

The police officer shook his head. "I'm sorry, sir, but there was no woman here, injured or otherwise, when we arrived. Only our officer, already dead."

Acton felt his world begin to spin as he reached out for Reading. Strong hands helped him to the ground as blood pounded in his ears. "She's dead," he mumbled as Reading took a knee beside him. "She's dead."

"We don't know that," replied Reading's reassuring voice.

Acton looked at his friend, his eyes blurred with tears.

"But why would they take her?"

Gabala, Cappadocia, North of Judea
45 AD, 15 years later

"Soldiers are coming!"

When the children had shouted the warning yesterday, it hadn't been the first time Longinus had heard those words, but he now knew it would be the last. Since their arrival years ago many had listened to their accounts and been swayed to their opinion that Jesus was indeed the Son of God and that His teachings should be followed. Many had been baptized and some had even left to spread the word or to seek out the Apostles that were now ministering the church the Messiah had died to establish.

And unfortunately for him and his friends, their success had become known. According to these men now sitting at his own table, oblivious to who he was, the rabbis in Jerusalem had heard of their location and demanded Pilate send soldiers to arrest them.

Pilate had ordered their beheading, clearly fed up with having to deal with the annoyance.

"He said if we were to return without Longinus *we* would be beheaded," said Gaius, the centurion leading them. He seemed like a good man, a dedicated soldier who treated his men with respect and seemed to lack much of the arrogance displayed far too often by Roman soldiers in their subjugated territories. And that example was reflected in his men.

When the soldiers had arrived in the city the warning had reached them quickly, the children spreading the word faster than any man even on horseback could.

So they had been ready.

Longinus had immediately sent Tiberius into hiding, he the youngest of them all with much life left to live—he shouldn't die for the transgressions of the elders. Though the younger man's commitment to their new beliefs, their new religion, was as strong as theirs, Longinus had argued, convincingly, that should they all die, the word they were trying to spread may die with them, but should at least one survive, there was still hope.

Tiberius had argued bitterly, but acquiesced in the end, now hiding in a nearby village, awaiting word.

It would be delivered by someone else.

Longinus looked at Gaius. "What will you do if you can't find them?"

Gaius shrugged, glancing at his men. "Keep searching, otherwise we lose our heads." He sighed. "I fear though we may never find them and soon our own comrades will be sent to find us with orders to return with *our* heads."

"That would be unfortunate."

"No kidding."

Longinus laughed as did the others, though the mood had clearly changed. Yesterday had been a celebration, a group of retired soldiers hosting these new arrivals in a bid to discover their purpose. They had treated them well, offered them food and drink and a warm, dry place to sleep, even the breakfast they were now just finishing.

But Longinus had one last thing to offer them, though it wasn't his alone to offer. He looked at Albus first, who nodded slightly, then Severus, who closed his good eye for a moment then opened it, agreeing to the unspoken question.

"Perhaps you will keep your heads after all."

Gaius' eyebrows furled. "What do you mean?"

Longinus smiled gently. "I am Longinus, the man you seek. This is Albus, and this Severus. The fourth man you seek, Tiberius, died several weeks ago in a rock slide."

The jaws of the men seated at their table dropped, and as if to further revive his faith in the basic goodness of these men, they looked horrified. Gaius broke the silence.

"You cannot be serious! Please tell us you jest, that this is just a bad joke at our expense!"

Longinus motioned toward his blessed weapon in the corner and Albus rose to retrieve it. Longinus took the spear and laid it on the table. "This is the spear I lanced the Messiah's side with, the spear that brought forth the blood and water from within that cured my blindness." He ran his hand against its rough surface, his eyes filled with tears. "It is the spear I wish to be buried with." He looked up at Gaius. "I am ready to die, so that you may live."

Albus returned to his seat, placing a hand on Longinus' shoulder. "As am I."

"And I," said Severus.

Longinus smiled at his friends. "We have all been preparing for this day and now that it is here, it does sadden our hearts, of that I can assure you. However there is no fear to be found in our impending deaths, for we know we have been blessed and will spend eternity in paradise with our Lord, our God." He reached out and squeezed the top of Gaius' hand. "And fear not, for there is no sin in what you do. You are following the orders of a soldier, and we give our lives willingly to you."

Gaius stared at the hand resting on his, his head slowly shaking back and forth. He looked at his men, then at the three condemned men seated across from them. "I can't," he finally managed to say. "I can't do it. You are such good people, righteous people. You took us into your home and

91

gave us food and drink, entertained us and provided us shelter. To repay your kindness with your deaths is unthinkable!" He shook his head, firmly this time. "I may not believe in your god, but I do believe in mine, and my gods would frown upon me should I ever commit such an atrocity."

Longinus took in a deep breath, patting the man's hand then leaning back. "I will tell your gods this: we die willingly, and though these men may wield the blade that removes our heads, they are merely instruments of the evil of this act, extensions of the blade itself. Think of them as the hilt the blade flows from, with no more guilt to be associated with them than the blacksmith himself who forged the blade so long ago. They are merely the arrow, loosed from Jerusalem by those who would have us dead, finding its mark here, on this day. We willingly give our lives to these men, so that their own lives may be saved." He looked at Gaius, leaning forward slightly. "All we ask is that our bodies be treated with respect, left here for those who know us to bury, and should it become possible, to return our severed heads so that we may enjoy our final resting place as whole men."

"Of course," whispered Gaius, his voice cracking.

"And one final thing."

"Anything."

"Live your lives well, free of guilt for what you have done here this day."

Gaius nodded, his eyes lowered, the shame he was clearly feeling too great to meet Longinus' kind gaze.

Longinus rose, picking up his spear from the table and taking one final look at its bloodstained tip.

"Let us be swift about this, so you may be far from here before the sun begins to set on this day."

He stepped outside, his friends following him, the soldiers, solemn, standing behind them. He looked up at the sky, clear, blue, the sun a little cooler here than in the harsh desert of Jerusalem. It was a beautiful city, a friendly city, a city where life was easier than the harsh one carved out of the desert so long ago.

It was a good place to die.

Outside Paris, France
Present Day

The helicopter bounced to the ground, the woman they had taken moaning in protest as the doors were pulled open. Dietrich jumped to the ground, ducking as the blades powered down, two black SUVs pulling up moments later. Dietrich pointed at the woman. "Load her in my vehicle and take her to the estate immediately. Phone ahead so the doctor is ready."

"Yes, sir."

Two of his men, including their medic, carried her to one of the SUVs, gently placing her in the back, it immediately racing from the farmer's field they were in and to a nearby country road. He strode toward the remaining vehicle as the pilot and his other two men cleared the helicopter of anything incriminating then doused it in gasoline. He climbed in the passenger seat, checking his watch. It had been almost thirty minutes since he had received the phone call from his mother.

He resisted the urge to turn on his cellphone, not wanting the cell tower ping to be traced. He just hoped his mother had used the secure phone to call him otherwise the police might eventually track them down should they decide to investigate every phone call made or received in the area during the time of the incident.

God, Mother, I hope you didn't screw up!

The pilot and his remaining two men jumped in the back of the SUV and the driver peeled away, skidding onto the road as they headed toward home.

A rumble reached his ears and he leaned forward, looking in the side view mirror at their helicopter as it erupted into flames, the aviation fuel igniting in a black and orange ball of fire.

He glanced over at the speedometer.

"Watch your speed, we don't want to draw any attention."

"Yes, sir."

The vehicle immediately slowed as Dietrich began to pick at his cuticles, a nervous habit he had never been able to break.

Especially in moments of stress.

Such as the possibility his father would soon be dead.

He looked back at the bags containing the relics, praying that these artifacts, the most famous Blood Relics in the world, might actually be genuine, but his pessimism was almost overwhelming, his faith shaken with the thought his father might be taken from him even sooner than previously thought.

A single tear rolled down his cheek.

He wiped it away with a finger, counting down the mile markers on the side of the road as they approached his family's estate purchased twenty years ago when his father moved the family business to France in exchange for generous government grants and a massive property tax break. He hadn't been happy to leave Germany and his friends behind, but he had adapted, never one to wallow in self-pity with the knowledge of how short a productive life he had left to live.

He frowned, the stray thought resonating.

Self-pity.

Was he upset because his father was losing his life, or that he was losing his father? His father had raised him for this moment, though it was coming sooner than expected, and he prayed his mother was wrong, simply overreacting to what might be nothing more than the common cold.

But if his father were to die, he would become the head of the family, responsible for carrying on the legacy, for running the business that would keep their search for a cure funded, so that one day, perhaps long in the future, the curse the men in his family had endured might end. It was the thought that drove them for generations, that someone, some distant descendent, might one day die of old age, his family at his side as he peacefully left this temporary existence to meet his maker, not a man broken in body and spirit, but a contented man who had lived a full life free from the ravages of a disease that had shown his family no quarter for over a century, mercilessly never skipping a generation, a sickening lottery won every time the next son was born.

A pain raced up his leg causing him to gasp.

No one said anything, all aware of his fate.

A fate he prayed might be avoided with the artifacts they had just spilled so much blood to retrieve.

Jerusalem, Judea
45 AD, Three Weeks Later

Gaius looked over his shoulder, making certain no one had followed him, still finding the alleyway empty. A foot scraped nearby and his head swiveled toward it, his hand reaching for his blade.

"Are you here?" hissed a woman's voice from the shadows.

"Did you find it?"

"Yes, it was on the dung heap, as you said."

Gaius stepped toward the woman, removing a pouch of silver from his pocket. He felt sorry for the wretched old creature as she handed him a canvas sack, the poor woman having recently lost her son. He had found her begging at the gates to the temple, mumbling about having had a vision in which his son appeared to her with what she called an angel who had promised to take care of him in paradise.

She was in need, as was he.

An offer was made.

Retrieve the head of Longinus, thrown on the dung heap by the rabbi earlier that day, in exchange for money to return home and give her son a proper burial.

Their return to Jerusalem had been triumphant yet solemn. They couldn't let on how they truly felt, instead forcing smiles on their faces as they were hailed as heroes for finding and executing the traitors. When the heads had been brought to Prefect Pilate, he had looked in the sacks then sat back in his chair, a chair Gaius could only describe as a throne.

"And the other?"

"Dead in a landslide several weeks earlier."

"Are you certain?"

Gaius nodded, though he couldn't say for sure. He really didn't care. "The locals confirmed it."

"Very well." Pilate motioned toward the three sacks. "Which one is Longinus?"

Gaius raised the sack he was carrying. "This one."

"Take it to the rabbi. Dispose of the others."

Gaius had bowed and left with his men, they agreeing to meet later once the head of Longinus had been retrieved, none having any intention of disposing of the other two as ordered. He had taken the head personally to the rabbi and watched in horror as the man insulted Longinus' memory then tossed the head onto a dung heap in the street.

He had dared not retrieve it himself, this mourning mother providing him his salvation.

He looked in the sack and frowned, his heart heavy at the sight of this good, brave man who had sacrificed himself to save men he had never met before. The acts of this man and his friends had been enough to convince him on the long journey back to Jerusalem that this god they worshipped must truly be worthy, and if the story of Longinus' sight being restored were true, which he had no doubt it was, then this god must truly be great.

He couldn't remember the last time *his* gods had performed a miracle, had answered a prayer.

He handed the woman the pouch of coins.

"Thank you," she said, patting him excitedly on the arm. "Now my boy will rest in peace."

She hurried off as Gaius strode with purpose toward the rendezvous point. He had already volunteered his men for a mission outside the city walls that would take them north for several weeks, and with their triumphant return his request hadn't been denied, instead eliciting praise for not resting before heading out once again.

As he marched through the evening streets, the city quickly settling in for the night, this honorable man's head making his arm grow weary, he came to a decision.

I'm converting as soon as my promise is fulfilled.

Notre-Dame Cathedral, Paris, France
Present Day

Reading hung up the phone, clipping it back on his belt, returning to the police car Acton was half sitting in, his feet still on the pavement. He looked at his friend, clearly in pain, having said very little since their rescue. Laura was gone, taken by their attackers for reasons unknown, and he knew it was tearing the man apart. He had seen the stomach wound and it hadn't looked good. He knew from too many years as a police officer and a soldier that she didn't have much time to reach an Emergency Room before bleeding out.

He wasn't optimistic.

Acton looked up at him. "Any word on Laura?"

Reading shook his head. "No. They've checked all the hospitals and clinics and there's no reports of a woman matching her description having been admitted."

"So they probably dumped her body somewhere."

Reading didn't want to admit to his friend that he was probably right, but it was the most likely possibility. If she had died, there was no reason for them to keep the body. If they were found with it, it would be irrefutable evidence they were involved.

But they'd probably also dump her where she couldn't be easily found.

Which meant his friend might never get closure.

Reading knew Acton well enough to know the man would go through the rest of his life blaming himself for her death. He understood the twisted logic the blame-game could take. He'd probably go all the way back to their original meeting, his sorrow suggesting if he had never met her she'd still be alive today.

But then she would have missed out on the happiest years of her life.

Reading and Laura had seen a fair amount of each other while she still lived in London doing the long distance relationship thing, so they had become good friends. And he knew she loved Acton more than life and wouldn't have traded those years together for anything.

Yet he knew any words now would be wasted on his friend. Instead, he needed to keep his friend's mind busy until he crashed, the man clearly exhausted.

"They found the helicopter outside of the city. They burned it so the police aren't optimistic about finding any evidence. The tail number indicates it had been stolen about an hour before the robbery. They just found the owner tied up in his charter office. Just vague descriptions and no security footage apparently."

"So no help."

"It at least gives us a geographical area to concentrate on."

Acton looked at him with a "give-me-a-break" look. "You and I both know they could be in a different country by now. Europe isn't the US. It doesn't take days to drive across."

Reading frowned. "You're right of course. But the police are at least trying. They're going all out on this with four of their own dead."

"None of them made it?"

Reading sighed. "Other than the one who surrendered, the rest were all dead before they made it to the hospital."

Acton pulled out his phone. "I need to make some calls."

Reading nodded. "Okay, I'm going to talk to the scene commander."

Acton grunted, already dialing. Reading looked for the officer he'd been dealing with, spotting him nearby, and as he began to walk away he breathed a sigh of relief when he heard Acton reach his best friend. Reading just wished Milton was here to comfort the grieving husband, but he knew no amount of consoling would help.

Not so soon after such a tragic loss.

He cursed.

Even I've lost all hope.

Mantua, Italia
47 AD, Two years later

Tiberius placed the spear gently beside the carefully wrapped body of his friend, tucked between the torso and the right arm, and by his left hand a jar containing the dried remains of a sponge Longinus had used to help clean the body of their Messiah after it had been taken down from the cross. He stepped back and nodded, all gathered bowing their heads in reverence to this great man who had helped convert so many to the teachings of Jesus during his time in hiding.

He had inspired many to great deeds, including Gaius and his men, who stood with him now, having fulfilled their promise to return the heads so his friends could rest in peace. Albus and Severus had been buried outside Gabala, their bodies made whole with the return of their severed heads, but it had been decided that Longinus should be moved lest his body be desecrated by those who would have him dead, the local authorities having already taken an interest in his burial.

They had snuck out of the city at night with the help of converts, heading for the only place Tiberius knew they might be safe.

His own hometown.

He hadn't seen Mantua in years, not since he had joined the Roman Army and been sent to the arid deserts of Judea and Syria. But there was little joy in his homecoming. Along the way they had forged documents for all of them so they might travel in peace without fear of arrest, and false discharge papers for himself, since he was known in his hometown.

His return, five years early, would cause questions.

He hated lying to his family, and though he had been elated to see them, the reason for his return, and the lies, had him secretly on edge the entire time.

Something his mother had noticed.

He had dismissed her concerns. "I'm still sad about the death of my friend."

"How did he die?"

"A martyr. He sacrificed himself to save the rest of us."

"Why? Were you in danger?"

The concern on his mother's face had warmed and worried him, just knowing she still cared as much as the day he had left twenty years before, barely a man, comforted him in a way he hadn't realized he'd been missing. "I have to tell you about something." He smiled, his heart filling with the warmth only true belief could bring. "Something wonderful."

His mother had listened patiently, asking many questions, and by the end of his accounts of that hot, horrible day in Golgatha, he knew he hadn't convinced her.

But he had intrigued her.

And that was the way it was with most conversions. Rarely, unless a miracle was seen as had been that day, did someone abandon a lifetime's worth of beliefs. People were convinced to convert over time as they realized that this new way of thinking, of a loving God as opposed to a vengeful one—or in his mother's case, vengeful *gods*—of a god who allowed His own son to walk among His creation and be destroyed by that very same creation, to die for their sins, was a message of hope that many in these times found they could cling to, no one in their memories having ever witnessed a true miracle from their old gods.

It also helped that the Apostles had spread throughout the region, preaching the new religion and performing miracles of their own to reinforce the message.

But here, in this small city in Italia, he and his new friends would have a difficult time of things, the Empire and its gods strong here. They would have to work in secret to protect themselves, determining who they could trust and who might be receptive to their teachings. He knew in time, not his lifetime, but perhaps that of his future children or grandchildren, they might be able to walk the streets in peace, without fear of persecution for their beliefs, surrounded by the converted.

It was a dream for now, the current reality one in which they had to be careful.

Which was why Longinus was being buried in secret, on his family's land, the grave to go unmarked, his desire to build a church on this very spot something already discussed with Gaius and the others.

All in good time.

He picked up a shovel and stabbed the mound of dark soil, tossing the first pile onto the sarcophagus fashioned by Gaius himself, a remarkable stonemason, his skills wasted in the army. The others picked up shovels of their own, making quick, solemn work of the pile, the grass, cut out carefully earlier, tamped back into place, there little evidence anything had happened here this day.

He hoped in time his friend could be publicly recognized for the remarkable man he was, but for now they had no choice.

Longinus, the first convert after the death of the Son of God to a new religion that would be persecuted for generations to come, would have to remain hidden from those who would denounce him.

Until such day as the beliefs he died for were no longer feared.

A day Tiberius feared would be so long from now, Longinus may very well be forgotten to the history he helped shape.

Kruger Residence, Outside Paris, France
Present Day

Dietrich rushed up the outside steps, two at a time, it having been over half an hour since they had left the cathedral. On the entire ride to the estate he had been consumed with thoughts of his father, his mind concocting vicious fantasies of finding the man dead in his chambers, his sobbing mother draped over the body, clinging to her husband as the nursing staff tried to pull her away.

It had driven him almost mad.

And he had renewed his vow that he would do whatever it took to save his father's life, he not ready to see him go, to take on the responsibility of leading the family.

He didn't want to lose his dad.

He looked over his shoulder at his men. "Get rid of the vehicles as per protocol and prep for the next mission." He shoved open the doors, crossing the threshold to the huge home. "And find out who the hell that woman is!"

Racing up the stairs to the second floor, he sprinted down the hallway, skidding to a halt before the French doors that led to his father's chambers, his mother having moved to a different room across the hall a few years ago to let him have his rest when the pain had become too great.

It had been an uncomfortable day for him, the very idea of his parents sleeping in separate rooms forcing thoughts of divorce and heartbreak to the fore. Even when he had looked it up on the Internet and found almost forty percent of couples sleep separately, it provided little comfort.

It was the continued affection they showed each other during the waking hours that had finally reassured him.

He tapped on the door and heard his mother's voice respond. "Come in."

Opening the door slowly, he poked his head inside to find his mother sitting on the side of the bed, holding his father's hand in both of hers, her eyes red and swollen. A nurse was checking numbers on a monitor, his father smiling gently as he looked over at him.

"Come inside, son, I won't bite."

He looks so weak!

A lump formed in his throat as he entered the room, the trepidation he felt at what was to come almost overwhelming. He approached his father, his mother reaching out a hand for his. He took it.

"How are you feeling?"

"Peachy. You?"

Dietrich shrugged, a slight smile breaking out for a moment. "Better than you apparently."

"I took a bit of a turn, but I'm feeling better now."

"Don't lie," admonished his mother.

His father patted her hand. "Alright dear, I'm feeling better than a little while ago, but not as good as yesterday." He looked at the nurse as she took his pulse manually. "But that's progress, right?"

The woman nodded. "Yes, Herr Kruger. Absolutely."

His arm returned to him, his father grinned. "See, and that's a professional telling you."

Dietrich grunted. "Uh huh."

"Enough dwelling on the inevitable. Whether it happens today or ten years from now, it is no matter."

Dietrich was about to protest when his father raised a finger, just a finger, the hand remaining on his chest, cutting him off.

"So what happened in Paris?"

"We retrieved the artifacts, they're being tested now."

"Excellent. Any problems?"

Dietrich desperately wanted to confess to his father what he had done, the sins he had committed, but he couldn't, he couldn't place any more stress on the man. "No problems."

"Excellent." His father frowned. "Unfortunately the tests on the Vienna relic were negative."

Dietrich wasn't surprised, it was after all a disputed artifact, previous carbon dating suggesting it was a thousand years younger than it should be if legitimate. But they were desperate and testing could be wrong.

"I think we expected that," he finally said, his father nodding. "I received word this morning that the Vatican is moving a collection of artifacts from various churches to their secure archives late tonight. Artifacts are being sent from around Europe."

"That could be a problem."

"Or an opportunity."

His mother looked at him. "How?"

"Everything will be in one place at the same time."

His father shook his head. "You'll never be able to breach the Vatican again."

Dietrich smiled.

"I have no intention of doing any such thing."

Laucala Island Private Resort, Fiji

CIA Special Agent Dylan Kane flushed the toilet for the umpteenth time this morning. It had been three days of nonstop drinking, eating, dancing and sex, but something had set his entire system off, leaving his gut in agony and his body protesting in ways he didn't care to think of.

It was nasty.

He looked at himself in the mirror and shook his head.

His face was a gray that belonged on the side of a naval vessel, not a CIA operator.

There was no way he was going to be able to go on duty tomorrow. He had wrapped up an op in Pakistan a week ago and after his debrief by his CIA handler in the region, had come here to be properly debriefed by several lovely ladies he had come to know over the years.

It had been an epic bender.

He stumbled into the hotel bedroom, several bodies strewn about—mostly naked—copious amounts of liquor bottles and glasses filling almost every horizontal surface.

He eyed his bed, two incredible looking women lying in it. He had no choice, he had to lie down, but the last thing he was up for now was anything that needed him 'up'.

He froze.

Please don't tell me...

He scanned the bottles, looking for the distinctive label of his favorite scotch, Glen Breton Ice, praying he hadn't been stupid enough to break that out of the private reserve he had in the basement of the hotel.

He sighed in relief. While he enjoyed partying with these people, some of whom he even casually knew, he wasn't about to waste something as fine as Glen Breton Ice on them or himself in such an inebriated state.

It was meant to be enjoyed in civilized company, or alone at the beginning of an evening when it could be appreciated.

He crawled into the bed and was greeted with two moaning women who draped themselves over him but thankfully fell back to sleep quickly when he didn't respond.

He closed his eyes and fell into a restless sleep, the fog of alcohol clearing enough for his usual nightmare to return, a nightmare he had been living with for years.

Raptor One, Sierra Four! Abort! Abort! Abort!

He woke up, drenched in sweat, wondering what had startled him.

His phone vibrated on the nightstand.

Gently extricating himself from the two beauties resting on his chest, he returned to the bathroom, locking the door behind him. He sat back on the toilet, his insides demanding a rerun, killing two birds with one stone, and pressed his thumb against the sensor, unlocking his phone.

He frowned.

It was an emergency relay message from his old archeology professor, James Acton. Acton had helped counsel him after 9/11 when he was debating whether or not to leave university and join the army. Acton, ex-National Guard, had encouraged him to follow his heart.

He had.

He had joined the army, made it into the Rangers then set his sights on Delta. It was after making The Unit that he was recruited into the CIA, a decision he had never regretted.

Unlike the raw oysters he had ordered last night.

That's it! The oysters!

He breathed a bit of a sigh of relief knowing he hadn't been poisoned, but his brain having reconciled things didn't help his digestive system.

He had given Professor Acton an emergency contact number after they had been reunited, Acton and his new lady friend seeming to be constantly getting into trouble. He had helped him when possible, or sent help when not. It was something he was happy to do, he having few friends, and fewer still who knew what he truly did for a living.

Besides the professor and Chris, there's really no one.

Chris Leroux was a high school buddy who had tutored him, getting him the grades he had needed to get into St. Paul's University. They had lost touch then bumped into each other years later in the CIA cafeteria, Kane now an operator, Leroux an analyst.

Leroux was one of the few people in the world he truly trusted.

As was Acton.

He dialed the phone number left in the message. A groggy voice answered.

"Hello?"

"Hey, Doc, it's Dylan."

The professor had clearly been asleep and Kane could hear the sounds of someone struggling out of bed followed by the click of a light switch. "Dylan, thanks for getting back to me."

"What's the problem, Doc?"

"It's Laura. She's been shot—"

Kane felt a pit form in his stomach, which was rather remarkable considering what his rebelling organ was doing to him at the moment. He had met Laura several times. She was a fantastic lady and it was clear the two professors loved each other deeply.

He counted her among the few he trusted.

"Is she okay?"

"I-I don't know. They took her, Dylan, they took her!"

Acton's voice cracked, his heartache clear, the fear in his voice palpable. "*Who* took her?"

"We don't know. Hugh's here with me, Hugh Reading, I'm not sure if you remember him—"

"Interpol. Yes, I remember him."

"The Vatican asked for our help, some Blood Relics had been stolen. We were in Paris trying to secure the artifacts at the Notre-Dame Cathedral when it was hit. Several police officers were killed and Laura was shot in the stomach. They took her with them and there's been no sign of her since."

Kane didn't dare say the obvious. Stomach wounds could be brutal, deadly, and the likelihood of her surviving was slim. But until a body was found, he knew the man would never be at peace.

Which meant he had to help find her, dead or alive.

"Keep your phone charged, Doc, someone will be in touch."

"Thanks, Dylan, it's appreciated."

Kane killed the call then doubled over, vomiting in the waste basket.

There's no way I'm going to be able to help.

Maggie Harris Residence
Lake in the Pines Apartments, Fayetteville, North Carolina

Command Sergeant Major Burt "Big Dog" Dawson rolled off his girlfriend, Maggie, both of them gasping for breath.

"My God, BD, it's like you were on a mission," she gasped, rolling half her body onto his, nuzzling his neck. "I don't think I'll ever get tired of that."

Dawson grunted, his eyes closing as he battled to stay awake, but it was a losing op. He was completely relaxed, every muscle in his body having been spent, and this was their reward.

Rest.

"Don't you dare fall asleep on me!"

He grunted again, forcing his eyes open. "Got toothpicks?"

"For what?"

"My eyelids."

She slapped his chest playfully. "What do you want to do now?"

"Sleep."

"You can do that anytime. I've missed you. You were gone for two weeks this time."

She was right, it had been a bit longer op, but nothing out of the ordinary. He and the boys from the Delta Force's Bravo Team had returned late last night and after a few hours of rest on post in his own bed, he had paid a visit to Maggie's as soon as she had got off work.

She was right. He could sleep later.

Like right now, after sex.

He never understood why men were sleepy and women seemed energized. After such complete release, it just seemed natural to want to rest, let the body go and drift into nothingness with your lover in your arms.

Maybe because they want more?

They had done it three times, which to him seemed enough. His record had been far more, but that was because it was his nineteenth birthday and his girlfriend had wanted to set some sort of record.

It had stood since then.

At least with him.

He wasn't sure about her.

But at his age three seemed pretty damned good, and he was spent.

Maybe she didn't…

Self-doubt began to creep in and he pushed himself up on an elbow, turning toward her. "Was it, you know…"

"Was it what?"

"You know…"

"What? Good for me?"

"Yeah."

She laughed, slapping his chest again. "Babe, if you're not sure, ask the neighbors."

He grinned, dropping back onto his pillow, closing his eyes.

"But I still want to do something."

He felt her jump out of bed, eliciting a groan from him. "Oh come on, Babe, I've been gone for two weeks, had almost no sleep, can't this wait a few hours?"

"I've been pent up in this apartment for two weeks, waiting for my man to come back and satisfy me."

"Which I apparently did."

"Yes, stud, you did."

"Three times."

"More, actually."

Ooh, I am a stud!

"Don't look so self-satisfied."

He grinned, swinging his legs out of the bed, stretching. "I guess I can take my totally satisfied woman out for dinner."

"That's more like it. Now let's take a shower."

"Isn't that how round three started?"

Maggie paused. "You're right. *I'll* take a shower, *then* you." He watched her fantastic body step into the bathroom, the door closing halfway.

I'm a lucky man.

He hadn't told her yet that he loved her, but he was pretty sure he did. It was a big deal for him. He couldn't remember the last time he had told a woman he loved her. When he was a teenager and in his early twenties he had said whatever he felt would get him across the goal line, but after breaking a girl's heart in his late twenties he had sworn he'd never say it again unless he meant it.

But you said you loved me!

Her cries still haunted him.

His phone vibrated. Somewhere.

He stood, eyeing the room, trying to narrow down the sound, finally finding his pants hanging over the dresser mirror, Maggie having pulled them off him and tossed them over her head when he had first arrived.

He was loving having a girlfriend, a serious girlfriend. There was some sort of stability there that he hadn't realized he had been craving all these years, The Unit providing him all the stability he had thought he needed.

He had been wrong.

He was finally beginning to understand why so many Special Forces operators were married, and why the brass preferred married men. It gave them something to fight for, something to come back to, an anchor in their uncertain worlds.

Maggie was quickly becoming his anchor, something he looked forward to coming home to, something he missed when away.

The boys had been ribbing him on the last trip about wedding bells in his future, but he had dismissed them. *Waay too early for that.* But he had to admit, he could see it someday.

He fished the phone out of its pocket.

"Go."

"Is that anyway to answer the phone?"

He smiled as he recognized the voice of an old comrade turned CIA Operator, Dylan Kane. A voice that didn't sound right. "You sound like shit."

"Funny you should say that, that's all I've been doing for the past six hours. That and the Technicolor yawn."

"Pleasant. You know I'm heading out for dinner in a few minutes."

"Don't get the pea soup. Or raw oysters."

"Ahh, trying to enhance the old sex drive."

"You should try it sometime."

"Apparently I don't need any help in that department."

"Good man!" Kane became serious. "I got a message from our old friend."

Dawson sat on the edge of the bed, pretty certain who Kane was referring to. "What's the professor gotten himself into this time?" he asked with a laugh.

"His wife's been shot"—Dawson immediately regretted his levity—"and to top it off, kidnapped. The Doc doesn't even know if she's alive."

117

"Christ, he must be going bat shit crazy."

"Wouldn't you?"

Dawson looked toward the bathroom, steam and happy humming rolling out the door. "What can I do?"

"I'm completely offline, I can barely walk. I'll contact my guy at Langley and get him working the data. Any chance you can get yourself over there to help?"

"Where's there?"

"Paris for the moment."

"Maggie will kill me. We've been talking about vacationing there."

"Take her."

"Riiight, I can picture it now. Honey, you go visit the Louvre, I'm going to go kill some people. Dinner at six?"

Kane laughed. "Up to you. Find Laura, take care of business, then fly her over for a romantic getaway."

Huh. Not a bad idea.

"I'll clear it with the Colonel. I'm assuming your Langley guy is Leroux?"

"Yup."

"Okay, I'll touch base with him and keep you in the loop."

"Thanks, BD, it's appreciated." He heard a grunt. "Oh shit, gotta go!"

Heaves erupted before the call ended.

Poor bastard.

He stepped into the bathroom, pulling aside the curtain.

"Hey, you were supposed to wait!"

He climbed into the shower, pulling her close.

"There's been a change of plans."

Kruger Residence, Outside Paris, France

Laura opened her eyes, immediately shutting them, the glare of overhead lights almost painful. With some effort she lifted her hand, shielding her eyes as she opened them again, blinking several times, her eyes dry. A monitor beeped to her left showing her vitals, weak but steady. Something moved to her right. She looked and saw a man in a lab coat swirling a large beaker, holding it up to the light.

It looked nothing like a hospital.

And everything like a laboratory.

"Wh-where am I?"

Her voice was raspy, her mouth and throat dry.

The man looked over at her, putting the beaker down. "So you're awake." He walked over, checking the monitors. "How are you feeling?"

"Water."

He reached for a glass on a side table, helping position the straw to her mouth. She took several sips then swished some of the water around, relieving her cotton-mouth.

"Enough?"

She nodded.

"Good. Now, how are you feeling?"

"Weak."

"Any pain?"

She reached for her stomach. "A dull ache, but that's about it. Where am I?"

"You're safe, if that's what's worrying you."

She looked around, it clear she wasn't in any type of formal medical care facility. "I doubt that."

The man laughed gently. "Yes, I suppose so. What I mean is that for the moment, you're not going to die, but you will need to be careful. I removed the bullet and stitched you up, but it made quite the hole and you lost a lot of blood. Fortunately we're equipped for that sort of event here."

"And where is here?"

"Let's just say 'the French countryside'."

"Uh huh. And I assume I'm a prisoner?"

"A horrible term, but for lack of a better one, yes. Once this entire exercise is over you will of course be free to go, but until it is, we can't risk you letting the authorities know where we are."

"Considering I have no clue, that's hardly a problem."

He smiled, patting her shoulder. Lifting a control pad attached to a wire, he placed it in her hand. "Bed controls. You can raise or lower yourself, whatever makes you comfortable."

She took the controls and looked at them. Pressing the button with an up arrow she felt herself start to rise and was soon in a reasonable sitting position, her wound a little tender but tolerable.

"Can I get you anything else? I need to get back to work. Feel free to chit-chat, I could use the company."

"I'm fine, thanks."

Her stomach rumbled, loud enough for both of them to hear it.

"I'll have a light meal brought for you. You don't want to stretch anything down there by overindulging."

He stepped away, placing a call for food, then returned to his workbench, lifting what she recognized as the Crown of Thorns. He swabbed several parts of it before gently returning it to the countertop.

"What are you doing?"

"Swabbing for DNA."

"Christ's DNA?"

"Ahh, so you're onto us."

"Multiple thefts, all taking only the Blood Relics? Not much of a stretch. Who's sick?"

"You're a bright woman, Dr. Palmer."

Her chest tightened. "You know who I am?"

"Your ID was in your fanny pack. I looked you up. Very impressive career. Oh! Congratulations on your recent marriage."

Her stomach leapt. *James!* "Where's my husband, is he okay?"

The man shrugged. "No idea where he is, but from my understanding only police officers were hurt during the retrieval, besides yourself of course."

She breathed a sigh of relief, watching as several vials were prepared and loaded into a machine that began to spin them. "Do you really think you can retrieve the blood of Christ?"

"Absolutely," replied the man, turning to face her while the machine did its work. "The only problem is finding an actual relic with DNA on it, then of course hoping that the DNA we do find is His."

"You sound confident yet not."

He laughed. "You're a very perceptive woman. I am confident in the science, just not the premise. First, finding an actual artifact with His blood on it I personally think is next to impossible. Second, should we actually find that blood, the only way we would know it was His is if it actually heals my employer. And third, if it weren't to heal him, he would insist we continue the search, because his assumption would be that it *wasn't* the blood of Christ." The man threw up his hands in exasperation. "I have no choice but to simply keep testing whatever they bring me."

"There's not a lot of relics left."

He frowned. "I know. It's unfortunate. He's a good man, he deserves to be saved if he can be."

Laura felt a slight rage build inside her. "A good man? I was shot, a priest was murdered, police officers are dead. A good man?"

"That, my dear, was not *him*. That was his son."

Laura bit her lip, silencing the retort she wanted to deliver. *Sins of the son?* "Was he responsible for all the thefts?"

The man nodded. "Yes, under orders from his father."

"He seems to have escalated."

"There's been a recent development."

Laura's eyes narrowed. "What?"

"My employer, the boy's father, took a turn for the worse today. I fear he'll die soon." The machine beeped. "Which makes my work all the more important."

"Don't you think you're on a fool's errand?"

The man chuckled as he removed the vials. "I may be, but if that man dies, I fear what his son might do."

"What do you mean?"

"He's a fine young man, but you've seen what he's capable of. If his father dies, he just might blame me." He paused, turning toward Laura. "Or you."

1st Special Forces Operational Detachment - Delta HQ, Fort Bragg, North Carolina
A.k.a. "The Unit"

Command Sergeant Major Burt "Big Dog" Dawson had taken a chance that the Colonel might be in and he had been right, his call answered directly since Colonel Thomas Clancy's secretary—or receptionist, assistant, whatever she was called—was now sulking on her couch back at her apartment.

She'll get over it.

In fact she already had, or at least partly. She understood the job and the fact he could be called away at a moment's notice. She understood that more than most since she worked with the Colonel five days a week. She was a little miffed at first that it was a favor for a friend, though when she had heard of Professor Palmer being shot and kidnapped, she had quickly whipped him together a quick bite to eat though he knew she was disappointed.

So was he.

But Professor Palmer had been instrumental in helping them with the Circle of Eight, and both professors had proven themselves to be good people, people who could be relied upon to always do the right thing, even if it meant risking their own lives for strangers.

And he owed them.

They all owed them.

Their first encounter had been ignominious at best. They had been given falsified intel, told Professor Acton was the head of a domestic terror cell and that he and his students were all on the President's Termination List.

He wasn't proud of what had happened and it still tormented him to this day, and when the dust had settled, he had tried to make up for all the innocent deaths by being a better person, and whenever possible, helping James Acton and Laura Palmer.

It had been tough at first. In fact, the first time Acton had seen him after those events he had swung a baseball bat at his head. He smiled. He liked to think that there was at least mutual respect there, and perhaps they might even be friends of a sort. The professors had even sent Bravo Team an invite to the wedding. They hadn't been able to attend, prepping for a mission to Afghanistan—and it probably wouldn't have been appropriate regardless—but Niner had sent a photo with them all standing against an unmarked wall.

With their faces all pixelated.

And a caption underneath.

Congratulations on your nuptials.
We're really happy we failed.
(To kill you that is.)

He shook his head. Niner was hilarious. Red was his best friend but Niner was definitely among his closest. All the guys were to varying degrees. He would die for any one of them, even the newer guys.

They were his brothers in arms.

His family.

And the head of that family was Colonel Thomas Clancy, a man he trusted implicitly, a man he knew always had their backs even if things were a total Charlie-Foxtrot and they were being disowned by their government.

Clancy would never give up on them.

He believed in loyalty, deeply, which was why Dawson was confident Clancy would give him the greenlight to head to Europe.

As long as the Colonel didn't already have plans for him.

He knocked on the closed inner office door.

"Enter!"

Dawson opened the door, stepping inside. "Good afternoon, Colonel."

Clancy grunted, jabbing toward a chair with an unlit cigar, his battle to give up his habit still ongoing.

It's going to get even tougher now that relations with Cuba are normalizing.

"What can I do for you, Sergeant Major?"

"I need a favor," replied Dawson, sitting in his chair. "Or rather, I need a green light to do a favor."

Clancy tore his eyes away from his computer screen. "Explain."

"I received a message that Professor Laura Palmer was shot and kidnapped in Paris just a few hours ago. I'd like to head over there, on my own time and dime, to see if there's anything I can do to help."

Clancy jammed the cigar in his mouth. "Those two are in trouble again?"

Dawson shrugged. "Their files make for entertaining reading."

"True. Someone should make a movie. We've got nothing in play at the moment for your team, but be prepared for recall just in case."

"Of course." Dawson started to stand then paused. "I hate to go on vacation alone."

Clancy shook his head. "Niner's newly single, isn't he? Take him, it'll keep him out of trouble."

"Thanks, Colonel." Dawson quickly rose, heading for the door. "Enjoy the rest of your weekend, Colonel."

Another grunt. "Cheryl's sister is in town visiting. If I could find a reason I'd be here 'til Monday."

Dawson chuckled. "Good luck, sir."

He closed the office door behind him and fished out his phone, putting an end to Niner's weekend.

Rome, Italy

Vatican Inspector General Mario Giasson watched as the last reinforced metal case was loaded into the back of the armored car. Half a dozen priceless relics had been flown under tight security to Rome, held under heavy police guard at the airport until they had all arrived. It would be a single transport to the Holy See, with an armed police escort.

Nobody would be stealing this shipment.

Not tonight.

He had been devastated to hear from his friend Hugh Reading that Laura Palmer had been shot and kidnapped. His heart went out to her poor husband and he had taken a moment to say a silent prayer. They were good people and unfortunately God seemed intent on testing them repeatedly.

But they were strong people, and he knew they would persevere, though his optimism relied heavily upon the hope Professor Palmer was still alive.

Unfortunately he had seen too many good people taken before their time, and though it hurt those who remained behind, he felt confident that it was the Lord's will every time.

"Let's go!" he shouted, the truck secure. He climbed into the passenger seat of his escort vehicle, young Francesco Greco driving. Two police vehicles pulled out first, lights flashing, the armored car next followed by their car and two trailing police escorts. The six vehicle procession was soon leaving the airport and moving through the streets of Rome.

He squeezed his phone in his hand as his fingers tapped on his knee.

"Relax, boss, there's no way they'd dare hit us. There's too many police."

"That didn't stop them in Paris."

"They weren't expecting them. That was an ambush."

Giasson grunted. "Until we're through the gates and back home…"

Traffic was light, it almost three in the morning, but he couldn't help but eyeball every vehicle they passed, or that passed them. The tension was killing him, his chest tight, his muscles contracted, his stomach protesting with a bit of acid reflux.

He reached for his antacids.

A light ahead changed and the procession slowed, Greco stopping just shy of the bumper. A horn honked ahead and Giasson leaned against his window to see what was happening.

And cursed.

"What the hell is that?"

He could see a man walking down the middle of the road, some sort of wide spray emitting from a nozzle he had aimed at the lead police car. He spun around, his side view mirror having revealed another man coming up from behind them, doing the same thing to the rear police cars.

Reaching for the door handle, he stopped as somebody jumped on the hood of their car, then hopped off.

"Get down!" shouted Greco, grabbing Giasson by the jacket and yanking him forward. Giasson caught a glimpse of something on the rear doors of the armored car just as his head dipped below the dash, a terrific explosion rocking the car. He sat up, taking stock of himself for a brief moment, then turned to Greco.

"Are you okay?"

The young man nodded then reached for his door just as two men passed them, spraying both sides of their car with some sort of foam. Giasson yanked on the handle and pushed the door open.

It barely gave.

He pushed harder, the door only opening about an inch.

"Try yours."

Greco pushed on his door, hard, to no avail.

Somebody jumped on the hood again then dove into the back of the armored car, the two officers inside tossed unceremoniously onto the hood of their car, the blast strong enough to have knocked them out cold. Giasson shoved on his door repeatedly, getting more and more frustrated with each futile push.

He roared in rage as the cases containing the priceless relics were handed out and loaded into the back of a van that had just pulled up.

"Goddammit!" he shouted, pulling his weapon, immediately beginning to recite a Hail Mary for taking his Lord's name in vain.

"Sir, no!" shouted Greco, grabbing for the weapon. "Bulletproof glass!"

Giasson bit his tongue, cutting off another curse, then slammed the butt of the gun into the dash repeatedly as the last case was offloaded.

And to add insult to injury, the final man out of the truck grinned and waved at them before jumping to the ground and climbing into the waiting van.

It was over in minutes, seconds even, the operation carried out with textbook efficiency, as if those involved were military trained. But it didn't matter anymore.

The relics were gone.

And with this theft, almost all physical traces of the Lord our Christ were missing, almost everything thought to trace back to those hours spent dying for our sins were gone, perhaps forever, for some unknown purpose.

And for the first time in years, he felt the burning desire to kill.

BLOOD RELICS

Hotel Astor Saint Honore, Paris, France

Reading groaned, stretching as he looked about the room. It was pitch dark, the blackout curtains doing their job, keeping the nighttime city lights from disturbing him. He looked at the clock, cursing.

His phone vibrated again.

Yanking off his CPAP mask—his doctor having told him to never leave home without it—he grabbed his phone and swiped his thumb.

"Hello?"

"Hi Hugh, it's Mario."

Reading grunted. "Waking me seems to be a habit with you."

"Sorry, mon ami, but there's been another theft."

Reading closed his eyes, drawing in a deep breath. "Where?"

"Two meters from my own nose. They hit the convoy transporting the bulk of the remaining Blood Relics."

Reading's eyes shot open. "You're kidding me! Any casualties?"

"None. Not a single shot fired."

"How the bloody hell did they manage that?"

"They used some sort of spray adhesive on the doors of the escort vehicles, trapping us inside, then blew the doors off the back of the armored car. If I hadn't seen it with my own eyes I wouldn't have believed it myself."

Reading shook his head. These guys were good. Too good. They had changed their MO again, back to non-lethal methods, which made him think what happened in Paris was an anomaly, there no reason for them to come in shooting like they had.

"These guys are too good to be just common thieves."

"They're not," replied Giasson. "We've had our first break. Three of the men caught on camera in Vienna have just been identified."

"Why the hell wasn't I notified?"

"Probably in your email," replied Giasson. "I guess they figured you needed your beauty sleep."

Reading grunted. "Details?"

"They're all known mercenaries, former KSK Special Forces."

"KSK?"

"German."

"German?"

"Yes."

"Interesting. One of them here sounded German. I think he was the same guy from the video in Vienna. Was he identified?"

"No, he's still a mystery. He didn't show up in any database."

Reading cursed. "So we've identified the hired help. I'll make sure my people are running down known associates, see if we can figure out how they're usually paid."

"Follow the money."

"Exactly. And these guys are clearly well-funded."

Giasson paused. "How's Jim doing?"

"Not good. He finally got to sleep a few hours ago, but until we find out what happened to Laura, one way or the other, I'm afraid he's going to be a wreck."

"Completely understandable. Listen, with pretty much the entire known collection of Blood Relics now in their hands, there's not much more that he can do to help us. This has turned into a criminal investigation. Tell him that we thank him for his help, and relieve him of any obligation to continue. He should be concentrating on himself now."

Reading laughed. "You don't know Jim very well. He'll never rest until he finds her."

He could hear Giasson breathe deeply. "If it were my wife, I would do the same."

"If it were mine, I'd go for a pint."

Giasson chuckled. "You're terrible."

"I'm divorced."

"I know, and you're still terrible."

Reading smiled. "I'm going to contact London and get an update. Then some sleep. Be safe, my friend."

"You too. Goodnight."

Reading opened his laptop, flipping through his emails then noticed one from Acton.

Kraft Dinner called. Help on way.

Reading had to think for a moment what he meant. *Kraft Dinner. KD. Kane, Dylan.* It was Acton's code name in his phone for his former student, now CIA operative. And if support of that nature was on the way, it opened up new options that might actually help them.

These guys don't wait for warrants.

Kruger Residence, Outside Paris, France

Dietrich sat in a chair at his father's bedside, his mother lying beside him, holding her husband gently, the turn his father had taken not improving. The doctor had suggested he had days, perhaps only hours.

It was the most gut wrenching experience of his life.

They were all waiting for Dr. Heinrich to report on the latest relics. It never took very long to determine if there was anything usable on the objects he retrieved, and so far, including the relics from Paris, nothing had shown any blood or DNA. He didn't understand the process, it wasn't his job, that's why they had Heinrich. The man was a genius in his field, and if he said the relics so far were of no use, then he believed the man.

But even if Heinrich did find usable DNA, it might still take days to replicate enough blood to save his father.

And he was certain the man didn't have that kind of time left.

Science would be what ultimately saved his family, not religion, of that he was certain. Once his father passed he would give up what he feared was a fool's errand, there no reason to continue it. He hoped he had at least another twenty years in him, and his own son, only two now, would have another fifty. Fifty years for modern medical science to find a cure.

Surely they can do it by then!

A cure for his son and future grandson.

It's what drove him.

It's what had driven them all over the years. To be as successful as possible in life so that the next generation could build on that success, for even one hundred years ago they knew money was the key to everything. Without money no doctors would help them, and as modern medicine came into being, they knew money was needed in order for doctors to research a disease as obscure as theirs, and to research why in his family it never seemed to skip a generation.

They had the money, medical science had reached the point where finding a cure was at least possible, meaning now was the perfect time.

But not for his father. His time was rapidly running out, there no cure for him.

Except for the Blood Relics.

He had been raised Catholic and believed in it all, deeply. There was something comforting about his faith, especially living his entire life with an hourglass quickly draining him of healthy years. He believed in Christ and that His blood could heal all man's ailments, but he didn't have his father's faith that His blood could be found.

The spear was the only thing he fervently believed would have blood on it and could have possibly survived. In his mind the cross would have been reused by the Romans, not left for the mourners to take with them. And how could they take it with them? It was massive and heavy. To claim to have actual pieces of the cross seemed ludicrous to him.

He could at least understand the Crown of Thorns. It made sense that someone might take that with them, but for it to survive two thousand years? Then there was the collected blood, the sponges, the cloths. None of it made sense to him, though he had never been witness to the death of someone he believed was the Son of God.

But the spear, the spear did make sense to him.

It was the one thing referred to in the Bible that irrefutably would have His blood on it and could conceivably survive. The tip that would have pierced His side was metal, which meant it would survive unless it was melted down for some other purpose, and if the legends were true and Longinus, the man who had stabbed Jesus, had actually converted to what was now known as Christianity, he would most certainly have preserved the spear.

But they had stolen all the purported copies of it, and none had tested positive.

It was lost to history.

As his father soon would be.

Maybe the other objects do *make sense.*

If the people with Jesus when he died truly believed he was the Son of God, then they knew that the occasion was momentous, historical, important. They would have treasured anything that remained of him, whether it be the Crown of Thorns, a sponge or a jar of his collected blood. Many ancient religious artifacts had been preserved for hundreds if not thousands of years.

Why not these?

What many people didn't realize was that after the Jewish-Roman Wars, the first of which happened within a few decades of His death, the Roman's slaughtered the Jews, destroying their towns and cities, decimating their populations and persecuting those who survived, forcing them to scatter from their homeland, not to return successfully until the mid-twentieth century.

And it had meant much of the written record was destroyed from that era, as it was for most cultures that were conquered.

But a spear would survive.

One of hundreds of thousands of spears probably made during that era.

But it wouldn't matter soon.

Soon his father would be dead, the Blood Relic search would be over, and he would put himself back into the hands of medical science in the hopes they could save him and his descendants from this curse.

There was a knock on the door.

"Come in," he said and the door opened, Dr. Heinrich stepping inside, his face telling them everything he needed to know.

"Any luck?" asked his mother, but he could tell she already knew.

Heinrich shook his head. "I'm sorry, but the only DNA I found was from the fresh blood of the woman who was shot. Some of it contaminated several of the objects."

Dietrich jumped to his feet, beginning to pace at the foot of his father's bed. "You're certain?"

"Yes, sir. I'll be rechecking everything just in case, but I'm not confident." Heinrich paused. "Are there any other objects to be tested?"

Dietrich shook his head. "No. The only ones that remain are ones even the Vatican doesn't believe are real otherwise they would have had them moved like the others." He cursed, his shoulders slumping. "It's over."

"No."

He spun toward his father, the voice the strongest he had heard it since his return from Rome. "Father, I'm not sure what else we can do."

"Find the spear."

"But we've got three already and they all tested negative."

"They weren't the real spear."

Dietrich grabbed his hair, pulling hard, trying to stop himself from saying something he might regret, his exasperation with his father about to send him over the edge. He needed to shout and scream and cry, but instead he was supposed to be the dutiful son who would immediately take over the moment his father died.

He walked over to the wall and punched it.

Immediately regretting it.

"Let me look at that," said Dr. Heinrich, walking over to him. Dietrich held out his hand, taking a deep breath.

"Father, I don't know where else to look."

"That's because we've been going about this all wrong."

Dietrich pulled his hand away from the doctor. "What do you mean?"

"Don't look for the spear. Look for Longinus himself."

Dietrich's eyebrows climbed his forehead. "You mean—"

"He's a saint. He was well respected in his time, and only his head was brought back to Jerusalem when he was finally captured. I guarantee you his supporters gave him a proper burial, and I also guarantee you he would have been buried with his spear."

Dietrich's head was bobbing up and down slowly as his father spoke. He was right. Countless soldiers from that era were found buried with their weapons, and someone like Longinus, who had become a leader among the newly born religion, would have been revered after his death. If they could find his body they might very well find the genuine spear.

The only Blood Relic he truly believed might have the blood of Christ on it.

"But how do we find him?"

His father smiled. "Don't we have an archeologist as a guest?"

A smile climbed up half his face.

Kruger Residence, Outside Paris, France

Laura opened her eyes, the pain killers she was on having knocked her out hours ago. The dull ache in her stomach continued, but a glance down seemed to show little blood seeping through the bandages.

She was going to live.

At least for now. She still had no idea what the endgame was. Her captors had clearly demonstrated their willingness to kill for their cause, and when religious causes were involved, fanatical believers quite often committed unspeakable atrocities.

But rarely were these things committed by Christians.

But there's always the exception.

Her conversation with the doctor that had saved her—a man she had learned was named Heinrich—suggested this man Dietrich, the son of the man behind it all, might be just crazy enough to kill her in a blind rage.

She spotted a man staring at her from the doorway and flinched.

"Dr. Palmer, I think it's time we spoke."

She nodded, pressing the button to raise her bed so she could at least feel like she was in a little less vulnerable position. She had been in situations similar to this before and she knew the key to survival was keeping her wits about her, to not panic, and to observe everything.

The young man crossed the room, stopping at the foot of her bed. She recognized him as the man from Paris who seemed to be giving all the orders.

Which ironically meant he was the man who had saved her life.

Perhaps only to take it away.

"My name is Dietrich, my last name is unimportant." She sighed silently, knowing that if the man gave his full name it was yet another reason to kill her to tie up loose ends. "I assume you've figured out what has been going on?"

She adjusted herself in the bed, wincing as the stitches stretched. "You're trying to recover Blood Relics in an attempt to extract Christ's DNA so your doctor here"—she nodded toward Heinrich, still working in the lab—"can use it to create blood to cure your family of a genetic disease."

Dietrich smiled slightly. "I see Dr. Heinrich is lonely again." He looked at the man, the doctor seemingly more preoccupied by his work than a moment before. "No matter, it simply saves me time. My father is dying, and will die soon. As I'm sure the talkative Dr. Heinrich has already told you, none of the artifacts we have managed to recover have any DNA on them."

"I'm not surprised," replied Laura. "Most of what you've stolen has either been shown to not be from that era, or never been tested at all."

Dietrich sat on the edge of her bed. "Do you mind?" he asked after the fact.

She shook her head.

Like I have a choice?

"We're a desperate family, Dr. Palmer. For over a century the males of my family have been born with an incurable genetic illness that seems to never skip a generation. I'm told it's an autosomal dominant disorder, a variation of Huntington's. Incurable. Once the symptoms start, we're dead within no more than twenty years, usually closer to ten."

"Do you…"

"Yes, I have recently begun to have spasms in my leg." He paled slightly. "I will be dead before I'm fifty, perhaps even forty."

"I'm sorry to hear that."

He looked at her, chewing on his bottom lip. "Yes, I think you actually are." He sucked in a deep breath. "My father may only have days. Which is why I need your help."

She wanted to laugh. *My help? You almost killed me and now you're holding me prisoner!*

She said nothing.

"We need to find Longinus."

Laura's archeological side's interest was irresistibly piqued. "The Roman soldier who legend has it pierced the side of Jesus with a lance?"

Dietrich nodded. "I see your reputation is well-deserved."

"What makes you think he can be found?"

"If we assume he's real—"

"Which is quite an assumption."

"—then we can assume those around him would have treated his body with respect."

"It's been two thousand years."

"And older have been found."

"Yes, but—"

"But nothing!" Dietrich ended the debate, his shouted words and change in facial expression suggesting the crazed irrationality Dr. Heinrich had alluded to. "He must be found."

"Why?" Her voice more subdued this time, deciding confrontation was not the way to go, and as she thought about it, if he *needed* her, then that meant she'd be kept alive.

Which meant more of a chance for James to find her.

"Because we're hoping the actual Spear of Destiny will have been buried with him."

Her head nodded irresistibly. It did make sense, a soldier in those days often buried with his weapons, especially if buried reverently, which if he were the man legend suggested, he would have been. She decided to give him a bone. "That's quite plausible."

"Good!" Some sense of optimism returned as Dietrich's face relaxed, his eyes opening a little wider, the corners of his mouth turning up slightly. "Then we'll need to get started right away, there's no time to waste."

Which is when the obvious flaw in Dietrich's plan was finally articulated. "I'm in no condition to go relic hunting."

Dietrich stood. "*You* won't be doing anything, Dr. Palmer. Your husband will be. And should he fail, and my father die, then so will you."

Hotel Astor Saint Honore, Paris, France

James Acton poked at his poached egg, moving it around the small bowl, the pierced yoke slowly oozing out, coating the bright white bone china. He knew he had to eat but he had no appetite. In fact, he felt sick to his stomach.

Reading sat across from him at the table, scanning emailed updates on the case, delivering the highlights between bites of heavily buttered croissants. The vehicles involved in the Rome robbery had been found abandoned with no physical evidence obtained and there had been no sightings of any vehicles leaving the helicopter landing site outside Paris.

The only lead so far was the names of several of the men involved, all of whom were known mercenaries.

At least it was something, something that Kane and his contacts might be able to work with.

He was tempted to call Kane right now, to find out if they had learned anything, but he knew that would just be a waste of time. If they had found something, they would have told him.

His phone vibrated on the table sending a ripple through the top of his untouched coffee.

Blocked number.

He answered.

"Hello?"

"Is this Professor James Acton?"

The German accent immediately set off alarm bells, Acton bolting upright in his chair, pointing at the phone to get Reading's attention. The former detective immediately jumped from his chair, making a call in hushed tones.

"Yes. Who is this?"

"My name is of no importance. What is of importance is that I have your wife."

Acton collapsed in his chair. "Is"—he hesitated, terrified of what the answer might be, hopeful of what it could be—"is she alive?"

"Yes, Professor, for now."

Relief swept over him and he forced himself to maintain control, tears of relief welling in his eyes. Then the last two words registered.

For now.

"Can I speak to her?"

"No."

"Wh-what do you want?"

"I assume you are aware of what we have been acquiring over the past several days."

Acquiring? Interesting choice of words.

"Blood Relics."

"Exactly. But there is one relic that has eluded us."

"Yes?"

"The *genuine* Spear of Destiny."

"You've stolen three of them."

"None of which are the genuine article as you are fully aware."

Acton frowned but said nothing, Reading returning to the table, pushing a pad and pen toward him with several words written on it.

Proof of life!

"We want you to find the genuine spear. In exchange, we will give you your wife."

Acton felt his chest tighten, his fingers gripping the pen tightly, the cheap blue plastic turning white as it threatened to snap. "How am I supposed to find that?"

"Find its owner."

Acton's eyes narrowed. "I beg your pardon?"

"Find Longinus, the man to whom it belonged."

Acton leaned back in his chair, his eyes popping wider for a moment in surprise. It was an intriguing idea. Find the body rather than the spear in the hopes that it had been buried with the man. It was at least within the realm of possibility that the body might still exist, preserved somewhere due to his stature among his followers.

Assuming he ever existed.

But at the moment he had to believe he did.

Or at least make this man think he did.

For every minute that he could delay things was a minute Kane and the others could use to find her.

"I'll need to speak to my wife before I agree to anything."

There was an exasperated exclamation from the man then the sound of footsteps echoing in what sounded like a large room. He jotted down everything he was hearing.

Footsteps echoing

Large room?

Steps ~~30~~/~~40~~/~~50~~/60

Door opening

Another big room?

"Hello?"

The sound of his wife's voice destroyed any blocks he had set up, the tears erupting as his shoulders began to shake in relief. "I-it's me."

"Oh God, James, it's so good to hear your voice!"

"Ar-are you okay?"

"Doctor Heinrich says I'm going to be fine. I'm in a really well-equipped lab here and I'm being treated well."

She never ceased to amaze him. Her voice was strong and he knew she was giving him vital clues, jotting down the doctor's name and the fact she was in a lab.

"I'm so happy to hear you're okay. I-I thought you were…" He couldn't bring himself to say it, her ordeal not yet over, and there no guarantee she would be returned to him. "I love you and—"

"That's enough." The man with the German accent replaced Laura's breathing and he felt the pit return to his stomach for a moment. "You will find us the genuine Spear of Destiny. Understood?"

"Yes, but what if it can't be found?"

"Then, Professor Acton, your wife dies."

The call ended and Acton placed his phone on the table, his mind a flurry of mixed emotions, terror at the prospect of his wife being killed should he fail, but elation in knowing she was alive and not dying from the gunshot wound.

"Well?"

He looked at an expectant Reading, still holding his own phone to his ear.

"She's alive."

"Thank God!"

"But they're going to kill her if I can't find the Spear of Destiny."

Reading's eyes narrowed. "Wasn't that one of the items they already stole?"

"Three of them, actually. And none were genuine."

"Do you know where it is?"

Acton shook his head. "Haven't a clue, but their suggestion—and I have to say it's a good one—is to find the body of Saint Longinus, the man who the spear belonged to."

"You mean the bloke who stabbed Jesus and got his eyesight back?"

"Yes."

"Any idea where *he* is?"

"I have an idea where he was about five hundred years ago."

"Well, that's a start." Reading's words dripped with sarcasm.

"I'm going to need help in finding this."

Reading nodded. "I'll do whatever I can."

Acton shook his head. "No, I want you concentrating on finding Laura. Find her and I don't need to find the spear."

"Did they give you a deadline?"

"No, but if they're going to all this trouble I'm assuming whoever they want to heal doesn't have much time."

Reading motioned toward the pad. "What's that?"

"What I was hearing. While I was waiting for him to bring the phone to Laura I heard about sixty footsteps in what I thought was a large room but I think must have been a large hallway, then a door open and more steps in another large room."

"So some sort of warehouse maybe?"

"Maybe. Laura though gave me some critical info that I don't know if the guy picked up on."

"What?"

"She said the doctor who treated her was named Heinrich and that she was in a well-equipped lab."

"Interesting. I'll run the name, see what we come up with."

"Good." Acton eyed his food, suddenly starving. "I'm going to eat then contact Mai. I need some research done." Acton grabbed his fork and tucked into his breakfast, now cold.

He didn't care.

His wife was alive.

And he was determined to save her.

BLOOD RELICS

Trinh Residence, St. Paul, Maryland

Mai Lien Trinh ended the phone call to her father, tears in her eyes. It was exactly twelve hours later in her homeland of Vietnam, which meant many of her phone calls were made in the middle of the night. If she waited until she got home from the university, either her friends were still asleep, getting ready for work, or at work. Then by the time they were done their work day, it was time for *her* to sleep or get ready for work.

The only way she could keep in touch was to make her calls in the very early morning, when her friends were getting home from work, or on the weekends.

She couldn't wait that long between calls.

In her culture families were extremely close, often several generations living within one home, her family no different except for her troubled brother who had left the family home as quickly as he could.

He had chosen a path of petty crime, a very dangerous vocation in Communist Vietnam, though it was that very lifestyle that had probably saved her life during the Hanoi incident where she first met Professors Acton and Palmer. She found now that she couldn't see him she was missing him more than she ever had before, despite seeing him rarely back home.

Home.

She wasn't sure if she would ever be able to call the United States home. She hadn't come here willingly, she was more of a political refugee, though she was grateful for being allowed to stay. The professors had taken her in, given her a home and a job, and she had to admit, with the exception of the loneliness, life was good.

147

She was working hard to improve her English by trying to only watch American TV and only surf English websites, though sometimes she yearned to hear her native tongue.

That was what the phone calls were partly for.

She could read and write English quite well, her challenge understanding rapid conversations and getting rid of her accent, though Tommy, someone she had met in the computer lab at the university, had said she sounded cute.

She flushed with the thought.

Cute!

She never thought of herself as cute. She didn't think she was ugly, just plain, though in America apparently there was something called Yellow Fever where a lot of American guys liked Asian girls.

Even the bookworms like her.

She didn't like the attention, which forced her to be even more bookish.

Her clothes were baggier, she wore her hair so that when she walked she could just lower her chin and her long black locks would act as blinders to the world around her.

She'd just have to get used to it.

Her phone vibrated with an email. She bolted upright in bed when she saw who it was from.

Professor Acton!

She had heard the horrible news yesterday, Dean Milton having called her to his office, plus it had made the late news reports. Professor Palmer had been shot and kidnapped, the news almost causing her to throw up in Milton's office, memories of the horrors they went through in Hanoi almost overwhelming her.

Milton had told her to go home and take a few days off.

She simply couldn't imagine being cooped up in her tiny apartment alone, worrying.

She needed to be doing something.

She opened the email, quickly reading it, exhilaration and fear filling her as she realized that Professor Palmer was alive but perhaps not for long unless they could find the body of this Christian Saint named Longinus.

And he needed her help.

She immediately replied, letting him know she was heading for the university now and would begin the research he needed.

She hit send then the shower, her stomach in knots with the uncertainty of the task ahead.

How can we possibly find a man who died two thousand years ago?

Chris Leroux & Sherrie White Residence, Fairfax Towers, Falls Church, Virginia

Chris Leroux stretched with a satisfied groan, his arms above his shoulders, one leg stretching far out followed by the other. He rolled over to hug his girlfriend but found the bed empty.

He frowned then heard the shower running.

He jumped out of bed, sporting a morning wood that had to be put down. He heard the faucet squeaking as Sherrie finished her shower. Opening the door, he peered through the cloud of steam, his girlfriend loving super-hot showers.

He preferred them to not leave first degree burns on his back.

The steam poured out the door and into the hallway, quickly revealing the most gorgeous girl he had ever set eyes on.

And she's all yours!

It was still rather remarkable to him that this woman loved him, but he was slowly realizing that she actually did. His recent revelation to her that he finally felt he deserved her had gone over like gangbusters, and though his self-consciousness and shyness were still well-entrenched personality traits, he at least wasn't constantly worrying that this girl he had always felt was way out of his league was preparing to leave him anytime soon.

"Is that for me?" she asked, nodding toward Mr. Happy.

He grinned.

"Get your laptop, you'll have to rub that out yourself. I'm leaving in ten minutes. Apparently I've got an op."

He sighed. Sherrie White was CIA, as was he, but she was on the operational side, an actual Agent. He was an Analyst. Senior Analyst now, with a team of eight reporting to him, something he was still getting used to. "How long will you be gone?"

"Don't know yet but I was told to bring my go bag."

"So at least overnight."

"Probably."

She tossed the towel at him then grabbed him down below, giving him a squeeze. "I'll miss you."

"I'll miss you too."

"I wasn't talking to *you*." She winked and laughed, swatting his flag pole, leaving him wagging and frustrated. "Your phone's vibrating!"

He rushed to the bedroom, Sherrie handing him the already answered phone. "Hello?"

"Hey buddy, it's me."

Leroux grinned as he immediately recognized the voice of his best friend, probably his only real friend, Dylan Kane. They were old high school buddies that had went their separate ways but found themselves later in life working at the CIA in very different capacities. "Hey, how are you?"

He wasn't sure how secure the line was so he avoided using his friend's name or asking any specifics whenever he called. More often than not Kane had a habit of just appearing in their apartment.

He never minded.

"I feel like shit. Some sort of food poisoning I think."

"Let's hope that's all it is."

"Well, I have pissed off the Russians a few times, so polonium is a definite possibility!" Kane laughed then groaned. "Quick call, I'm going to be hitting the head in sixty seconds to test the plumbing here again. I sent you an encrypted email that I need you to read right away. See what you can do, okay?"

"Sure," replied Leroux, flipping open his laptop and logging in with the facial recognition software. "Just give me two seconds." He opened up his secure email, entering another password and a thumb scan. He clicked on the email from Kane, quickly reading it. "Them again?" He had been involved before in helping these two professors, he usually Kane's go-to-guy when there was off-the-books trouble.

Kane laughed. "Yeah, those two were doomed to find each other. I've got a buddy who's going to provide support on the ground, details are in the email. I need a data guy. Can you help?"

"Should be able to." He didn't mind helping, it was just that his boss, Director Leif Morrison, seemed to always know exactly what he was up to. Which he supposed wasn't a surprise considering he was the Chief of Clandestine Operations. "Can I get it cleared?"

Kane moaned in what sounded like excruciating pain. "If you have to." The words sounded forced, the pain clearly getting worse.

"You should see a doctor."

"It'll pass. Literally and figuratively."

"Still…"

"Gotta go. Keep me posted on what happens, I'm just not going to be able to get hands-on with this one." He grunted. "Oh shit, gotta go."

The call ended and Leroux tossed his phone on the bed beside his laptop, concern for his friend apparently etched on his face.

"What's wrong?"

He looked up at Sherrie who was fully dressed, standing at the foot of the bed. "Dylan's sick. Food poisoning. He wants me to help out with those two professors."

"Acton and Palmer?"

He nodded. "Yeah, apparently Palmer was shot in Paris and kidnapped."

"Holy crap! Do they know who did it?"

Leroux shook his head. "Doesn't look like it. I'll know more once I start digging."

Sherrie leaned in and gave him a peck on the lips that turned into a lingering kiss. "Mmm, I'm going to miss you," she finally said, her eyes closed, her forehead pressed against his. "Love you."

"Love you too. Be careful."

"Always am." She looked at her watch. "I'm going to be late. Gotta go!"

She hurried from the bedroom and he heard the alarm system chime as the door to their apartment opened then closed. Turning his attention back to his laptop he began firing off data requests to the Langley databases, the results of which would be waiting for him when he got back to work.

On a whim, he pulled up the morning intel briefing and as he read bullet after bullet that seemed to involve the two professors, his eyebrows slowly migrated up his forehead.

What have they gotten themselves into?

Hotel Astor Saint Honore, Paris, France

Acton looked up from his laptop as Reading entered from one of the suite's two bedrooms, freshly showered. He motioned toward Acton's computer.

"Any news?"

Acton nodded. "I've got the first chunk of research from Mai."

"Let me guess, there's no map with an arrow pointing to a spot marked X?"

Acton chuckled as he leaned back in his chair, stretching with a groan. "Nope. If we believe the legends, he fled Jerusalem a few days after the crucifixion, got himself baptized along with a few other soldiers that fled with him, then went north to modern day Turkey where he lived for fifteen years before finally being found and beheaded."

Reading pushed the sheers aside, looking at the Paris skyline. "So, I suppose we're not looking for his head. Where'd his body go then?"

"Well, the head went to Jerusalem where the Roman Prefect Pilate had it sent to the senior rabbi who had demanded these men be killed. The rabbi then tossed it on a dung heap where it was retrieved by an old lady who claimed to have seen a vision of Longinus telling her he would take care of her recently deceased son and told her where the head was. It was then reunited with his body in Cappadocia."

"Modern day Turkey."

"Yes."

"I sense a 'but'."

"I'll make an archeologist out of you yet."

"Not bloody likely." Reading sat down at the table, across from Acton.

Acton smiled, happy to have his mind occupied with something other than worry. He had a mission, a task that needed to be completed with the most precious of rewards at the end.

And the most heinous punishment should he fail.

Despite the scant evidence of where the man might be buried, he had to keep a positive attitude. He had discovered unbelievable things in his years as an archeologist and this would just be one more to add to his list of achievements.

There was no way he could accept failure.

He pointed at the notes he had made on his screen. "There're numerous reports that his body was moved after his death which makes perfect sense. The Romans and the Jewish leadership in Jerusalem were persecuting the new Christians vigorously so Longinus' followers would most likely have hid his body, and with most soldiers being from Italia—"

"Modern day Italy?"

"Very good."

"Who needs a doctorate and twenty years of experience?"

"Apparently not you. *As* I was saying, with most soldiers being from Italia, it's very plausible that he was moved there by his companions since Christianity had barely reached the homeland. In Italia they most likely wouldn't be actively hunted."

"So he's not in Turkey."

"Unlikely."

"Good. I doubt we'd get the necessary clearances to go gallivanting around there especially with what's going on in Syria."

"True. So if we assume he was moved from there, the question is where."

"Italy's a big place."

"Indeed. But there're clues. The oldest stories have him being taken to Mantua, an ancient island city in Italia—Italy—and buried there. Why, we're not sure, but a Christian following did develop in the area ahead of much of the rest of Italia, which suggests followers of the new religion travelled there for a specific purpose. That there was an early Christian presence there has been proven, just not why. The stories that Longinus was moved there would certainly provide a reason for this early toehold."

"But…"

"But history, legend, folklore, whatever you want to call it, suggests he was moved yet again."

"Of course he was. Where?"

"Anywhere from Rome to Sardinia to Greece."

"Lovely."

"But!"

"Ooh, a good but?"

"Possibly. He apparently turned up in the Basilica of Sant'Agostino in the fourteenth or fifteenth century, but the records of him actually being there have been lost."

"But could possibly be found?"

Acton threw his hands up with a sigh. "I've started with less."

"Where's this basilica?"

"Rome."

There was a knock on the door, startling Acton, his nerves still keeping him on edge.

Reading rose. "I'll go." He strode to the door quietly, evidently feeling an abundance of caution was necessary, making Acton feel a little better about his own anxiety. Reading peered through the peephole and stepped back, smiling. "Help's arrived."

He pulled open the door and Acton jumped up in excitement as Command Sergeant Major Burt "Big Dog" Dawson and Sergeant Carl "Niner" Sung entered the room, dropping heavy duffel bags in the entrance as Reading closed the door behind them.

"Am I ever glad to see you guys!"

Acton pumped their hands, ushering them toward the comfortable chairs the two-bedroom suite offered. "Good to see you too, Professor, I just wish it was under better circumstances," replied Dawson as the two men, obviously tired, dropped into the well-padded seats.

"Thirsty?"

They both nodded and Acton headed for the fully stocked fridge in the kitchenette, pitching them each an ice cold bottle of water.

"Thanks, Doc," said Niner as he twisted the cap off. "And thanks for those first class tickets. You've spoiled me. I'm never flying coach again."

Dawson grunted. "I'll never hear the end of it the next time we're in a Herc."

"Shoot me now!" cried Niner, grabbing his seat cushion and pretending to vibrate. "I'm having flashbacks of Afghanistan!"

"Don't tempt me." Dawson nodded toward the bags near the entrance. "We arranged for a few supplies."

"Weapons?" asked Reading.

"Are you asking as a cop?"

Reading smiled. "Never mind."

Niner grinned. "Good choice." He looked at Acton. "Any word on your wife?"

"You got my last update about the phone call?"

They both nodded.

"Then that's about it. I'm heading for Rome shortly to begin my search for Saint Longinus, but I'm not overly optimistic, especially with the time constraints I think we're under."

Niner put his water bottle on the table. "You're still convinced this is all about the blood of Christ and healing some sick dude?"

"Yes. The German guy confirmed it's about the blood, or at least the Blood Relics, but not why. The only thing I can think of is its purported healing properties. And Laura did refer to a doctor and a lab."

"We'll operate under that assumption," said Dawson. "You said you're going to Rome?"

"Yes."

"Then one of us will go with you—"

"No," interrupted Acton, shaking his head. "I want the three of you looking for Laura. It's a hell of a lot more likely you'll find her than I'll find some two thousand year old corpse. The Vatican Inspector General—"

"Giasson?"

Acton nodded. Dawson and the others on his team had dealt with Giasson during the storming of the Vatican they had all become mixed up in. "Yes, Mario's agreed to provide security for us while we're there."

"Us?"

"I've got some academic help arriving this afternoon."

"Okay, we'll leave the relic hunting to you. As long as our hostiles think you're useful to them, you're probably safe. We'll focus on finding your wife. I've forwarded all the intel we've got to our contact at Langley, and if I know him, he'll come up with something. In the meantime I think we need to run down the one lead we do have."

"What's that?"

"These KSK guys."

"That's exactly what I was thinking," said Reading, shaking a sheaf of papers. "They all used to work for Renner Security based in Stuttgart, Germany."

Acton's eyes narrowed, Stuttgart not exactly where he would have thought a band of mercenaries would be headquartered. "Stuttgart?"

Dawson drained the last of his water. "Yeah, the German Special Forces are headquartered about twenty miles from there so they use it as a recruiting center."

"Are they reputable?" asked Acton.

"They have their usual bit of dirty laundry like most of these types of outfits that provide private security, but nothing that's made headlines."

Reading grunted. "Just means they haven't been caught."

Dawson chuckled. "I've already set up a meeting with their CEO for later today. You're welcome to come along."

Reading shook his head. "No, I'm going to stay here and coordinate things."

"Sounds like a plan," replied Dawson, turning to Acton. "What time is your flight for Rome?"

Acton looked at his watch then jumped from his seat. "I've gotta get ready. I'm leaving here in fifteen."

Dawson rose. "Okay, you said you arranged a room for us?"

Acton pointed toward two keycards sitting on the table. "Those are yours. Your room is across the hall."

"Is it anything like this?" asked Niner as he stood, taking in the large room.

"All the rooms on this floor are suites and I figured it was best we were all close. You'll each have your own room."

"Thank God," replied Dawson, motioning toward Niner. "He's newly single and horny. I was afraid I'd have to share a bed with him."

"And I like to spoon."

"He's not joking."

Acton laughed, the first time since Laura's kidnapping, and it felt good.

These men were the best in the business, and with their contacts, Laura just might stand a chance.

Because he could see no way he was going to find the body of Saint Longinus.

Not without a miracle of my own.

St. Paul's University, St. Paul, Maryland

Mai Trinh flinched as a hand waved in front of her face. She ripped the earbuds free as she spun around in her chair, cringing on instinct at whatever might be about to assail her.

It was Tommy Granger.

She smiled, covering her heart. "You nearly scared me to death."

"You had your Katy Perry cranked so loud I don't think you'd have heard a herd of elephants stampeding behind you."

"Why would there be elephants behind me?"

Tommy laughed, dropping into a chair beside her. "We need to work on your sense of humor." He wagged a finger at her. "I bet back in Vietnam you were considered very funny."

She blushed, turning away slightly. "Not really."

"Ahead of your time, then." He nodded toward the screen. "What are you working on?"

"Something for Professor Acton."

Tommy leaned forward quickly, his knee suddenly bouncing rapidly. "Did you hear what happened in Paris?"

"Yes, that's what I'm working on."

Tommy's eyes narrowed. "I don't understand."

"Professor Palmer has been kidnapped—"

"You mean she's not dead?"

Mai shook her head. "Thankfully, no, apparently the kidnappers called Professor Acton. They want him to find the Spear of Destiny."

"What's that?"

"The spear that stabbed your Jesus Christ."

"Oh yeah, like in that Mel Gibson movie. Have you seen that? The Passion of the Christ?"

She shook her head.

"My parents took me to see it when it came out. The theatre was packed. There's this scene where they torture him—" His voice cracked and he shook his head. "I remember crying out at one point for them to stop. It was the first time I saw my dad cry, and he's not really big into religion."

"Sounds like a good movie."

He nodded. "I watched it again just a few months ago…" His voice drifted off as his eyes glistened. Mai desperately wanted to reach out and comfort him, this boy, this young man, who had helped make her feel a little less lonely, clearly needing it.

But she held back.

It wasn't her way.

She decided distraction was the easier way to go.

"The kidnappers want the professor to find the body of Longinus, the Roman soldier whose spear it was."

"They want him to find the body of some dude who died two thousand years ago?"

Mai nodded. "He became a bit of a revered figure from what I've read, so it's definitely possible."

"I suppose. But what if he can't find this guy?"

"Then Professor Palmer will be killed."

"Jesus Christ!" Tommy quickly made the sign of the cross. "Sorry, I guess that wasn't the right choice of words considering."

Mai shrugged, not sure why.

"Do they have any leads?"

"I just sent a bunch of research on Longinus to Professor Acton. My best guess at the moment is Rome."

"No, I mean the kidnappers. Any leads?"

"They've apparently identified some of them, mercenaries I think, but not the lead guy. According to the email update I just got he hasn't shown up in any databases yet."

"Maybe they're looking in the wrong databases."

Mai's eyes narrowed. "Sorry?"

"If this guy doesn't have a criminal record, then he's not going to show up in their databases. What do we know about him?"

Mai brought up the document she was using to track just that, the amateur sleuth in her already fantasizing about doing what the authorities couldn't. "Not much. He has a German accent, spoke perfect English to the Professor and perfect German at the museum in Vienna. This is his picture from the security camera." She scrolled down, showing a clear image of the man holding a hostage from behind. "And that's about all we know."

Tommy shook his head. "There had to be something in the phone call. Too bad they didn't record it."

"They didn't, but the Professor did take notes." She brought up a photo of the pad sent in the email update to her and several others including Dean Milton.

Tommy quickly read the scribbled notes then leaned back, his fingers tapping the arms of the chair. "Sounds to me like he's in some sort of warehouse or a large home."

"Home?"

"Yes. My grandparents have a large estate and when you walk on the floors there, the scale of the house is so large, everything echoes. It's just as possible that this is a house and not a warehouse. Think about it. A long quiet walk where all he hears is footsteps echoing, then a door, then more footsteps in another large area. That area we know has Professor Palmer in it because she's put on the phone and says she's being kept in a lab with a doctor named Heinrich." He paused. "Have they found any record of him?"

"Not that I know of."

"Well, he's probably easier to find if that's his real name. Anyway, the caller could have been walking down a long hallway then entered a room where they've got a lab set up. Some of the rooms in my grandparents' house are huge—easily enough room for a small lab."

"I guess it's possible." Mai wasn't nearly as convinced of the possibility, but then she thought Professor Acton's home was large, though apparently it was quite modest, especially compared to some of the homes she saw on television.

They were unbelievable.

Maybe it is possible?

"My point though was that *if* it is a large house, then it could be *his* house. Remember, these guys have committed robberies in Spain, Rome, Vienna, Paris, then Rome again, all in four or five days, which means they're well-funded. I doubt they're flying commercial, especially after Vienna where they were caught on camera—which if you look at the footage they were showing on TV last night certainly suggested they weren't concerned about being seen—which means they're probably flying chartered jets. And that means money."

Mai's head was nodding the entire time, Tommy making a lot of sense. "And they don't appear to be stealing for money," she added. "Apparently there were other very valuable objects including gold and jewels that could have been taken at the same time but weren't."

"Right, right! Money isn't their motive. And if these mercenaries aren't concerned about being caught on camera, then they obviously aren't concerned about working again or going to prison, which means they're expecting huge payoffs that will allow them to disappear and live out the rest of their lives in comfort."

"Which means money."

"Yes! Lots of money. So if we assume there are huge amounts of money involved, and that people who do this sort of thing usually have some sort of criminal record before they try something this big, then the fact the lead guy has *no* criminal record suggests he's the moneyman and the mercenaries are his hired muscle."

"So we're looking for a millionaire?"

"At least, maybe even billionaire. But the fact nobody has recognized him suggests he's reclusive."

Mai turned to her keyboard, quickly making notes. "So he's very rich, probably German—"

"Or Austrian, perhaps Swiss, they speak German too."

"Oh, okay. He's probably a recluse, but he's apparently quite athletic and certainly didn't seem shy to me."

"Not like us!" laughed Tommy, putting his hands on Mai's shoulders and shaking her gently. She froze for a moment, trying to regain her focus, it the first time she had been touched physically by a boy in over a year.

She hadn't realized how much she had missed it.

And she didn't mean intimate contact, it was just contact of any type. Professor Palmer always gave her hugs, which she craved, and Professor Acton would give her a quick hug when she would arrive for dinner, but beyond handshakes, this was the first time someone had put their hands on her in a familiar way.

"Oh, I'm sorry," said Tommy, removing his hands, apparently noticing she was still frozen.

"No," she whispered, her head dropping slightly. "It's okay."

She glanced slightly over at Tommy who was beaming, the meaning of her words thankfully not lost on him. She smiled awkwardly then turned back to the computer. "So he's probably not in the computer business?"

Tommy laughed. "Probably not! My guess is it's family money."

"Why?"

"He's too young to be that rich and not all over the Internet. My guess is he was born into the money and therefore learned how to keep a low profile."

"So how do we find him?"

"High society."

"Sorry?"

"For fun I wrote a program for my senior thesis to show how the government could track our movements through other people's social media posts. The program pulls photos from Facebook, Instagram, whatever, then using facial recognition plot points, uniquely tags the people in the photos then crawls all of the friends' accounts that had everything set to public viewing. I can follow those plotted people through their friends and acquaintances, use the geocoding embedded in the metadata—another thing most people don't know about—and then just through data analysis, identify which Facebook accounts belonged to what face."

"So you could trace someone through their friends' photos back to their original account and know where they had physically been?"

"Yes, it was a piece of cake!"

"Huh?"

"Sorry, an expression. It means it was easy."

"Oh."

"Can you do that with this photo?"

"Sure, I can plot his facial recognition points no problem. Then we just need to write a program that pulls as many photos from the Internet as possible dealing with high society—and I don't mean Hollywood, I mean the truly rich—where somebody like this might show up and be caught on someone's camera, a press photo, whatever."

"Do you think you can do it?"

"Yes. But it might take some horsepower. We're talking a lot of data, a lot of bandwidth."

"Meaning?"

"We're going to need Dean Milton's permission to use the lab."

Mai smiled. "You get to work, I'll go talk to the dean."

Hotel Astor Saint Honore, Paris, France

"Do you have enough money?"

Niner's shoulders slumped, a frown creasing his face. "I'm an E-5 in the army, Doc, which means before allowances and bonuses, I make about thirty-three thousand. Of course I don't have enough money."

Acton flushed, stammering out an apology. "I didn't mean that, I meant—"

Niner rubbed a tear from his eye. "It's so hard, you know, trying to get by on so little. I send every spare penny I can to help out my folks. Then there's my family in South Korea. You know it's really hard there; that country's so primitive, so poor." He shook his head. "I can barely make ends meet. D-do you have enough money?"

Acton's eyes narrowed. "Wait a minute, South Korea is one of the richest countries in the world. You're bullshitting me, aren't you?"

Niner grinned. "You should have seen your face, Doc!" He laughed, his head shaking. "Don't worry about me, I do just fine. And I know what you meant and yes, the account you provided has more than enough. We tapped it for our flight here along with the equipment delivery and vehicle when we arrived. We're good."

"Okay, just let me know if you need more, and don't hesitate to use that entire line if you have to. I don't care what it costs to get Laura back."

The elevator doors opened. "I completely understand. I don't know if there's anything I'd stop at if it was somebody I loved."

A doorman bowed to them slightly as they pushed through the revolving doors, and as Acton stepped into the fresh air he was greeted by a gentle breeze and car horns blaring.

"Taxi, sir?"

He didn't bother asking how the doorman knew he spoke English.

Must be how I'm dressed.

He glanced at Niner who was surveying the area, probably for threats, his eyes hidden behind sunglasses, his eyeballs doing most of the wandering rather than a turning head.

Maybe it's because I'm with an Asian guy?

He doubted it. With the number of former French colonies in Asia—not the least of which was Vietnam—there were plenty of Asians in France.

Just good at his job.

"We've got a car waiting for us." Acton looked at the empty laneway in front of the hotel. "Or supposed to be."

The doorman pointed to the road. "Everything is blocked by that ridiculous automobile. You'll have to go to the street then to the right. All of the cabs and limos are there. We have staff there to help."

Acton nodded. "Thanks." He and Niner walked the few yards to the road and past a Jaguar XK-8 cabriolet, its owner in a shouting match with several people including what appeared to be his wife.

"I cannot move the vehicle, it is broken down!" he shouted in a thick French accent at an angry tourist. "What part of that do you not understand, you imbecile!"

"Don't be calling me an imbecile, mate, you're the one that bought a Jag!"

The exchange continued, the entire electrical system apparently having failed. Acton spotted the chauffeur that had picked them up at the private airport the day before near the end of the street, waving.

"It *is* a new battery, I'm not an idiot! When I say the car is always doing this, it doesn't mean I'm not trying to get it fixed."

"Shoot the piece of shit, put it out of our misery."

"I had a Jag once, cost over two hundred euros for a new battery!"

"Must have been blessed by the Queen!"

Roars of laughter replaced the angry shouts for a moment, leaving Acton wishing Reading was with him to hear the exchange. The chauffeur rushed toward them, taking Acton's carryon bag he was rolling behind them.

"Allow me, Professor."

"Thanks, Andre." He turned to Niner. "I think I'm good from here, thanks for the escort."

"Nothin' doin', Doc." He extended his hand and Acton took it, shaking it firmly, not risking any type of limp wristed display with this warrior. "Good luck in Rome and make sure you keep us posted on your movements. If you need help, you've got our numbers."

"Thanks, Niner. Find Laura for me."

"We will."

Acton climbed in the back of the Mercedes S600, Andre closing the door, the shouts and horns immediately silenced, and within moments they were underway.

On an expedition he was certain was doomed to failure.

Dean Gregory Milton's Office
St. Paul's University, St. Paul, Maryland

"Mai Trinh's here to see you."

Gregory Milton's eyes widened slightly. *Odd.* He hit the button on his phone. "Send her in, Rita." Milton rose from his chair as the door opened and the tiny Asian girl that had helped save his friends in the Hanoi incident entered, shy as ever.

"Good morning, Miss Trinh," he said, motioning toward the couch. "What can I do for you today?" He was certain it was about what was happening in Paris right now. He had received a call from Acton late last night and hadn't got a wink of sleep, powerless to help.

It was frustrating.

With his back in recovery mode he wasn't able to hop on a plane and go help, though even if he were perfectly healthy he wouldn't be much good beyond moral support.

But sometimes that's all that was expected. He was certain Acton wouldn't expect him to solve the problem, just be there to help him through this difficult time mentally.

He had already made the offer last night but Acton had saved him by telling him he needed somebody stateside to coordinate things should it become necessary.

He had agreed.

And he had seen by the CC list on the email updates that Mai had been informed and enlisted to help in the archeological aspect of this crisis.

And now she stood in his office for only the second time, the first when he had formally hired her several months before.

He took his seat after Mai, wincing slightly as a pain shot up his spine.

Sitting up all night wasn't smart.

"I need your permission to use one of the labs," she said meekly. "One of the computer labs."

"What for?"

"Well, Tommy Granger—"

"The whiz-kid who was arrested as a minor for hacking the DoD mainframe?"

Mai's head shot up, her eyes wide. "He's a criminal!"

Milton smiled. "Some might say so, though he claims to have gone straight. Anyway, continue."

Mai seemed uncertain as to what to say.

"You said you needed a computer lab. Why?"

She smiled slightly. "Tommy came up with the idea of trying to find the German using the Internet. He wants to use facial recognition to crawl the web and find his face in photos of high society."

"High society? Why?"

"We think he's rich." She quickly gave him a rundown of why, and it seemed solid. Very solid, in fact. And the idea she and Tommy Granger had come up with was fascinating. He remembered reading about his software, even allowing himself to be used as a guinea pig.

It was frightening in its abilities.

He had immediately gone home and updated his privacy settings on Facebook and disabled the geocoding on his phone.

"So do we have your permission?"

Milton nodded.

"Use whatever resources you need. Keep me posted."

A broad smile broke out on Mia's face as she jumped to her feet, he a little slower. "Thank you so much!"

"You're welcome. But don't forget your primary job is to help Jim out with his research."

"Of course, sir. It will be Tommy who does most of the work. I'm not very good on computers, not like him."

"You'll learn. Just make sure you put it to good use," he said with a wink.

She blushed.

He opened the door for her, making a mental note to check if winking in Vietnam meant something different than here.

He closed the door as a spasm of pain shot through his spine. He gasped, grabbing at the small of his back, collapsing to one knee. Dropping to all fours, he rolled over, clutching at the epicenter of his agony.

He closed his eyes, focusing on his breathing. It wasn't the first time this had happened, and it probably wouldn't be the last, but it was the first time it had happened at the office, and it was the first time it had happened without Sandra around to help him.

He cursed.

"Rita!"

The door opened within seconds and Rita cried out. "Oh my God! Are you okay?" She rushed to his side, kneeling down beside him.

"It's my back." He pointed to his desk. "Top drawer, right hand side. Pills."

She jumped up, rushing around the desk, pulling open the drawer with trembling hands, the bottle shaking in them. "How many?"

"Two. And calm down, you're making me nervous. It's not like I'm having a heart attack here."

"I-I'm sorry, sir, just the sight of you on the floor."

She poured out some pills on the desk—all of them by the sound of it—then plucked two from the pile, rounding the desk with his bottle of water.

He took the pills and popped them in his mouth as she propped his head up. He sipped some water and swallowed, lying back down, the pain already beginning to wane without the muscle relaxants having had a chance to work their wonders.

"What can I do?"

"Get me a pillow and two strong students." Rita nodded, grabbing a throw cushion from the couch and placing it under his neck. She hesitated.

"Students?"

"To get me up."

"I'll get Oscar. You don't want the students seeing you like this. It will undermine your authority."

He chuckled, regretting it. "Whatever you say, Rita."

Rita disappeared to get one of their maintenance workers while he tried to relax every muscle in his body, battling the temptation to give in to self-pity. He had spent too many hours, too many days, crying about what had happened to him, usually when the house was empty, his wife at work and his daughter at school, unwilling to let them see what he had become.

A paraplegic wreck.

But in time he had overcome the emotional aspects, at least enough to move on with his life, and once he realized he could actually be fairly independent even if in a wheelchair, he began to appreciate he could still live a full life.

But when the one toe had been spotted by his daughter, tapping to music, it had changed everything.

But not completely.

His doctors would say the fact he was feeling this pain was a good thing, it something he couldn't have felt after the shooting, but right now part of him, a tiny, infinitesimal part, wished for momentary paralysis to kick back in and take the pain away.

Stop feeling sorry for yourself.

He thought of his best friend and the agony he must be going through with his wife being held for what was, for all intents and purposes, ransom.

At least she's alive.

Which was something his newly pessimistic nature had convinced him she wasn't.

He frowned.

Maybe I should see that shrink they keep offering me.

He had always thought seeing a psychiatrist or psychologist—he'd have to look up the difference—meant you had failed as a man. He wasn't sure where the thinking came from, probably his father, maybe even his grandfather. Both were vets, his grandfather a former Marine who had fought in the Pacific during World War Two, his father a draftee in the Vietnam War. Both had done their duty and survived, and never spoke about what they had seen or done.

PTSD wasn't something acknowledged back then. Back then they called it shell-shocked, and it was frowned upon.

Neither had ever sought counselling—at least as far as he knew—and he thought they had lived out full lives. But it was a new age, where men were more likely to express their feelings rather than keep everything bottled up inside, even soldiers encouraged to speak out if they were in trouble.

It was something he had embraced as an educator, but never thought he'd be in the position to actually need that help himself.

Perhaps it's time.

The door opened and Oscar entered, the shocked expression on his face causing a wave of shame to sweep through Milton's body, almost overwhelming him as he felt immediately emasculated.

I'm making the appointment today.

CIA Headquarters, Langley, Virginia

Chris Leroux pushed back from his keyboard in frustration, kicking his foot out to send him into a spin as he leaned back, staring at the ceiling tiles. He had spent two hours trying to gain access to the Renner Security network and had failed.

He didn't like failure.

But from what he could tell, beyond a couple of computers connected to the outside world that contained nothing but their external website and a contact form, there seemed to be nothing else.

Which he knew was BS.

What it most likely meant was they had a completely segregated internal network which was rare in the corporate world, most companies having their networks connected behind firewalls to the outside world, relying on security hardware and software to keep the bad guys and governments out.

Though some would equate the two.

What he *had* found out was interesting. By hacking the German government's public benefits system, he found that the intel indicating the identified gunmen were former employees wasn't exactly correct. In fact, he had discovered something quite fascinating. It appeared that Renner Security had a habit of firing and rehiring their German-born employees, and that those employees, when fired, had sometimes been tied to what might be described as questionable activities around the world.

Plausible deniability.

He could just imagine the conversation going to occur later today when Dawson named the identified shooters.

"They did what? It was just that type of thing that got them fired!"

By firing their personnel before sending them out on a questionable op, the company could deny involvement. Once the op was finished, and assuming everything went smoothly with no blowback, they'd be rehired so they'd be entitled to their generous government benefits upon retirement.

He assumed that the same was being done with their contractors, though deniability there was much easier.

Just pay cash.

But this was a German based company that specialized in giving former KSK personnel jobs. They seemed to have an excellent reputation and had never made the papers. It was the off-the-books ops that had garnered some attention, but only from the intelligence community.

Until now.

If this current op was actually part of a Renner Security contract, then it marked the first time they were involved in something clearly, blatantly untoward.

Which made him think they had no idea what their "former" staff were doing.

Whether they knew or not however was irrelevant in the end. It was who had hired them or their former employees to carry out the job that was. And the best way of finding that out was to follow the money.

He had already found the rather modest bank accounts of the identified men, and there was no unusual activity going back two years, which meant they most likely had private accounts for the nefarious activities.

But he had found a mistake.

One of the men, who was an employee for the better part of the past two years, had no salary deposits in his accounts for the entire time.

Which meant his money was going somewhere else.

And only the internal computer network at Renner Security would tell him where.

But how the hell do I get access?

There was a knock on his door, startling him out of his continued spin. He grabbed the side of his desk.

"Enter!"

He still felt like Captain Picard every time he said that.

The door opened and his heart leapt into his throat at the sight of his boss, Director Leif Morrison, the National Clandestine Service Chief for the CIA.

He jumped out of his seat. "Sir, can I help you?"

"May I come in?"

"Of course!"

Morrison stepped inside, closing the door behind him. Leroux motioned to one of the chairs in front of his desk. "Please, have a seat."

"Thanks." Morrison sat down, crossing his legs and folding his hands in his lap. "What are you working on?"

Leroux stole a quick glance at his screen. "Umm…"

A slight smile broke out on Morrison's face. "Spill."

How does he always know?

"I got a message from Dylan overnight asking me for some help. Actually, the help is for Professor James Acton."

"The man whose wife was shot and kidnapped in Paris yesterday."

It wasn't a question, it was a statement of fact, which meant Morrison knew full-well what was going on and was just here to confirm it.

"Yes." Leroux wasn't sure what to say. "You see, he—the professor—got a phone call from the kidnappers. Apparently she's alive and they're holding her until he finds some ancient body, Longinus, I think."

"Saint Longinus, the Roman soldier who lanced Jesus at the crucifixion to make sure he was dead, and had his blindness cured when the blood touched his eyes."

Leroux's eyebrows popped. "Umm, yeah."

"While I do enjoy reading the Bible, I also enjoy reading the Apocryphal texts as well. Quite enlightening."

Leroux made a mental note to download the Bible onto his eReader that night. He had tried reading on his tablet but it made his eyes too tired. There was nothing like a dedicated eReader. There was no backlight to strain the eyes, and it read just like a book—if not better. He often wondered why "the jungle" had released their tablet and called it the same thing as their eReader. The devices were so completely different in function and purpose, that he felt it actually dissuaded people from buying eBooks since they weren't a pleasant experience on a backlit tablet.

It was like using the microwave over the oven. Sure it was faster, but it never tasted as good.

"Chris?"

"Huh?" He suddenly realized his mind had wandered like it so often did, as if trying to convey some bit of critical information to whom, he didn't know. "Oh, sorry, sir. Well, I was asked to help try and find Professor Palmer."

"As I expected."

Expected, not suspected.

Leroux's cheeks flushed and he dropped his chin slightly. "I'm sorry, sir, I know I should have cleared it with you first—"

Morrison held up a finger, cutting him off. "Let me save you from having to come up with some lame excuse on the fly. Are you using your team?"

"Of course not, I'd never do that. And I'm not neglecting my duties. And I'll make up any time I do spend on this."

Morrison chuckled, rising from his chair. "Which is exactly why I trust you, Chris." He waved off Leroux's exit from his own seat. "Tell me next time, you might just be surprised what happens, like right now." Morrison's hand gripped the doorknob. "This is now an official task. Use whatever resources you need."

"Th-thank you, sir!"

Morrison nodded and left the room, leaving Leroux to kick off from the desk, sending his chair into another spin.

All the resources. Officially.

He smiled.

Now that this is official…

He needed access to the internal network at Renner Security, and until a moment ago, he had no way of actually doing it.

But now he did.

He picked up the phone and dialed.

James Acton smiled as he descended the steps of the Gulf V charter, his single carryon brought behind him by an insistent and gorgeous flight attendant. The woman had paid an uncomfortable amount of attention to him, she probably under the false assumption he was rich and unhappily married, the flashing of his wedding band doing nothing to deter her.

He hadn't wanted to be rude so he had ended up feigning sleep, which had worked.

I should have brought Niner, he's single now.

"Professor Acton, so good to see you again. I wish the circumstances were better."

Acton shook Mario Giasson's hand as the head of Vatican security glanced over his shoulder at the blonde bombshell descending the steps in six inch heels.

"Monsieur Acton, 'ere ees your bag!" she cried, her thick French accent making her even more gorgeous. She pressed a piece of paper into his hand. "And should you get bored, 'ere ees my hotel."

"Umm, thanks." Now he knew why she had insisted on bringing his bag down herself—it gave her the excuse to give him her number.

She rushed off, the wiggle causing even Giasson's eyes to wander to and fro. "New friend?"

Acton chuckled. "Never fly a private jet alone. They think you're rich and looking to score."

Giasson laughed as they loaded his bag into the trunk. "To resist such a lady's advances proves just how much you love your wife."

"I know, and if I ever told her about how well I did, somehow I think I'd still lose."

Giasson tossed his head back with a good belly laugh then climbed in the back seat with Acton. "Too true! Fortunately in my line of work I deal with very few women so my wife doesn't have much opportunity to get jealous."

"I teach at a university. Lots of opportunities. Luckily Laura isn't the jealous type." His face clouded, Giasson picking up on it immediately.

"Has there been any further word?"

"From her or the kidnappers, no. I've enlisted some help though that will hopefully find her soon, but just in case, I have to start my search."

"Do you think they're watching you?"

Acton paused, the thought having not occurred to him until just now. "I suppose they could be." He felt his spine tingle. He turned in his seat, looking out the rear window, seeing nothing but heavy traffic. "Do you think they could be?"

Giasson shrugged. "It's possible. They've been in Rome twice before so we know they have a reliable way in and out, probably a private plane just like the one you flew in on. They don't attract the same type of security, and from within Europe, almost none." He looked at his watch. "Where would you like to go first? Your hotel—"

"No, there's no time to waste. Let's go to the basilica right away."

Giasson smiled. "I thought you might say that. Father Albano is expecting us."

"Excellent." Acton looked out the window again, his heart leaping into his throat as he saw a black car with tinted windows directly behind them as they began to pull away from a red light. The car turned and he shook his head, letting out the breath he had been holding.

You have to focus! Even if they are *following you, you're safe as long as you're looking.*

He just hoped that was true.

These people seemed desperate, as if whoever they were trying to save didn't have much time.

And if that person should die?

Laura might be next.

Konigstrasse, Stuttgart, Germany

Dawson found himself admiring the beauty that was Europe, pretty much every street having a building on it older than America. It was the history he loved, the stories behind the buildings, the towns, the castles that dotted the hilltops. He just wished he had more time to play tourist when he was here.

I'm going to have to bring Maggie to Europe on an actual vacation.

He couldn't remember the last time he had been on a real vacation. In fact, he couldn't remember actually *ever* being on one. Visiting family didn't count, decompression leave after an op didn't count, and weekenders in Atlantic City *definitely* didn't count.

Maybe Dylan's idea of bringing her here after we're done isn't such a bad idea after all.

"Watcha thinkin'?"

Dawson closed his eyes for a moment, shaking his head. "None of your business."

He felt Niner's arm curl around his elbow. "But honey, communication is the corner stone to any good relationship."

"Don't you dare start your gay couple act like you did in France that time."

"I'm hurt."

"Remove your arm before I break it." Dawson continued to admire the timber frame buildings lining the pedestrian mall they were waiting in. Niner's arm worked its way loose.

"You're not getting any tonight, Mister."

"Thank God for small miracles," muttered Dawson as he tried to keep a straight face. Going on an op, especially one like this, was always fun with Niner.

You're never bored.

He shivered.

But you can get cold.

"See, you're cold, we should snuggle."

"I could gut you and climb into your still warm corpse."

"Ooh, I love it when you go all Jedi on me."

Somebody bumped into him and he felt a hand reach briefly into his jacket pocket.

"Entschuldigung," said the man as he stumbled past, slipping slightly on the cobblestones lightly dusted with snow.

Dawson said nothing, instead reaching into his jacket pocket, his fingers wrapping around a small package. "I'm getting cold. Let's head back to the car."

Niner nodded, swinging a shopping bag filled with some souvenirs they had bought as part of their cover of two tourists out shopping for their girlfriends back at the hotel. It hadn't been part of their plan, but plans always seemed to change on ops like this, and when the CIA analyst Leroux had called him with an idea, he had immediately agreed.

Niner climbed in the driver side, firing up the still warm engine, heat immediately beginning to pour out. Dawson looked at the pedestrian traffic, waiting for Niner to pull out into traffic before removing the package from his pocket.

Leroux had informed him that Renner Security's computer network seemed to be completely isolated so there was no way to access the data he needed to trace the former employee's financial data.

He needed them to tap the network.

A brush pass had been arranged.

Moving now, he pulled the small package out of his pocket. It was a tiny envelope, something newly cut keys might be placed in. He tore it open, dumping the tiny device into his hand.

Just plug it into any USB port.

Leroux's instructions sounded simple, it was the execution that would be difficult. It was truly a tiny device, the smallest memory stick he had seen, the standard USB connector actually longer than the rest of the nub containing all the electronics. Apparently it would be able to bypass any security and establish a two-way connection with the Internet using the cellular network.

Assuming they're not jamming cellphones.

Niner turned right, glancing in the rearview mirror.

"We've got a tail."

Dawson's lips pursed. "I'm not surprised. These guys are good."

"Very good. That means the hotel in Paris was being watched."

"Agreed."

"Which means the professor probably has a tail too."

"Agreed."

"He's probably safe for now, though."

"Agreed."

"You're very agreeable today."

"Agreed." Dawson pulled out his phone, firing a text message to Reading to let him know about the probable surveillance.

Niner glanced in the mirror. "Tail's still with us."

"If these guys are as good as we think they are, they probably witnessed the brush pass."

"Probably. They'll definitely search us before they let us into that meeting."

"True. Still wearing your special shoes?"

Niner turned left, accelerating slightly. "Oh yeah."

"Good. I've got a bad feeling about this."

"You too?"

"Let me know when we're out of sight."

Niner nodded, making another turn. "Now."

Dawson quickly tried to stuff the tiny device in a small pocket embedded in his belt, behind the buckle. He was doing it blind, not wanting to risk anyone seeing him look down, giving them a target area to search.

"Need any help?" asked Niner, raising his eyebrows suggestively while glancing over at Dawson's crotch.

"I'll break your fingers."

"Who said anything about using hands?" Niner clicked his teeth then licked his lips.

"We definitely have to get you a new girlfriend."

St. Paul's University, St. Paul, Maryland

"And we're off!"

Mai smiled as Tommy clicked the button on the first machine, the screen jumping to life as image after image appeared, the software picking out the faces then mapping the facial recognition points, "No Match" appearing over and over.

She already felt disappointed but said nothing as Tommy rushed around the lab, starting up the process on all forty machines. He plopped into a chair beside hers, slightly out of breath.

"Poor man's parallel processing!"

He had explained it to her. His software would use a centralized database to coordinate the effort, and the networked machines would poll this database to see what photo was up next for analysis. With the combined horsepower in the room, they were able to process far more data than any one machine could. Now it was up to them to keep plugging in possible sites and search results for the program to crawl and pull images from.

She had been at it all morning and afternoon as Tommy prepared the modifications to his software. She had hit every respectable newspaper site, every type of event she could think of from polo matches to car races— anything rich people might be at.

She was ashamed to admit her contributions had been minimal, her experience with rich people and the Western world so limited, she had never even heard of Formula 1 racing and thought polo was something played in a pool. It was Tommy who kept shouting out ideas as he worked tirelessly.

He's remarkable.

She caught herself stealing a glance at him as he leaned in to look at the display on the machine coordinating things.

He is kind of handsome.

His hair was messy, but apparently that was a style here. She had never really found white guys attractive, but then again her exposure had been limited to the odd tourist and conference until her arrival in the United States.

Now, in Maryland, she mostly saw white guys and black guys with very few Asians and some Hispanics—something she had never seen before.

It was sort of exciting, seeing all these different types of people in the same place.

It was also a little scary.

But as she got to know the professors and their circle of friends, and Tommy along with other staff at the university, she was slowly learning to shed her distrust of those different from her—a distrust ingrained by the Communist Party as part of her upbringing—and expose herself to the new cultures surrounding her.

Tommy was looking at her, smiling.

She flushed, dropping her head, ashamed she had been caught staring.

"You looked a million miles away." Tommy turned his chair toward her. "Thinking of home?"

She nodded, not unaware it was a lie. She wondered if he knew it was too.

"How about we get to work?"

She nodded, turning toward the keyboard, thankful for the opportunity to focus on something other than Tommy's smile.

I wonder what father would think if I dated a white guy?

One side of her lips curled up in a slight smile.

He'd kill him.

Leonardo da Vinci Airport, Rome, Italy

"Oh, pardon me, I'm so sorry."

Terrence Mitchell froze, having bumped into three people in it seemed as many seconds. He wasn't good in crowds, especially crowds in a hurry. He was even worse if he was in a hurry too. His wife Jenny put a hand on his shoulder.

"You okay, love?"

He nodded. "Uhuh."

"There's a chap over there holding a sign that says Mitchell. Could that be for us?"

Terrence looked where his wife was pointing and shrugged. "I don't know. They didn't say anything about sending a car."

"But how many Mitchells could there be here in Rome?"

Jenny led the way, Terrence was sure to try and clear a path for her clumsy husband. As he watched her pleasantly plump frame in front of him he felt a warm feeling rush through him. She was pregnant with their first child and he couldn't be prouder—he felt like a man.

A terrified man.

What did he know about being a father?

He was barely a man, nowhere near thirty yet. Yes he had a wife, but that didn't make you a man, especially when she was a career woman herself so didn't need him to support her.

But a child would be completely reliant on him.

He wouldn't be alone in it, however. Jenny was an amazing woman, was ecstatic about being a mother, was buying all the books and preparing the nursery and chatting with her two sisters about their experiences, she the last of the three to fall pregnant.

But he was an only child, had never babysat—his parents had been terrified he'd hurt someone with his clumsiness—and was certain he had no parental instincts whatsoever. This was proven to him in spades last year when he had tried to reason with a five year old about why he shouldn't drop Jenny's iPhone in the toilet. Ten minutes of the kid holding the phone over the bowl with nothing but his thumb and forefinger, lowering it every time he would try to get closer.

It was when he tried reverse psychology that things took a turn for the worse.

Fine, go ahead and drop the phone.

Plunk.

They had bought a new phone the next day.

Jenny stopped in front of the man holding the sign, giving Terrence a profile shot of her swollen belly.

This baby is in serious trouble!

I'm *in serious trouble!*

He just didn't know how to react. He had insisted that Jenny stay at home, it too dangerous for her to come and help out Professor Acton. There had been quite the fight, mostly one-sided, ending with him conceding he was a daft bastard, but it hadn't really changed his mind.

He was terribly worried about her.

The professors seemed to get themselves into violent trouble over and over, and it wouldn't be the first time they had been dragged in. In fact, it would be the third time, the last time having them kidnapped in the Amazon.

I should have just told Professor Acton no.

But then he'd never be able to live with himself if anything happened to Professor Palmer.

He loved her.

It was a crush, an infatuation never to be mutual, but it was there, despite his being married to a fantastic woman. He had fallen for Professor Palmer the first day he had laid eyes on her seven years ago. She was why he had become an archeologist rather than taking economics as he had planned. It was a stupidly rash, teenaged thing to do, but he had done it, hadn't told his parents until his third year, and discovered he not only loved his teacher, he loved the subject matter as well.

It was a decision he had never regretted.

And though his love would always go unrequited, and he was completely in love with Jenny, Professor Laura Palmer, the wife of the luckiest man alive, Professor James Acton, would always have a special place in his heart.

And it was the one secret he could never reveal to anyone, especially Jenny.

It would crush her.

He knew she wouldn't understand, nor did he expect her to. He could only imagine how hurt and jealous he'd be if she confessed she was secretly in love with Professor Acton or some other man.

But don't worry, love, because there's no chance of me ever being with him, our *love is secure.*

He nodded to the man as Jenny motioned toward her husband. "We're the Mitchells."

Those three words caught him off guard, causing a wave of shame to rush over him, a knot to form in his stomach.

The Mitchells.

He was pretty sure it was the first time he had ever heard it said.

And it suddenly struck him, in the middle of an airport in Rome, the reality of his situation.

He was married, married to the most wonderful woman he had ever met, a woman who accepted all his faults and made him feel better about himself than he had ever felt before, because this woman, this woman who he shared the love he had to give with some fool's infatuation, loved him completely and unconditionally.

This woman, this incredible woman, who was about to be the mother to his first child.

And she deserved his complete and utter devotion.

He sucked in a deep breath.

And that's what she's going to get.

"Yes, we're the Mitchells," he said. "Were you sent by the Vatican?"

The man nodded. "Yes, let me get your bags."

"Oh, that's not nec—"

Jenny cut him off. "You better take his before he kills somebody with it."

The man nodded, Terrence was certain suppressing a smirk. He was about to protest when Jenny took his bag, rolling it over to the chauffeur.

"Follow me, please."

Terrence shot Jenny a look but she just grinned at him and tucked her arm in his, rolling her bag in front of him. "Would you, love?"

He took her bag, flipping it over by accident then righting it with a kick of his foot that stubbed his toe. He winced. She leaned her head on his shoulder as they began to follow their driver and it melted his heart, any anger at her emasculation gone as he realized she had been joking, she now free of the load she had been pulling.

Free to pat her stomach.

"I think he just kicked."

"He?"

She shrugged. "You never know. If *he* keeps kicking like that, he could make a good center forward."

A son!

It would be incredible.

A center forward?

A pit formed in his stomach.

How the devil am I going to teach a boy how to play football! I can't even kick a ball!

"Or it could be a girl."

"Could be," agreed Jenny cheerfully as she rubbed her stomach. "Either way is fine by me."

Jenny whistled as they walked up to a stretch limo. "Is this for us?"

"Complements of the Vatican," replied the chauffeur as he loaded their bags in the trunk then opened the rear door. Terrence helped Jenny inside with a held hand, and as he started to climb in himself he heard her cry out. He paused as he felt the grip on his hand tighten, but before he could question what was happening he was shoved from behind. As he tumbled onto the floor the door slammed shut behind him plunging them into near darkness. He pushed himself up and into the seat to find himself sitting across from a man holding a pistol in his lap.

He wrapped his arm around Jenny protectively, his entire being focused on the weapon not five feet from his unborn child. "Wh-who are you? What do you want?"

"You are Terrence and Jenny Mitchell?" asked the man, his voice thick with what sounded to Terrence like a German accent.

"Yes."

"You have been called here to assist Professor Acton in the search for the body of Saint Longinus."

Terrence felt his muscles begin to slacken as the terror of the situation overwhelmed him. This man knew everything and memories of the torture he had undergone in the Amazon began to flood back, his mind shutting down to protect itself.

Nails dug into his thigh, yanking him back to reality as Jenny must have sensed what was happening to him.

"Yes," she replied.

She's so much stronger than I am!

"My employer has asked me to convey a message. You are being watched. Should Professor Acton actually succeed, you are to call this number immediately." He leaned forward, a business card in his hand.

Terrence couldn't bring himself to reach for it.

Jenny took it, holding up the card.

It had nothing but a phone number.

"Should Professor Acton lie to my employer, or try to deceive my employer, you are to contact us immediately. Should you fail to report any deception or failure on his part, you will both be killed."

Terrence's head swam, everything blurring in front of him, the thought of his wife dying too much to handle, the thought of his unborn child never seeing his mother's smile, never seeing even the light of day, unthinkable.

An ember of burning rage ignited within him and his eyes immediately focused on the man, his world snapping back into focus. "If you harm my wife, I'll kill you."

The man smiled, leaning forward with the gun not a foot from Terrence's chest.

"I would like to see you try."

Terrence's hands darted out, one hand smacking the inside of the man's wrist, the other slapping the top of his hand, immediately causing the gun to fall to the floor as the surprised man jumped back in shock, nursing a tender wrist.

Jenny grabbed the gun, pointing it at him.

Terrence just sat, stunned the training Professor Palmer's ex-SAS security team had provided actually worked.

And that he had had the balls to actually use it.

If he was being honest with himself he knew that it had been rage driven instinct, not any sort of courageous act that had caused him to disarm the man, and their victory was most likely temporary, as was evidenced by the smile on the man's face.

"I underestimated you, Mr. Mitchell." He leaned forward. "But make no mistake, this changes nothing. I am part of a team. Even if I am eliminated, my team will still kill you. And no tricks, taught to you by former SAS Lt. Colonel Cameron Leather, will help you—you will never see the man who fires the bullet through the belly of your wife."

Terrence wanted to reach out and grab the gun from Jenny and shoot the bastard. He glared at the man instead, raising his finger when suddenly the gun fired, shot after shot belching from the barrel, Terrence watching in horror as Jenny emptied the magazine into the man's chest.

The car screeched to a halt sending them tumbling forward, Terrence's outstretched hand slipping on the bloody chest of their now dead kidnapper. Pushing himself to his knees, he turned to Jenny, his mouth agape.

"Oh my God, what have you done?"

Jenny said nothing, instead just staring at the dead man, the shocked expression on her face mirroring his own. That's when Terrence noticed the gun still in her hand. He reached down and gently took the weapon away from her as the front door opened then slammed shut.

Oh shit!

He leapt forward, quickly searching the man for a spare magazine when a cellphone began to ring in the man's pocket. He glanced over at Jenny, still sitting on the floor, shaking, her eyes staring into those of the man she had killed. Terrence pulled the phone out of the inner jacket pocket and answered it.

He said nothing.

"Mr. Mitchell?"

Terrence felt his chest tighten, a lump forming in his throat as his mouth went dry. "Yes?"

"I assume my colleague is dead. This changes nothing. You still have your assignment. The man you killed was part of a team. You and your wife will be executed should you fail to follow your instructions."

The call ended and Terrence collapsed on the floor, his arms at his side as his entire body began to shake. He dropped the gun and phone, both hitting the carpeting with a thud that seemed to jolt Jenny out of her trance. He felt her hand on his.

"I need to get out of here."

Somebody rapped on the window, causing them both to jump, then the door was yanked open, the sunlight pouring in blinding them for a moment. Something was shouted in Italian as Terrence held up his hand to shade his eyes.

"I'm sorry, do you speak English?"

"Police. What is happening here—pistola!" The man jumped back and Terrence moved to shield his wife from whatever was about to come. "Get out of the car with your hands up!"

Terrence looked back at Jenny. "I'll go first and explain."

She nodded. "I'm sorry."

He shook his head. "You were protecting the baby."

Her eyes closed. "By making his mother a murderer."

"There's no way it was murder. We struggled for the gun, it fell on the floor, you grabbed it and shot him when he lunged at you. Understood?"

She looked up at him, her eyes wide, then nodded.

"Come out, now!"

He flinched from the barked order, the sounds of sirens in the distance getting closer. He squeezed Jenny's hand then crawled toward the open door. "I'm coming out! I'm unarmed!" Stumbling through the door he was suddenly grabbed by the back of his jacket and yanked forward, hitting the asphalt hard. "Take it easy! I'm the victim here!"

"Don't move."

He was quickly patted down then his hands were handcuffed behind his back before he was pulled to his feet, there now at least half a dozen police officers on the scene and hundreds of onlookers.

"Come out of the car, now!" ordered one of the men.

"That's my wife," said Terrence. "She's pregnant so take it easy!"

Jenny's hands appeared then her foot and finally her entire body as she stepped out. Two officers rushed her, grabbing her arms but thankfully not throwing her to the ground as they had him. She was patted down and handcuffed.

"Is there anyone else in the vehicle?" asked the officer who appeared to be in charge.

"There's one dead man who held us at gunpoint. The driver ran away. I don't know if there was anyone else in the front with him."

"What happened?

"We were kidnapped. We thought we were being picked up by the Vatican, but instead it turned out to be the same people who shot and kidnapped my professor in Paris."

"Paris?" The man's eyes narrowed and words were exchanged in Italian, one of the officers getting on his radio.

"Who were you supposed to meet?"

"The name is on my phone. Mario something."

"Giasson," said Jenny. "He's the head of Vatican security."

"Inspector General Giasson?" It didn't sound like he believed them. "Why would you be meeting with him?"

Terrence pulled at his handcuffs. "We're here to help with the recovery of a Blood Relic."

"Blood Relic?"

"You know, like the artifacts that have been stolen over the past few days that have the blood of Christ on them."

Excited utterances erupted from the crowd, it clear this was a hot topic at the water cooler in Rome.

An officer approached with a phone, giving it to the man in charge. Words were quickly exchanged then he motioned toward Terrence, an order given. The handcuffs were removed and the phone put in his hand.

"For you."

"Hello?"

"Terrence Mitchell?"

"Yes."

"This is Inspector General Giasson. I have someone here who will confirm your identity. One moment."

Muffled noises then a familiar voice answered.

"Terrence? This is Professor Acton."

Tears of relief filled his eyes as his face lit up at the sound of Acton's voice.

It's almost over.

"Hello Professor. We seem to be in a spot of trouble."

"So I've heard. Are you two okay?"

"A little rattled, but we're uninjured." He lowered his voice. "Jenny shot one of them."

"I know. Listen, sit tight, we're coming to get you. We should be there within twenty minutes."

"Thank you, Professor."

"You're welcome. Now hand the phone back to the police officer."

"Okay, bye."

He handed the phone to the cop and more words were exchanged in Italian, Terrence assumed with Giasson. A few minutes later the call was ended and the handcuffs were removed from Jenny's wrists.

A phone rang, the distinctive ringtone immediately drawing Terrence's eyes as he recognized his own phone ringing. His eyes focused on a pile of personal effects sitting on the sidewalk.

"May I?" he asked, and one of the officers picked up the phone, handing it to him. He looked to see the blocked number message then swiped his thumb. "Hello?"

"If you tell them anything about your instructions, your wife dies."

"Listen—"

"Look at your wife's stomach."

Terrence turned and nearly vomited, a red dot bouncing on Jenny's stomach for a moment, then disappearing. He could feel all the blood drain from his face.

"Do we understand one another?"

"Y-yes."

"Then say, 'I can't talk now, mom, I'll call you later'."

"I-I can't talk now, mum, I'll call you later."

The call ended and Terrence put the phone in his pocket, turning to Jenny.

"What's wrong?" she asked as he reached out and gripped the side of the police car she was resting against.

"It was them," he whispered. "They said not to tell anyone about the instructions they gave us."

"I hardly think they're in any posi—"

The red dot reappeared and he held up a finger, motioning with his eyes toward her stomach. Jenny stopped and looked down. She gasped as her hands covered her stomach protectively, the light dancing across her hands then disappearing.

How could they have possibly known what we were saying?

Renner Security, Stuttgart, Germany

"Is all this really necessary?"

Dawson held his arms out as a man in a crisp gray uniform wanded him. They had already had to sign in, get their photos taken and have their ID's scanned. Mr. White and Mr. Green, both FBI agents stationed at the American Embassy in Paris, were being thoroughly documented.

It's an intimidation tactic.

"Standard procedure," said a man observing the proceedings that had introduced himself upon their arrival as Michael Kellner. His English was perfect and Dawson had no doubt he was ex-military, probably KSK.

The wand whistled at Dawson's crotch.

"Ooh, man of steel," grinned Niner.

"Ha ha." Dawson tapped his belt buckle. "Buckle."

The man continued on and waved him through, repeating the procedure with Niner who cleared with the same whistle at the belt buckle.

"Very good, gentlemen, I'll show you to Herr Renner's office. If you'll follow me?"

Kellner swiped his pass and a glass door leading deeper into the building slid open. Dawson stepped through, noting that it appeared to be some sort of ballistic glass at least three inches thick. The door immediately slid closed behind them. They walked along a hallway with an impressive view of the city from a bank of windows, all the offices wisely on the interior of the building so prying eyes couldn't see any computer screens or read any lips.

It was suggestive of a company keen to keep its secrets.

And a tad bit paranoid.

"Master race?" whispered Niner as yet another gorgeous well-built blonde passed them with a smile. Everyone they had seen so far was a physical specimen worthy of the cover of any romance novel, even Kellner's v-shaped physique was obvious despite his Hugo Boss suit.

I wonder how many people know of Hugo Boss' ties to the Nazi party.

He didn't for a second think that these people were Nazi's, not in the slightest. Intelligence files suggested many of them were former German Special Forces which would have thoroughly screened these men before ever admitting them to their ranks, and with many being ex-military, they being in terrific shape was to be expected.

And as to the women, eye-candy was quite often employed by macho-companies like this to titillate the mostly male clientele.

And if we were in any other country, the thought wouldn't have even crossed your mind.

He always found it fascinating how preconceptions would sometimes enter the subconscious simply by knowing someone's cultural background or nationality, especially how one's opinion of someone could immediately change the moment you found out that little tidbit that your subconscious told you was important not because of anything the person in front of you had done, but because of what people like them had done, sometimes decades or centuries in the past.

Will whites always feel nervous when a young black man approaches them on a lonely street? Will black men always feel fear when a police car pulls in behind them?

He never felt much sympathy when a criminal died, and even less when that criminal was held up as a poster boy to justify rioting and looting. But when somebody innocent was killed because of preconceived notions, his heart went out to the victims and his heart grew a little colder toward the perpetrators.

In his business unfortunately he dealt with preconceived notions daily. He naturally didn't trust Russians, even though he knew many that were perfectly fine people that he did trust, and he always kept a wary eye on anyone who 'looked' Muslim merely because people of the same faith had tried to kill him on too many occasions to count. He had Muslim friends, though he had to admit they were few and all what he would consider moderates, most privately admitting Islam needed its own Reformation before peace could truly be had.

Only they were too terrified to say it publicly.

I wonder if Luther felt the same way when he went up against the Catholic church.

Kellner rapped on a door and Dawson slipped the transmitter from his belt, palming it. A muffled shout from the other side and Kellner opened the door. They entered and another perfect specimen, this one with salt and pepper hair, rose from behind a glass and chrome desk, a broad smile on his face.

"Herr Renner, may I present Special Agent White and Agent Green of the FBI."

Dawson extended his hand, Renner's handshake firm and dry. "Sir." They were shown to two sleek chairs in front of Renner's desk, Dawson noting there wasn't a hint of wood in the entire room.

Or an earth tone.

Grays, blacks and stark whites dominated along with brushed chrome and graphite.

Ultra-modern.

The only personal touches were a series of frames on one wall with medals and photographs, several showing Renner with various dignitaries he vaguely recognized and others with him in fatigues, arms around other soldiers.

Rather than sit, Dawson stepped over to the wall as Kellner left the room. "Kosovo?"

Renner stood to his right, Niner to the left. He opened his left hand, palm up and felt Niner's fingers take the transmitter. "Bosnia, actually."

"Nasty business from what I've been told."

"It was. Nothing like Iraq or Afghanistan, though."

"No, I suppose not." Dawson decided to use the psych profile he had read on Renner. "Funny how we don't get any credit for trying to save Muslims from the Serbs."

Renner grunted. "No, we're apparently all anti-Muslim at war with their religion." He sighed, pointing at two of the men in a photograph with him, all smiles, all young. "These two died in Kabul. Suicide bomber."

"So killed by the same people he was trying to save."

Renner turned and looked at him. "Exactly. For an FBI agent, you have a curiously refreshing way of looking at things."

Dawson smiled slightly. "We're a long way from Washington."

"Indeed you are." He motioned to the chairs and Dawson went to take his seat, but before he did he paused, turning back to the wall as Niner sat.

"Is that an Iron Cross?"

He immediately stepped over to the wall, admiring the rare medal, noting the Swastika in the center.

"My grandfather's. Awarded to him personally by Rommel."

"So serving the military runs in the family."

"It skipped a generation, my father instead focusing on business." Renner waved his hand as he started to turn, Dawson spotting Niner sitting back down in his chair, adjusting himself to disguise the fact he had been standing. "In fact, he helped me start this company when I left the army."

"I read the profile before coming here. Quite impressive."

"Thank you." Renner sat behind his desk, leaning back in his chair, steepling his fingers in front of him as Dawson sat. "Now, how can I help you?"

Dawson pulled an envelope from his inside pocket and slid it toward Renner. "The men on this list are all wanted in connection to recent thefts of archeological artifacts in Spain, Italy, Austria and France."

Renner took the envelope and pulled out the papers. "And what does that have to do with us?" he asked as he unfolded the pages. "Ahh, I see." He flipped through them. "I recognize the names. We terminated them recently."

"May I ask why?"

Renner folded the pages back up, returning them to the envelope. "I'm afraid that's an internal matter." He slid the envelope back toward Dawson with a single finger. "I can assure you however it was nothing serious, mostly salary disputes."

Dawson took the envelope, returning it to his pocket. "Salary disputes. None showed a desire to go private, perhaps take contracts outside of Renner Security?"

Renner shrugged. "Not while here, though I'm sure they're in need of an income, so I wouldn't be surprised if they took a contract."

"True. Do you know where we can find them?"

Renner smiled. "About the only thing I can tell you is that they are *not* at the addresses we have on file for them, otherwise you would have already found them."

Dawson smiled. "True."

Renner pressed a button on his desk then stood, ending the meeting, the song and dance merely a pretense for them to plant their transmitter, and for Renner to officially push the company line that these were *former* employees.

Dawson and Niner rose.

"Thank you for your time, sir," said Dawson, shaking Renner's hand as the door opened and Kellner entered.

"Always a pleasure to help out the FBI."

Dawson nodded, noting the slight smile on Renner's face at the mention of the FBI. Dawson suppressed the frown desperate to break out.

He at least knows we're not who we say we are.

"This way, gentlemen," said Kellner, holding his hand out and toward the hallway.

As they stepped out into the late afternoon sunlight shining through the bank of windows an alarm sounded, red lights mounted in the ceiling at regular intervals flickering on and off. Kellner touched an earpiece, his eyes opening wide as he turned toward them.

"Trouble?" asked Niner.

Kellner reached into his jacket and Niner's hand darted forward, crushing Kellner's windpipe, his other hand quickly retrieving the weapon the man was reaching for.

Dawson looked behind them to see the hallway starting to fill with personnel. "Get his pass." Niner nodded, yanking the badge and reel off the gasping man's belt. Dawson sprinted toward the reception area, Niner on his heels.

"Halt!"

Dawson dropped his shoulder and tackled the man confronting them, nailing him square in the chest. They both hit the ground, Dawson pulling the man's weapon and rolling to a knee, aiming down the long corridor causing most to jump back into their offices. Niner took a knee beside him and slid the heel of his shoe aside, pulling out a small square of C4 with a detonator.

Renner stepped into the hallway and Dawson took a bead on him, pulling the pass off his man's belt.

"Gentlemen, you're not getting out of here. Why don't you just surrender?"

"Ready?" asked Dawson.

"As I'll ever be."

"Let's go."

Dawson rose, retreating toward the door, his weapon trained on Renner as Niner whipped the small bundle at the closed glass doors, counting down the delay he had programmed into the timer.

"And down!"

Dawson dropped to a knee, lowering his head so any glass or shrapnel would hit his back and not his neck, Niner doing the same behind him. He covered his ears and squeezed his eyes shut.

The blast was deafening and too close for comfort. His head was ringing a bit but it was nothing he hadn't experienced hundreds of times before. He jumped to his feet, doing a self-assessment on the fly as they continued their retreat through the now shattered door.

"Our stuff, now!" shouted Niner, Kellner's weapon pointing at the receptionist. Her hands shaking, she placed two plastic trays on the counter. They quickly filled their pockets as Dawson kept his weapon trained on the hallway.

Renner began walking toward them.

"You aren't getting away, gentlemen."

"Stairs?" asked Dawson, the receptionist pointing to their left. "Let's go!"

Niner led the way, Dawson covering Renner for a few extra seconds then following Niner, his weapon aimed at the cowering occupants of the Renner Security reception area.

"It's locked!" Dawson glanced over his shoulder to see Niner swiping Kellner's pass to no avail. Dawson pointed the weapon at the receptionist.

"Open it!"

"I can't! Everything is locked down!" she cried, her hands up, most of her body hidden behind the counter as she ducked.

"Cover me," ordered Dawson as he rushed to the door, Niner taking his place. He retrieved the small block of C4 from his own shoe and placed it on the lock. "Fire in the hole!" The blast made quick work of the door and he pushed it open, checking the stairwell, finding it empty. "Let's go!"

Niner retreated toward the door and they were soon rushing down the stairwell toward the ground floor, the sound of heavy footfalls above them keeping them motivated as their pursuers refused to give up.

Niner shoved through a fire exit, another alarm going off as they found themselves outside and at the side of the building. Two men suddenly appeared from around the front corner of the building, weapons drawn.

"Halt!"

Dawson shot the man on the left in the leg, Niner doing the same to the one on the right. Both men dropped, writhing in pain as Dawson sprinted toward them, his weapon still trained on his target, ready to take him out should he be foolish enough to try and raise his weapon again.

It fell to the ground, his partner doing the same as they instead grabbed their wounds. Dawson jumped over them, turning the corner to see civilians running away from the sound of the shots.

Good. Makes it easier to spot the hostiles.

Several men burst from the main entrance of the building, giving pursuit as Dawson located their car parked wisely on the street rather than in the underground parking that had been available to them.

"Start the car!" shouted Dawson as Niner put on a burst of speed, key fob in hand, the lights of the Ford Mondeo flashing as he unlocked the doors. Niner yanked open the driver side door as Dawson slid across the hood, weapon still extended toward their pursuers, more now pouring from the side entrance they had just come from. Niner's door slammed shut as the engine roared to life.

"Let's go!"

Dawson climbed in as Niner gunned the engine, sending them into traffic. Dawson hit the button for the sunroof then pushed himself through, his gun leading the way as he kept a bead on the lead pursuers just in case anyone had the idea of shooting.

Niner turned the corner just as Dawson spotted their tail from earlier. "We've got company!" he shouted, dropping back into the passenger seat.

"Buckle up! It's going to be a bumpy ride!"

Dawson reached for his seatbelt as Niner jumped the curb to avoid the stopped traffic ahead, sending pedestrians screaming and fleeing, Niner laying on the horn to warn the less observant. As they barreled down the wide sidewalk Dawson checked the side view mirror to see the black Mercedes gaining, it not having to wait for pedestrians to get out of the way.

"They're getting a little close!"

"Stop backseat driving!"

Dawson's eyes popped wide as he turned his attention forward, a café patio rapidly approaching, people still sipping their coffee. "Umm, you see that, don't you?"

"Don't make me pull this car over." Niner pumped the horn, the closest patrons beginning to abandon their drinks and seats. He adjusted their trajectory slightly, favoring the side closest to the road with about half a car width of depth available. "It's not gonna work!" shouted Niner as he apparently noticed the same thing Dawson just had.

An iron fence lining the side of the patio facing the road.

If they took the line Niner was on now they'd hit post after post, and depending on how hard of an impact, the airbags might just deploy, cutting off their engine.

"Clear!" Niner jerked the wheel to the right, lining them up with the center of the patio just as they hit the first table, abandoned coffee cups and assorted snacks firing out in every direction including up the hood and onto the windshield.

"Where the hell are the windshield wipers?" yelled Niner, grasping at air, finally finding the stalk and turning them on.

He locked up the brakes as the sidewalk came back into view, the thick cream infused coffee cleared away, a small child with a balloon in her hand standing in the middle of the sidewalk as her mother rushed toward her, screaming.

Niner cranked the wheel to the right, sending the car into a skid as he yanked on the emergency brake then released it, gunning them down an alleyway, missing the little girl by only a few feet.

"Still on us!"

Dawson leaned forward, checking the mirror and cursed as the Mercedes pulled into the alley. "We've gotta lose them then this car. Cops all over the city are going to be looking for this thanks to your lane choices."

"Hey, we're trained to always take the lane with the least cars in it."

"Remind me to revise the training manual to define what a lane actually is."

Niner cranked the wheel, directing them into another narrow street then hammered on the brakes, the car shuddering to a halt as a large garbage truck rumbled toward them. Niner slammed the car in reverse and floored it, the engine whining as they shot backward and past the alley they had just come from, the Mercedes about to reach them. Dawson pointed at the one way sign and was about to say something when Niner glared at him. "Not a word from the cheap seats."

Dawson shrugged, palms upward at the garbage truck driver, giving a "Hey, what can *I* do" look at the irate man shaking his fist at them and seemingly not too concerned over how close he got.

The Mercedes burst out of the alleyway, the driver cranking the wheel to the left to follow, just as the garbage truck arrived at the same spot, slamming into them, shoving the driver side into the corner of an old timber framed gasthaus, shattering the first floor windows with the impact.

Dawson waved at them.

Niner spun the wheel, reversing their direction as a small courtyard opened up and gunned them from the scene, quickly turning up another lane, leaving their pursuers behind. Dawson fished out his phone and sent a message to Langley.

Need pickup.

"Let's ditch this thing before you get someone killed."

Niner sniffled. "I save your life and all you do is criticize. You're such a man."

Dawson pointed at an open parking spot. "Park it there, princess."

Niner nosed the car in, popping up on the curb then back down. Dawson climbed out, checking to make sure their pursuers didn't have friends, then blended in with the late afternoon pedestrians, Niner beside him.

His phone vibrated with a message.

Pickup in 15 minutes at these coordinates.

He touched his thumb on the GPS coordinates and the map application launched with instructions on how to get to the rendezvous. He showed it to Niner.

"Let's boogey."

Renner Security, Stuttgart, Germany

"What did they get?"

Renner was glaring at the tech as the young man's fingers flew over the keyboard, expertly checking log files as another examined the device that had been found inserted into the back of his laptop computer. The network security software had detected the hack but he had no idea how long the device had been active before the alarm had been triggered and the internal network shutdown.

"I'm not sure yet, but they got a lot."

"Sir!"

Renner looked toward the door, Kessler poking his head inside. "Our guys lost them, one is injured pretty bad."

"Scheize!" Renner's fist slammed into the desk.

"They were hit by a garbage truck. Karl has a broken arm and leg, but he'll live."

Renner batted the words away. "I don't care about that. Do we have any idea where they are?"

"The tracker we put on their car has them stationary the past two minutes so we're assuming they've left it. We have men heading to the area now."

"They downloaded our employee records!" exclaimed the pimpled geek at his desk. "It looks like they pulled the entire file."

Renner paused.

That might not be so bad.

Their employee files were all legit, and if these guys were CIA like he suspected, nothing in there would really be secret. All off-the-books projects were staffed by "former" employees, and no records were kept on the network, instead everything in a vault with an electromagnetic pulse safeguard that would wipe all of the data in the event of a breach.

"They got nothing," he finally said, looking at Kessler. "Nothing of value, at least."

Kessler smiled. "So our security software worked."

Pimples raised his hand. "Umm, no, it looks like they had already broken their connection."

Renner's eyes narrowed, not liking the implications. If they were the ones that broke the connection, then that meant they had what they wanted. "But why would they want personnel files?"

Kessler stepped farther into the room, arms folded across his chest, one hand rubbing his chin. "We keep tombstone data in there like name, address, phone number, date of birth."

Pimples' head bobbed. "Employee history, banking information, emergency contacts—"

Renner snapped his fingers. "Banking information." As soon as he heard it he knew what they were after. Due to the nature of his employees' work he was quite certain the CIA would have thick dossiers on them all including all of their biographical information and current contact information. But they might not have their financial data, and if they did, they almost certainly didn't have any buried accounts. "I want every single employee file checked, starting with recent layoffs. I want to know if any of their bank accounts are private."

Kessler lowered his voice. "What are you thinking?"

Renner ignored him for a moment as he contemplated the consequences. If one of his men had used a Swiss or Cayman account instead of a regular account at a German bank, he might also be using that same account for the off-the-books work. And if he had, then the CIA might be able to track who they were actually working for.

Which might mean they'd actually catch the moneyman and possibly tie his company to half a dozen murders.

And that meant prison time.

He looked at Kenner.

"We need to talk."

Kienestrasse, Stuttgart, Germany

Niner looked at the postcards on display, one with a large Porsche logo catching his eye. He plucked it from the rack and flipped it over.

Porsche Museum? Cool!

He returned it to the rack and casually glanced over his shoulder as the chimes over the door rang, a new customer entering the tiny kiosk filled with souvenirs. Dawson looked at his watch. "It's time."

Dawson pulled open the door and stepped outside, looking both ways as Niner nodded to the store owner behind the counter then followed. Dawson turned left, the rendezvous just around the corner, as Niner looked right, a black sedan rounding the corner, travelling just a little too slow to be natural. He reached out and grabbed Dawson, yanking him around and into his arms as Niner planted his lips on his commander's.

Dawson did the same, not reacting like he might at The Unit, instead going along with the only cover Niner could think of on the fly, for there was one thing he knew ex-Special Forces types wouldn't want to pay too much attention to, and that was two men making out.

He slowly turned their intertwined bodies so he could see the car slowly make its way past them, the two occupants eyeballing everyone on the street, including them for a moment before continuing on and around the corner.

Niner let go. "Mmm, Maggie's a lucky girl."

Dawson wiped his lips. "I'm assuming you had a reason for that other than the desperate desire for an ass whooping."

Niner nodded toward the corner where the car had turned. "Friends of Herr Renner's, I believe." They resumed their walk toward the rendezvous point. Niner looked over at Dawson. "Can I ask you something?"

Dawson grunted. "I'm already terrified. What?"

"How was I?"

"Huh?"

"How was I? You know, as a kisser. It's not something you can ask a girl. I've been told I'm a good kisser, but you can't always believe what a girl's telling you, sometimes they're just trying to get into your pants so they'll tell you anything."

"That ass whoopin' might just be back on the agenda."

"Aww, come on, BD, tell me, if you were gay, would you have been turned on by that kiss?" Niner grinned. "I know I would be. You're a *very* good kisser!"

Dawson shook his head then looked up at the sky. "Why God hast thou forsaken me?"

A parked car flashed its lights ahead ending Niner's fun. "That must be them."

Dawson looked and nodded, tapping his watch twice with his right hand. The lights flashed again. "That's them. Thank God."

Niner grinned and clasped his hands behind his back, skipping the final few steps to the car. He opened the back door, motioning for Dawson to get in.

"After you, sweetheart."

Dawson climbed in then backhanded Niner's balls causing him to double over in pain.

"If I had of known you were going to go all Fifty Shades on me, I'd of tried kissing you sooner."

He climbed in and closed the door as Dawson cursed.

"I can't win."

Basilica of Sant'Agostino, Rome, Italy

"I trust everything has been resolved?"

Acton nodded at Father Albano as they took their seats in the cramped rectory. "For now, at least." Precious time had been lost, too much time, but he knew Laura would never have forgiven him if he had left Terrence and Jenny, two of her favorite students, to twist in the wind with the Italian authorities. And the bottom line was he needed them. Their extra sets of eyes would save him far more time than had been lost.

He was just thankful that Giasson had been able to grease the wheels, assuring the Italian authorities that he would take personal responsibility and make certain they showed up for full depositions in the morning.

It's good to have friends in high places.

Money greased the wheels outside the Western world, but within it, it seemed to only grease political wheels, and that usually in the form of some sort of donation.

It never really expedited those things that needed extreme haste.

But power did, and Giasson had it, at least in Rome, the deeply religious community giving the Vatican a lot of respect. And latitude.

"As you saw earlier, we have hundreds of remains in the catacombs beneath these buildings, and they are among many thousands in the city. These catacombs have been closed off to the public for centuries, in fact, most don't even know they exist. Until today, I myself have only been in them twice before. It's simply too dangerous."

Acton nodded. "It did look like there had been some recent cave-ins. I agree it's too dangerous to simply search without knowing at least where to begin or what we're looking for."

Father Albano looked relieved. "I'm glad you feel that way. I would hate to see someone hurt in what I believe to be a fool's errand."

"You don't believe in the spear?" asked Terrence.

Father Albano held up his hands, waving them and shaking his head. "No! No! No! Don't misunderstand me. I believe in it, absolutely, after all it's in the Gospels. I simply don't believe that Saint Longinus is buried here. I know there are rumors that his body was taken here in the fourteenth or fifteenth century, but a search of church records conducted in the early twentieth century failed to find any reference to this."

Acton pursed his lips as he thought of the reference material Mai had sent him. A Vatican historian had conducted a thorough search of the archives and found nothing to suggest Longinus had ever been moved to the basilica, and the body was considered officially lost, if it had ever existed, though the church would never admit to that part since there was a prominent sculpture of the saint in St. Peter's Basilica.

To them he was real.

Just lost.

And for Laura's sake, Acton had to assume he was real.

And findable.

"Can we assume since your records were gone through less than a century ago that they've been organized in some way?"

Father Albano shook his head. "They were, but during the Nazi occupation everything was seized. Hitler was obsessed with finding any and all religious artifacts including the Spear of Destiny which meant his archeologists came here and seized all of our records."

Acton grabbed his forehead, massaging his temples. "*Please* tell me they've been returned."

"Oh, absolutely. After the war the Americans found crates filled with our documents and relics and they were returned. To be honest, other than removing the artifacts and returning them to their rightful places, the documents have been left pretty much untouched, the Nazi's actually having done a better job at preserving them than we could."

This piqued Acton's interest. There might actually be manifests associated with them if the crates were returned complete, the Nazi's fanatical with their paperwork. Hitler's obsession just might help them. He stood.

"It's getting late and we better get started."

And Laura is running out of time.

Renner Security, Stuttgart, Germany

"Our men weren't able to find them, sir. They'll keep looking, but…"

Renner wasn't surprised by Kessler's report. These men were good, most operators were, no matter what country they were from. He was good too, and so were his men, but he had been foolish.

Over confident.

He had wanted to show that he wasn't concerned about meeting the FBI—or CIA—about anything. He had known full-well what this was about, it was the top news story across the world. It shouldn't have been, but things had gone off the rails with the killing of a priest in Spain, then the massacre—for lack of a better word—in Paris, especially coming on the heels of the cowardly Charlie Hebdo attacks.

He had been at home when news broke of the Islamic attacks, arguing on the phone with his ex-wife over alimony of all things. He had told her to shut up and turn on the news. After an initial outburst she had turned on her television and they had both watched it together, over the phone, as the events unfolded live, it the longest, most civil conversation they had had in years.

It hadn't lasted.

The payday he had received for allowing his men to be used on this relic hunt was massive. He hadn't even needed to negotiate, the number offered upfront so large he couldn't be bothered trying to get more. The offer had been sent to him anonymously with instructions on how many men were needed, what they would be needed for, and where they should show up. His men were all receiving huge paydays themselves with the understanding they would all be disappearing permanently after the job was done.

He had selected single men with no wives, ex-wives, children or surviving parents or siblings. It was a disturbingly large pool of candidates.

The pool became much smaller when they were interviewed by him for the job and told they would have to disappear when it was done.

It was one thing to live alone, it was another thing to actually *be* alone, to start over, under the radar, not only giving up everything you had built over a lifetime, but the work you loved as well.

It hadn't taken long though to find enough men motivated by the money, and he sent them to the rendezvous with the understanding he would never see or hear from them again.

He hadn't expected to see their faces on security footage leaked to the press.

He had immediately phoned Kessler to make sure everything was in order with their internal records. There was no point in purging the records, that would simply raise suspicions, he just wanted to make sure there were no typos in the termination dates and that all the proper paperwork had already been sent in the event court orders were to arrive.

Everything had been done properly and on time, well ahead of their faces hitting the news services.

Renner Security was good at its job.

Including its paperwork.

And it had given him a false sense of security. It had never occurred to him they would actually try and hack their system, and even if they had, their data retention protocols weren't supposed to reveal anything worth stealing.

But it had been confirmed that one of those on assignment had used their Swiss bank account for their regular paychecks. And Renner had no doubt that any payment for this job had been made to the same account, which meant the payment might be traced back to its source.

And that same source had paid *him*.

He looked at Kessler, still waiting in the doorway. "I'm screwed."

Kessler stepped inside, closing the door behind him. "How so?"

"They're going to be able to follow the money all the way back to me."

"Perhaps we need to clean up the mess?"

Renner's eyes narrowed. "How?"

"Eliminate our former employees and their new employer."

Renner had always known Kessler was cold; it was what made him so good at his job. But to actually hear him talk about killing their own in such a calm fashion sent a chill down his spine.

He shook his head. "No. The problem is electronic, not soft. You could kill them all, the banking records would still lead back to me."

Kessler nodded. "Then what will you do?"

Renner frowned. "I'm not sure." He waved Kessler away. "I need to think."

"Of course, sir."

Kessler left the room and Renner turned toward the wall adorned with the memories of better times.

It's over.

Hotel Astor Saint Honore, Paris, France

Reading massaged the bridge of his nose, squeezing between his tired eyes, his phone on the hotel room table, the speaker doing a disservice to the man he was talking to. "A wound like that, how long could she last without treatment?" he asked.

"That depends, do you mean how long until she would die if not treated at all, or how long she would have before treatment would need to be started in order to save her?"

"The latter."

"Well, that depends."

"You're not being much help, Arthur."

Dr. Arthur Goodman laughed. "No, but I'm trying to be precise." Goodman was an old friend of Reading's from his Scotland Yard days, a coroner from London he had dealt with on far too many occasions.

"I'm not the Crown Prosecutor preparing the case, I'm a copper trying to narrow down a search radius."

"Okay, okay. From what you've told me of the wound, I'd say she'd have as little as fifteen minutes and as much as an hour, perhaps even more if your characterization of it is completely wrong."

"There was a fair amount of blood."

Goodman grunted. "To your untrained eye, perhaps, but looks can be deceiving."

"I've seen my fair share. It looked bad."

"Too bad Chaney wasn't with you, he'd have been able to tell."

Reading felt a dark cloud settle over him at the mention of his former partner, Detective Inspector Martin Chaney. He had disappeared after the events in Venice, never to be seen again, at least by him. He was still officially on medical leave, but no one knew where he had disappeared to. Reading was certain it had everything to do with the Triarii, an ancient cult Chaney was part of that had caused Reading and his friends a lot of grief over the years, and with the number of bodies that had piled up due to their beliefs, he feared the worst for his friend.

But he had another friend that needed him right now, and thinking of Chaney would just be a distraction.

"Well, he's not here, so you're going to have to deal with my amateur assessment."

Goodman chuckled. "Glad to see you're as pleasant as ever." He became serious. "From what you've told me, I'd cap your radius at no more than one hour from the moment of the shooting. If it was really bad, she never would have survived that helicopter ride. How long was it again?"

"Fifteen minutes."

"Right. If she were bleeding out, she'd have been too far gone to be saved. But the fact she was means she was bleeding slowly, so an hour is reasonable."

"But it could be more."

Reading could almost hear him shrug. "Could be, but from what you described, I doubt it." There was a pause. "You're sure they didn't just transfer to another helicopter?"

Reading's head dropped. "I hadn't even thought of that." He rapped his knuckles on the table top. "No, that's right, there were two sets of tire tracks, four-by-fours, and no evidence of any other vehicles. Another helicopter would have left evidence behind."

"You sound tired, my friend."

Reading sighed. "You have no idea. I'm getting too old for this shit."

"You and me both!" laughed Goodman. "Now I'm going to let you go, my wife tells me I can't afford to lose any beauty sleep. You call if you need me for anything."

"I will. Thanks, Arthur."

He ended the call and looked at the map laid out before him showing concentric circles radiating out from the helicopter landing site. He looked at the circle for the 45 minutes of driving time they would have had.

It's hopelessly huge.

About the only good thing was it was mostly countryside and small villages.

But it was still huge.

There was a knock at the door.

He looked at his watch and frowned. *Who the hell would be calling at this hour?* He checked the peephole and smiled, opening the door. "Gentlemen."

"I'm guessing you don't associate with a very good crowd if you're calling us that," said Niner as he and Dawson entered the room.

"Success?" he asked as Dawson closed the door behind them.

Dawson nodded. "We planted the transmitter and got the data, but they're onto us."

Reading dropped into a large, plush chair, his sore buttocks and back thanking him. "How so?"

"They objected quite strenuously to us leaving," replied Niner, pointing at the fridge. Reading nodded and Niner grabbed several bottles of water, firing one at Dawson who caught it handily, the other bouncing off Reading's chest and onto the floor, his arms not having moved an inch. "Sorry."

Reading shook his head slightly. "I'm dead."

"You catch like it," said Niner, picking up the bottle and placing it on the table in front of Reading. "Good thing I wasn't throwing beer bottles."

Reading grunted, his head lolling over to the side in Dawson's direction. "So what do they know?"

"Only that someone is looking into things. They probably also know what data we stole by now."

"Which means if they're involved they're going to be disappearing into the woodwork."

Dawson took a long swig of his water. "I would. But if someone's actually dying from some incurable disease as we've surmised, then it might not be that easy for them to just up and leave."

Reading frowned. "But not impossible."

Niner flipped his already empty water bottle in the air. "Which means we don't have a lot of time."

Reading's eyes drooped as he began to fade fast.

He heard the two much younger men rise and his eyes opened, Dawson waving off his attempt to get out of his chair. "We'll leave you to get some rest. We're going to do a quick debrief then get some rack time. Hopefully Langley will come up with something by the morning."

Reading gave a tired wave of the hand without removing it from the arm of his chair, his eyes already closed as he drifted off to sleep.

Kruger Residence, Outside Paris, France

Dietrich's phone vibrated in his pocket as he paced in front of his father's bed. He fished it out and frowned, looking at his mother, his father having passed out from medicine administered earlier by Dr. Heinrich.

"I have to take this."

She nodded, her slumped shoulders and the dark circles under her eyes indicating just how exhausted she was. He had urged her to get some sleep while his father was resting but she refused to leave his side.

She knows he's going to die soon.

A lump formed in his throat and tears welled in his eyes as he looked at his father, his breathing labored, his fluid filled lungs causing a heavy rasp with each intake of breath.

He swiped his thumb and held the phone to his ear as he stepped out into the hallway.

"How did you get this number?"

"I have my connections."

Dietrich scowled at himself in a large gold framed mirror. "You were never supposed to call me."

"It's become necessary."

He had never spoken to Karl Renner, all contact done through an intermediary, but obviously someone had spoken.

Probably one of his men told him how to reach me.

His blood began to boil at the thought of the breach in protocol.

"You have sixty seconds."

"The CIA was here asking questions."

This piqued Dietrich's interest, his chest tightening slightly. He looked around. "What do they know?"

"It's hard to say, but it's clear they've tied my firm to your actions."

'Your' actions?

"So? You've been compensated very well for just that possibility."

"It's not enough."

"It was before."

"Well, not now. Not after you started killing people. Before my firm was simply involved in providing *former* personnel who would have been accused in involvement with several robberies. Now there are multiple murders. That means a very powerful microscope is going to be focused on me and my firm. I have to disappear."

"Then disappear. I paid you millions. I'm hanging up now."

"Wait! I need another ten million euros."

"That's ridiculous. Good bye."

"I'll have to go to the authorities and tell them everything I know, otherwise I'm going to go to prison."

Dietrich's free hand curled into a ball, his nails digging painfully into his palm. "I'll call you tomorrow. Be at your house at nine a.m."

He ended the call, pacing in front of the mirror several times as he tried to control his rage. He had never been extorted before.

And he didn't like it.

But there was another takeaway from the phone call.

The CIA was getting close.

If Renner was panicking—and his background research into the man suggested he *never* panicked—there was more going on than he was letting on. The CIA paying Renner Security a visit shouldn't have been unexpected to the man, after all it was his men being used and there always was the possibility they'd be caught on camera. That was why their paydays were so huge—they would need to disappear for a long time.

Which meant the CIA must have said something that panicked Renner. And if Renner was panicked, it must be significant, and the only thing he could think of was that they had somehow tracked him down.

But that didn't make sense. If they knew who he was, then why weren't they here, now, breaking down his door? No, they didn't know who he was.

But maybe they're on the right track.

His face on camera hadn't been ID'd yet, which wasn't a surprise. His family was very reclusive. They never entertained, and when they went anywhere it was under assumed names. His father's name would appear in the business section of the newspaper from time to time, but photos were never made available.

The only way the CIA could trace him would be some sort of paper trail, which meant a money trail. Everything had been done through wire transfers from secret bank accounts to what were supposed to be equally secret accounts. Nothing would lead back to him.

But it could lead back to Renner.

He smiled. That's what it was. Renner was worried that the money paid to his men would be traced back to a single source which also sent him money. Court orders could unseal those accounts, no matter what assurances the Swiss might have provided when opening them, and it would all tie back to Renner.

Herr Renner and the CIA will be quite surprised to find out who's financing the entire operation.

Dietrich speed dialed a number on his phone, it immediately answered.

"Yes, sir?"

"I have a job for you."

Basilica of Sant'Agostino, Rome, Italy

Terrence Mitchell stretched and yawned. He was tired, but every time he closed his eyes the image of the red dot on his wife's stomach appeared, forcing him to keep going. He felt terribly guilty not telling Professor Acton the complete truth, but he had no choice. He couldn't risk the life of his wife and unborn child, and besides, what difference did it really make? His instructions were to tell their abductors if the professor discovered anything, or strayed from his own instructions.

And Professor Acton would never do that.

He was on a mission to save his wife, and the only way he could do that was to find the body of Saint Longinus, which he was then going to hand over to Professor Palmer's captors.

It makes no difference.

He kept telling himself that, but the fact he had to repeat it over and over meant he wasn't convinced. On several occasions he had wanted to whisper the full truth to Acton but he couldn't be certain they weren't being listened to.

Somehow they knew what Jenny and I were talking about.

They must have been reading their lips from a distance, or had some sort of parabolic microphone. They obviously had a line of sight on them because they were able to aim a laser scope at her.

Twice.

Which meant that here, in this dingy old storage room, they should be perfectly able to converse with nobody eavesdropping.

But for some reason he just felt they couldn't.

These people are good. Maybe they've planted a bug of some type.

He instinctively began to pat himself down but stopped.

Focus!

The best way out of this situation was to actually succeed, and amazingly enough, he actually thought they might. The Nazi records had indeed been in the crates, tucked neatly into a pouch on the inside of each, itemized lists of all the documents and artifacts confiscated decades before. There were almost two dozen crates and they had only gone through a few of them so far, none of the documents helpful as of yet, but as Acton had said, it was going to save them probably days if not weeks of searching, especially considering the state of so many of the documents, scrolls of paper now so brittle they couldn't risk opening them.

A concern the Nazi's didn't appear to take as seriously.

Their haste is our gain.

He looked over at Jenny, her head lying on the table top she had been working at, a gentle snore emanating from her exhausted form. Professor Acton had left several hours ago to get some sleep in the sparse guest quarters Father Albano had provided for them. Terrence had been too wired at the time to join him, it clear the poor professor hadn't slept properly in days.

He rubbed his eyes and flipped to the next page of the manifest, his list of Google translated document types opened on his laptop. Tracing his finger down the list, he didn't find the words he was now reading. Flipping over to Google Translate, he entered the words and felt a surge of excitement at the result.

Interment Certificate.

It was the closest they had come. He scanned across the page to the date.

May 3, 1482 AD.

He smiled.

It's the right timeframe!

Even if it had nothing to do with the body they were looking for, it was an indication that records of the proper type had indeed survived from that period.

Which meant their search may not be futile after all.

"Have you found something?"

He turned to see Jenny looking at him, her eyes half closed, head still on the table.

"An interment certificate from the fifteenth century."

She sat up, clearly picking up on his excitement. "Is it for him?"

He shrugged. "I don't know, I just started looking at it." He began to type the text from the Notes field of the manifest, the translation updating with each press of the spacebar. He frowned. "Just some priest who died a few weeks before." He quickly scanned down the page and saw several more Interment Certificates. "There's more here, though."

Jenny joined him and together they began the painstaking process of translating each one, and it wasn't until several dozen failed efforts that he paused, looking at the translation.

"Woah."

"What?" asked Jenny, leaning over to look at the screen.

"This is dated fifteenth century, but it indicates the body is for a 'first century monk'."

"That wouldn't be the first we've found."

"No, but listen to what it says. 'Note in margin indicates mistaken identity'. It says his actual name was Quintus."

"So not Longinus."

"No, but remember, somebody went through all this paperwork in the early twentieth century and found no mention of Longinus."

Jenny frowned. "I know. That's why I think this is a waste of time."

235

"Don't you see? They were looking specifically for a reference to Longinus. But what if he was moved here, and the record was changed for some reason?"

Jenny's tired eyes narrowed slightly. "You mean he actually *is* here, but the record was changed for some reason, by mistake perhaps?"

"Exactly. We're seeing lots of records of interment here, and I'm sure we'll find many more in these boxes. And I'm equally sure we'll find no references to Longinus."

"Thank you!" she said, throwing her hands out at him. "I'm glad I'm not alone in thinking this. I didn't want to say anything to Professor Acton, but I think this is a complete waste of time."

Terrence frowned. "I think you're missing my point."

Jenny sighed. "I'm too tired not to."

"What I mean is this: if we assume that the records are complete, and we assume that Longinus was indeed brought here as history suggests, then his record must have been altered in some way."

"Interesting theory." Terrence spun toward the voice to find Professor Acton standing in the doorway. "What prompted it?"

Terrence nodded toward the translation on the screen. "There's reference to a monk named Quintus being interred here in the fifteenth century, but it says there was a note in the margin of the document suggesting a mistaken identity."

"And Quintus was the actual identity?"

"Yes."

Acton pursed his lips. "If we assume our priest from ninety years ago was diligent, then we should find no reference to Longinus in these records." Terrence opened his mouth to mention he had said exactly that when Jenny punched him in the leg under the table, cutting off his boast. "So we should be looking for anomalies."

"Like this."

"Exactly." Acton looked at his watch prompting Terrence to glance at the time on his computer.

3:42am.

I need sleep.

"Here's what we're going to do. You two keep going through the manifests, looking for anomalies. As you identify them, I'm going to try and find the actual document and examine it. Hopefully we'll get lucky." Acton looked at Terrence and smiled. "But first I want you two to go get some sleep. We can't risk you making a mistake."

Terrence nodded. "Thanks, Professor. We'll see you in a few hours."

"Take as long as you need." Acton paused. "I wonder." He stepped out into the hallway, Terrence and Jenny following. There were two guards provided by the Vatican standing nearby. "Do either of you speak German?"

Both men nodded. "Yes, Professor, I do. It's pretty common in Switzerland."

"I do as well. Actually, it's my mother tongue."

Acton smiled at Terrence and Jenny. "How many more of you speak German?"

The first guard shrugged. "A lot?"

"Do you think they'd be willing to help?"

"Doing what?"

"Translating old German manifests."

The man smiled. "Absolutely."

Acton sighed, looking at Terrence, a look of restored hope on his face.

"You two go get some rest. Hopefully we'll have reinforcements soon."

CIA Headquarters, Langley, Virginia

Chris Leroux flinched in his chair at the knock at his office door. He glanced at the time. After midnight. Again. He loved his job, especially when he was making progress, especially when lives were at stake and he had a chance to actually save them, but even he needed rest.

Which was why Morrison had given him a team that could work nightshifts if needed.

But with an off-the-books project like this he never used official resources beyond himself, though this time Morrison had greenlighted him to do so, so tonight he'd have to plead complete and utter absorption in his work.

"Enter!"

The door opened and a grinning Sherrie entered. "Hey, baby!"

Leroux leapt from his chair, rounding his desk and grabbing the love of his life in his arms, picking her up off the floor in a bear hug. He put her back down then kissed her, long and slow, the way he had learned she liked it, Sherrie pretty much the only girl he had ever kissed more than once.

She moaned.

Apparently I'm getting better at this.

She broke away, placing a hand on his chest and looking up at him. "I had a feeling you'd be here."

"You're home early." He sat on the edge of his desk, motioning toward one of the office chairs. She waved it off.

"I'm only here for a minute, I'm exhausted. The op wrapped up a little early so I caught the red-eye here so I could see you." She nodded toward his computer. "How much longer are you going to be here? I see a team sitting outside twiddling their thumbs." She lowered her voice. "But don't tell them I said that."

He smiled, knowing full-well that his team was busy though to the untrained eye, it might appear they weren't. An analyst's job quite often involved a lot of waiting as databases were scoured by sophisticated algorithms or data requests were actioned by other teams. Too often they were left in a holding pattern while waiting for others.

But if they're waiting for stuff…

"Twiddling their thumbs, eh?"

"But you didn't hear that from me."

"I think I'll hand off some of this work, I'm exhausted too."

He returned to his seat, quickly whipping off several emails.

"What are you working on?"

"Professor Palmer's still missing. We managed to hack the security company's network—the one that provided the resources for the thefts—and now I'm trying to track the money. I found one of the guys involved has been using a Swiss account for his regular salary deposits, so I'll have my guys trace all the activity on that account and see if it leads anywhere."

"Are the Swiss cooperating?"

Leroux grinned. "What they don't know can't hurt them."

"Don't you just love working for the CIA?"

Leroux logged out of his computer and rose.

"Best job anywhere."

Basilica of Sant'Agostino, Rome, Italy

Professor James Acton massaged the back of his neck, his single, poorly angled hand a poor substitute for the real thing his wife was so expert at giving.

God I hope she's okay.

But praying to God might not be the proper thing to do right now considering the work he was doing certainly wasn't *His*. He was on a quest to ultimately find the blood of Christ so that it could be used to save the life of a murderer.

But surely saving Laura's life justifies this?

Carefully examining document after document had left him with plenty of time for his mind to wander during the downtime, and he had twisted his logic to justify his actions, the sad fact of the matter truly being that he felt he needed to. He didn't truly believe that the blood of Christ could heal—it defied the science he had relied upon his entire adult life.

But then there was the Vault.

The Vault had been terrifying, the things contained within it enough to shake the beliefs of the faithful, and to thrust the greatest skeptic into the arms of God.

It had changed him.

It had changed *them*, Laura too never quite the same.

But as time marched on and the events of those days slowly faded into distant memories, it was easy to forget what had been discovered. And it was moments, like now, alone with his thoughts, that brought those memories back to the fore, renewing his shaky faith.

And in his mind, no matter what he did today, God would punish those responsible, regardless of whether or not he succeeded in finding the Spear of Destiny and the blood it was purported to be stained with.

"Any luck?"

Acton looked up to see Terrence and Jenny standing in the doorway, the room a bustle of forgotten activity around him, half a dozen off-duty Swiss Guards quickly reading through the Nazi manifests and bringing any that raised red flags to Acton for evaluation.

It was saving them days.

He nodded, pointing at his computer screen. "Almost a dozen documents so far that indicate changes to the original or ambiguities at least. I've been pulling the originals but they're so fragile they'll need to be examined in a proper lab." He pointed at one scroll sitting beside him. "Especially this one."

"Why that one?" asked Jenny, leaning in for a closer look.

"It refers to the body of a Christian martyr from the first century, originally buried in Mantua, eventually interred here in the fifteenth century. It fits the timeframe, and Longinus is considered a Christian martyr since he died for his beliefs."

"What's the name?"

"Tiberius."

Kruger Residence, Outside Paris, France

Laura woke, her mouth dry, whatever drugs she was on causing some dehydration. She opened her eyes to find curtains set up around her bed and the lights overhead turned off, though the morning sunlight and the lights of the lab were enough to almost overwhelm the thick white sheets. Reaching for her glass of water next to her bed she felt her stitches stretch and she yelped in pain, easing back to her lying position, not willing to risk making things worse.

Thirst she could live with, a torn open abdomen, not so much.

The curtain moved aside and Dr. Heinrich greeted her with a smile, the sunlight streaming in from behind almost silhouetting him like an angel.

Angel of death, maybe.

"Good morning!" he said, his ever cheerful self not having taken leave despite his apparent continued failure in finding blood on any of the artifacts. She had to admit he did seem like a genuinely nice man, though she wondered how anyone could work for murderers.

Maybe he's a prisoner too?

"Good morning," she mumbled, her dry mouth making it difficult to talk.

Heinrich laughed, stepping toward her bed and getting her glass of water, helping her position the straw. She took several long sips, swishing it around her mouth to loosen it up, then nodded. Heinrich returned the glass to the tray table then moved her sheet aside. "Let's see how the bandages are looking."

She looked down and the dressing looked clean, an improvement over yesterday when it had shown thick blotches of dark red having soaked completely through.

Heinrich nodded, satisfied. "We'll change those in a few minutes, but it's already looking better." He pressed on the wound gently and she winced. "How's the pain?"

"Still there," she gasped.

Stop pushing, you sadist!

He immediately lifted his hand. "That's to be expected, it will take time, but I want to start weaning you off the pain killers, they're not good for you. Besides, being aware of your pain helps prevent you from doing anything stupid like trying to go to the bathroom by yourself."

"Or escaping."

Heinrich chuckled, patting her arm. "Now now, you shouldn't be even *thinking* of something like that. Not that I care, you being here or not makes no difference to me, though I do enjoy the company. I'm more concerned with that wound reopening before you could get yourself to a hospital. Or worse."

"'Worse' meaning they'll shoot me if I try to escape."

Heinrich's face clouded over and he sat on the edge of her bed, lowering his voice. "It wasn't always this way. In fact, until a few months ago, this was a happy home though with a heavy weight upon it. Herr Kruger, Dietrich's father, took a rapid turn for the worse triggering Dietrich to follow through on what I thought was a passing fancy, this entire notion of the Blood of Christ being used to heal his father. We had always hoped that medical science would progress fast enough that a cure would be found, God knows he has the money to put behind the research, but unfortunately time has run out." He lowered his voice further still. "I don't think Herr Kruger will last the week."

"I'm sorry to hear that."

She wasn't.

Heinrich seemed to sense it. "Herr Kruger, *senior*, is a good man. So is his son, unfortunately his son loves his father so much he's lost sight of the values his father raised him to believe in, and now even his father has grown desperate, compromising his own values." He shook his head, sighing. "Do any of us truly know what lengths we would go to if we were in the same position?"

"I know I wouldn't kill anyone."

"Wouldn't you?" Heinrich raised his hand, cutting off her reply. "I know, I know, *you* wouldn't. And neither would I. But then, if there was something out there that could have saved my son from his cancer, and someone stood in my way…" He shook his head. "I don't know, I just don't know."

Laura didn't say anything as she wondered herself what she would do to save James, or their future children. She would like to think she wouldn't kill, but she couldn't be sure. Killing an innocent? Absolutely not, but killing someone standing in the way of her saving someone she loved?

She too didn't know.

"You lost a son?"

Heinrich nodded, biting his lip.

"How old was he?"

"Sixteen."

She reached out and squeezed his hand. "I'm so sorry. I can't imagine what it would be like to lose a child."

Heinrich sucked in a deep breath, the corners of his mouth turning down deeply.

"What's wrong?" asked Laura, her chest beginning to tighten in anticipation of something horrible about to be said.

"I've analyzed the scans I took from yesterday and I'm afraid I have some bad news for you."

Laura's hands gripped the sheets, tight.

"What?"

And when she heard what it was her stomach flipped and her chest tightened, her heart slamming into her ribcage as blood pounded in her ears, Heinrich's words growing distant as her entire future changed with a single sentence.

She leaned over the edge of the bed and vomited.

Renner Residence, Feuerbach, Germany

Karl Renner looked at the security panel near his front door, debating on whether or not to set it. He sighed, taking one last look back into the living area of his large home, a home that held many fond memories for him, though few recent. He and his ex-wife had designed the home themselves, it custom-built almost five years ago.

They had only lasted another three.

He ran his hand along the chrome banister leading upstairs then gripped it tightly, not wanting to let go, for it wasn't just a home he was leaving, it was a life.

He was about to disappear.

Forever.

The authorities would be closing in soon and he needed to disappear fast. He was heading to a private airport where he'd fly to the French Riviera then take a boat to Morocco where passport checks were a little more lax. Forged identity papers would get him to the Dominican and he'd live out his life in the sun, possibly never to see his homeland again.

It was heartbreaking.

But necessary.

And with the amount of money he had stashed away before this, and with the payday he was about to receive, it was going to be a good life.

Just a sedate one.

He held in the Away button on the security panel, it chirping three times at him as the indicator light changed to red. He stepped outside, locking the door behind him, there still some hope deep down that it might all blow over and he'd be able to return someday, someday hopefully soon, but it was *deep* down.

Face it, you'll never see this place again.

He reached into his pocket for his key fob when his phone vibrated. Pulling it out of his pocket instead, he checked the display to see a blocked number.

Maybe it's him again.

The mastermind behind all his troubles had called as promised, agreeing to a payout of another ten million euros, there little argument, little discussion at all in fact.

It must be nice to have ridiculous amounts of money.

He had given his solemn promise there would be no further requests for payment, and that he would be leaving the country immediately.

Only the latter promise did he intend to absolutely keep.

He tapped the button to take the call.

"Hello?"

"You should have never betrayed us."

Renner froze, quickly scanning the street for hostiles as he stepped back toward the door. A black SUV caught his eye.

"Good bye, Herr Renner."

He held out his hand and saw the red beam of a laser scope play across his skin for a moment. His head dropped as he looked at his chest, the bead dancing on his crisp white shirt.

The sequence of events was strange, part of him certain he heard the vehicle squeal away before he actually felt the impact, but he knew that wasn't right. What *was* certain was the pain wasn't really what he had expected, the shot hitting him in the heart, the vital muscle torn open as the bullet pierced his skin, shattering a rib, sending shards of bone off in every direction to cause even more damage.

He dropped to his knees, the phone clattering to the interlocking brick porch as his arms sagged to his sides, his chin on his chest as he continued to stare at the rapidly increasing red stain, the hole made by the bullet so tiny it was hard to believe the damage it had done.

He gasped for breath but could feel his body failing him, his gasps now short, rapid inhalations, growing more infrequent with each quick intake. Tipping over, he fell on his side, his face slamming against the cool stone as bright spots began to flicker in front of him, his breaths now seconds apart as his mind tried desperately to hang on for one last moment of lucidity.

He focused on his rose bushes.

And wondered who would take care of them.

Sapienza University, Rome, Italy

James Acton stood impatiently outside the lab where their documents were being analyzed by some of the most advanced scanners in the world. It had been this very spot where he and Laura had stood when the document buried with a Templar knight discovered under the Vatican had been read for the first time in nearly a thousand years.

And it had led to chaos worldwide.

Today the only life he was concerned about was that of his wife. Terrence stood beside him, his hand resting on Jenny's shoulder, she having pushed a chair up to the glass. He glanced at her rather obvious baby bump and smiled.

One of these days.

He and Laura had been discussing children for some time, and with her now working in the United States and both of them under the same roof, it was finally a possibility. And having a child would mean little adventures like this would have to end, though it seemed even going on vacation now was wrought with peril for them.

China! What a nightmare that turned out to be!

Having a little boy or girl running around the house would definitely be a change of pace, but a good one, one he was ready for. He loved gallivanting across the globe, and if it weren't for Laura's predicament, this would be an incredibly exciting time. If his hunch proved true, they might be about to find evidence that one of the Apocryphal texts was actually accurate, and that the Roman soldier Longinus did indeed exist.

Laura would be loving this.

He took a deep breath, fighting the tightness that threatened to trigger a bout of anxiety when Vatican Inspector General Mario Giasson entered the room.

"Good morning, Mario."

"Professor."

"Jim, please."

Giasson smiled. "Jim." He nodded toward the scientists on the other side of the glass. "Anything yet?"

"They just started. They've prepped the first document I want them to examine and are scanning it now. We're trying to see what was scratched out."

"Do you think they'll be able to?"

Acton nodded. "As long as it wasn't done at the same time—meaning the same ink would have mixed together and dried at the same rate leaving probably nothing discernable—then there's a very good chance."

"You sound optimistic."

Acton frowned. "I have no choice."

"To that end, I just spoke with Hugh. Did you get his update last night?"

Acton nodded. "Hopefully they'll be able to find something in the data they pulled."

"I think they just might."

Acton looked at Giasson, finally tearing his eyes away from the screens displaying the document. "Now *you're* the one who sounds optimistic."

"They just found Karl Renner shot to death on his doorstep. He was packed, heading for a private airstrip when he was shot."

Acton's eyes popped wide as a feeling of exhilaration raced through him.

Innocent men don't run! And innocent men don't get assassinated.

"Any idea who did it?"

Giasson shook his head. "Not yet, but it's early on. I just got the word on the way here."

"Look!" Acton turned to see Terrence pointing at one of the screens, various filters being applied to the scanned image, the dark band of heavy ink quickly changing colors and shades as the computer flipped through thousands of different scanning wavelengths.

"Oh my God," whispered Jenny as she rose from her chair, pressing against the glass.

"It's working!" Acton leaned closer as writing began to appear, faint at first, but as the experts behind the glass continued to manipulate the scanner, tweaking the settings as some wavelengths improved things and others made things worse, the handwritten words slowly took form.

"Does that say 'Sancti'?" asked Terrence, squinting for a better look.

Adrenaline rushed through Acton's veins as he grabbed Giasson by the shoulder, shaking him. "It absolutely does."

"Saint," gasped Giasson.

Acton was mouthing out the letters following it, the handwriting still not clear, though individual letters were. "That's definitely an L, isn't it?"

"It looks like an L. And an O," agreed Jenny.

Terrence turned to Acton, his eyes wide with excitement, a smile spread across his face. "It says Longinus, doesn't it? Sancti Longinus!"

Acton was still shaking Giasson by the shoulder, there no doubt in his mind now, the hand written words recorded by some long forgotten records keeper centuries before, were now clearly displayed on the monitors.

Sancti Longinus.

"You found him!" exclaimed Giasson, turning toward Acton. "Congratulations, Professor."

Acton shook his head in disagreement, though there was no suppressing his smile. "No, we haven't found *him*, but we've found why he was *thought* to have been moved here almost five hundred years ago."

"So what now?" asked Terrence.

"Now we go back to the basilica and see if we can find the actual body this document refers to. Somehow they found out it wasn't Longinus and updated their records. That could be because they discovered something with the body that proved it wasn't him, they received some sort of documentation after the fact proving it wasn't, or they found the actual body elsewhere."

Jenny returned to her seat, holding her stomach. "If there was some documentation, wouldn't it have been with the records we found?"

"Possibly, but any such documentation would have his name figured prominently in it and we know that the Vatican's own historian didn't find any references to the name."

Terrence perched on the chair, putting his hand on the back of his wife's neck, giving it a gentle massage. "So *if* there was documentation, then it has either been lost or destroyed over the years."

"*If.*" Jenny moaned at Terrence's ministrations. "We know for certain now that there *was* a body in the catacombs once thought to be Saint Longinus. What would they have done with the body if they found out it wasn't him?"

Acton shrugged. "There's probably little doubt the person was Catholic, so they would have treated the body with respect, regardless. And considering the fact that there appeared to be many bodies listed of relative commoners, I'd say there's a good chance they kept it."

"If they were going to get rid of it, wouldn't they have indicated that on the document when they were updating it to say it wasn't him?"

Acton turned to Jenny, a slight smile on his face, her conclusion so obvious it had been missed by all including him. "Of course they would have." His smile turned into a grin. "Up for getting a little dirty?"

Both Terrence and Jenny's heads bobbed eagerly.

"Then let's go."

Chris Leroux had a smile on his face, Judy Garland's Good Morning playing on his mental radio, not because he had watched Babes in Arms but purely because it had been used in a Viagra commercial at some point.

In other words, he had got some last night.

And this morning.

He *loved* when Sherrie came back from assignment.

"Hey, boss, you're looking chipper."

Leroux blanched as he looked at Marc Therrien.

Is it that obvious?

"Good morning," he managed, unlocking his office door. "Any success?"

"Some, but there's been news. Not sure if you've read your flash updates yet."

Leroux shook his head. "No, I was, umm, busy this morning."

"Alright boss!" Therrien raised a hand for a high five, then thought better of it after Leroux's shocked look. "Umm, sorry, boss. Anyway, Karl Renner is dead."

Leroux stopped, his eyebrows rising as he turned toward Therrien. "Dead?"

"Yeah, looks like a professional hit. Single shot to the chest. On the man's doorstep no less."

Leroux hung his jacket on the hook behind his door then sat down, logging into his computer. "Any leads on who did it?"

"None yet, it just happened a few hours ago. But it looks like he was heading to parts unknown."

"What do you mean?"

"Car was loaded with suitcases and he was apparently heading for a private airport for a flight to the French Riviera."

"Maybe he was going on vacation."

"Don't think so. Everything was last minute, flight just booked this morning. I think he knew we were onto him and he was planning on disappearing."

"And somebody didn't like that."

"Apparently not," said Therrien as he sat in one of the office chairs. "But that doesn't really make much sense, does it? If he's disappearing, isn't that what we were expecting his men were going to be doing as well? Why would somebody shoot him for that? If he disappears, then he can't be interrogated."

Leroux logged into his secure email, quickly scanning the update on Renner. "Maybe his plans and theirs have nothing to do with each other. Maybe they were just tying up loose ends."

"But this isn't over. Killing him now sort of confirms he was involved, doesn't it? Now we'll focus on him, and since he's much more high profile than his men, we might just be able to track things back to the source."

"I don't think that will be happening, at least not yet."

They both turned as Sonya Tong poked her head into the office. She was one of Leroux's best analysts and had been part of the nightshift team tasked with following the money.

He was also pretty certain she was sweet on him, despite Sherrie being clearly in the picture.

It was kind of flattering, though awkward.

"What makes you say that?" he asked, trying to avoid eye contact, he having *zero* experience with office crushes other than his own.

Tong nodded toward his computer. "I just sent you the update. It took a little doing but we gained access to the bank files of that employee who was sending his salary to Switzerland—"

"Already? Excellent work!"

Tong blushed.

Uh oh, easy on the compliments.

"Thanks, Mr. Leroux." Flustered, she fumbled for her train of thought.

"You accessed the bank files?" prompted Leroux.

"Oh, yes! And we found regular deposits that matched up with his employment record perfectly, plus monthly withdrawals of about five thousand euros a month which we assume he used to pay his bills. *But*, we found two *very* large deposits, one for a million euros three months ago, and another for the same amount just a week ago."

"Just before this all started."

Therrien whistled. "Two million euros, that's a lot of coin. A man could disappear for a while on that."

Leroux nodded. "And the usual pattern on these types of payments is a final lump sum when the job is done."

"So we can probably assume another one to two million."

Tong sat down beside Therrien, crossing her legs, her skirt hiking up an uncomfortable amount. "And they found six motorcycles in Vienna, which suggests at least six people involved, so we could be looking at a twenty million euro payout."

"That's like, what, twenty-five million dollars?"

Leroux nodded. "Close enough. Not to mention equipment, helicopters, vehicles and what not. This is an extremely well-financed operation."

"There's not a lot of private individuals who could finance this type of thing," said Therrien. "We're sure it's not government?"

Leroux shrugged. "I doubt it, but you never know. We need to find the moneyman."

Tong leaned forward. "And that's what I was about to tell you. We traced the payments from our suspect's account back to the source."

Leroux smiled, Therrien grinning as he turned toward Tong. "And?"

"And the account was opened by Karl Renner three months ago, a single deposit of fifty million euros made upon opening, in bearer bonds, so untraceable. Ten million euros were transferred to another account in Renner's name, opened years ago."

Leroux closed his eyes, pinching the bridge of his nose. Hard. It made no sense. Renner was the mastermind, the man behind the entire thing? No, something was wrong here. You don't kill the mastermind.

Unless the mastermind turned on the men he hired.

These men were capable of killing, of that there was no doubt. The fact they had participated in two crimes where people had died showed they had set their morals aside, their motivation now a hefty payday, and if Renner were to jeopardize that in some way they might eliminate their own boss.

But it still didn't fit.

"Why would Renner be behind this?" he finally asked the room. "It makes no sense."

"No it doesn't," agreed Tong. "That's why I'm digging deeper. Personally..." Her voice drifted off and she looked away, as if uncertain whether or not she should continue.

"What?" asked Leroux. "Spit it out, you know the rules, never hold back when you're brainstorming."

Tong blushed slightly. "Well, I think he's been set up."

Leroux nodded. "So do I. I can't see how he'd have accumulated fifty million euros on his own."

"Could *he* be the middleman? Somebody gave him the bonds, he opened an account and distributed the money?"

Leroux nodded at Therrien's suggestion. "That's definitely a possibility. Either way, we need to know where that money came from, and we just hit a major road block."

"I just hope it's not a dead end," agreed Therrien.

"If it is, then the entire Stuttgart op was a waste of time."

Leroux shook his head. "No, we rattled somebody's cage. Renner was running, and somebody felt he knew something he shouldn't have. That means Renner either knew who the real moneyman was, or knew how to reach him." He pointed at Therrien. "Start tracing his phone records. I want to know about any incoming or outgoing calls, especially after the transmitter was planted. I think he panicked and made a call he shouldn't have that got him killed."

"Will do."

"And Sonya, I want you to try and find out who actually opened that account. That kind of money means they live differently than us. If it was bearer bonds, it was done in person, so find out where. Then find out about any private planes, first class tickets, whatever, for the same period. See if you can find any CCTV footage that might have caught him on camera."

"How do we know what he looks like?"

"We don't," replied Leroux. "But I'm willing to bet it's our mystery German from Vienna."

Basilica of Sant'Agostino, Rome, Italy

"You're absolutely certain you need to do this?"

James Acton smiled reassuringly at Father Albano. "Yes, Father, it's the only way. We need to find the body referred to in the document if we have any hope of finding Saint Longinus himself."

Father Albano made the sign of the cross, looking to the stone ceiling of the catacombs dug under the church centuries before. All around them dozens upon dozens of alcoves contained bodies, some wrapped, some in coffins, others simply piles of bones. Acton prayed there was some sort of organization here, at least by era. He wouldn't know until they started.

"If you do find him, it would indeed be a great discovery."

Acton nodded. "Absolutely."

Father Albano glanced at Jenny, lowering his voice. "Should she be here in her condition?"

"I'm perfectly capable, thank you very much."

Father Albano grimaced at Acton, keeping his expression hidden from Jenny before turning toward her. "I meant no disrespect, young lady, I was simply thinking of the safety of your child. There have been several collapses here over the centuries."

"Perhaps he's right," said Terrence, the words eliciting a scowl from his wife. "Well, love, it *is* dangerous, and you're carrying our child, and—"

"And it doesn't matter for now, regardless." They all turned toward Giasson's voice as he descended the ancient stone staircase. "You're both due for your deposition."

"Can't that wait?" asked Jenny, a little whine in her voice.

"I made a promise to the Roma Polizia and I keep my promises."

Jenny frowned, Terrence taking her by the arm, a relieved look on his face as he had an excuse to get her out of there.

And himself.

Terrence never came across as the brave type, more the reluctant hero at times, his clumsiness preventing him from actually being reliable in a fight, but he had never shied away from danger when it was absolutely necessary, and after his torture in the Amazon, Acton had gained a newfound respect for the young man.

Despite him having a crush on his wife.

It was quite plain to anyone, except he hoped Jenny, that Terrence was smitten with Laura. Laura thought it harmless, and Acton was secure enough for it not to bother him, especially after Jenny entered the picture, clearly capturing Terrence's heart.

Just not 100% of it.

He smiled at the husband and wife as they stopped in front of him.

"Sorry, Professor. We'll get back as soon as we can."

Acton nodded at Jenny. "Do what you need to do. With any luck, I'll find him before you get back."

Jenny frowned. "That would be disappointing." Her jaw dropped. "I'm sorry, Professor, I didn't mean it the way it sounded."

Acton laughed. "Don't worry, I know what you mean. I'd hate to miss a discovery like this too. Now go. The sooner you're gone, the sooner you're back."

Jenny followed Giasson up the stairs, Terrence behind her, as Acton turned to survey his surroundings once again.

"Would you like me to help?" asked Father Albano, the trepidation in his voice clearly suggesting the answer he hoped for.

"No, Father, I'm certain you have more important duties to attend to. I'll be fine on my own."

Father Albano placed a hand on Acton's shoulder, smiling slightly. "Thank you, my son." He looked up the stairs, quite narrow by modern standards, shaking his head. "I don't think it was wise of me to come down here at my age."

"Let me help you," replied Acton as the old man climbed the first of many steps, hugging the wall, any railing that might once have been there long gone.

"Bless you, my son," said Father Albano as Acton positioned himself one step behind him, holding up his left arm to act as a railing for the man to push on, his other hand pushing gently on his back to keep him steady and help him up. They took the steps one at a time, both feet firmly planted on each before continuing to the next.

Acton found himself getting slightly frustrated with the pace, but knew it wasn't the poor man's fault. Acton was used to harrowing staircases and tunnels, caves and caverns, it his job to crawl about where none had gone in years.

I wonder what I'll be doing at his age.

Certainly not gallivanting across the globe, crawling around ancient ruins and getting shot at by terrorists, cults and criminals.

How old was Harrison Ford in Indy 4?

Father Albano began to take the steps a little faster, leaving only one foot on each now as Acton continued to picture his retirement.

Kids and grandkids. That's what I want.

He could imagine no better reward after a life of hard work than to be surrounded by family with the woman he loved at his side. He'd keep up his academic work but send out the younger generation to get their hands and knees dirty.

I wonder if my kids will become archeologists like their parents.

As they neared the top of the stairs Father Albano reached out for a railing, installed more recently, this portion of the structure at least several hundred years newer than the catacombs below.

"I think I'm good now, my son."

"Are you sure?"

The old man nodded as he pulled himself up the final few steps, much quicker now, Acton backing off to give him space, but keeping a wary eye on him until he cleared the door. "I'll check on you in an hour," said Father Albano, looking back down at him.

Acton smiled. "Just call me from there and I'll come up to see you, deal?"

Father Albano chuckled. "Deal."

Acton turned and rushed down the stairs, eagerly surveying his surroundings, his flashlight playing across the catacombs.

I'm going to need more light.

St. Paul's University, St. Paul, Maryland

Mai Lien Trinh opened her eyes, a ceramic Taz coffee mug staring her in the face. She lifted her head off the table, quickly wiping away the small puddle of drool as she looked over at Tommy, sound asleep with an impressive pool of his own. She stared at him for a moment, pondering whether or not she found it disgusting or cute.

She settled on cute.

In a disgusting way.

Something was beeping and she looked at the screen, it flashing a message repeatedly.

Match Found!

"Tommy, wake up."

Nothing.

"Tommy, wake up!"

Still nothing.

She reached over, hesitating a moment before pushing on his shoulder.

He grunted but remained asleep.

She punched his shoulder.

Tommy jumped up in his chair. "Huh? What?" He looked around, disoriented, then adjusted his glasses, wiping his mouth with the back of his hoodie. "Good morning," he mumbled at Mai, clearly not a morning person.

She pointed at the screen. "What does that mean?"

Tommy scrambled for the keyboard, his fingers flying, his mouse scurrying as he clicked several links before a photo was shown of a group of people, all clearly well-heeled in their tuxedos and evening gowns.

263

"That's him!" exclaimed Mai as she pointed to one of the men tucked into the back, his face barely visible, his neutral facial expression contrasting sharply with the rest of the group.

"It definitely looks like him," agreed Tommy. He pointed to the metadata associated with the photo. "This was taken after the Monaco Grand Prix five years ago."

"Where?"

"I think it's the palace, which means this was a formal event."

"So?"

"So that means guest lists."

"From five years ago?"

"It's the best we've got. It's *all* we've got."

Mai leaned closer to the photo, not sure what to do. All they had was a photo of a man with no name taken five years ago. How they could possibly find out who had attended that party was beyond her.

Then she smiled as something dawned on her.

"What?"

She looked at Tommy. "*We* don't need to figure out who was there."

"We don't?"

She shook her head. "No, *we* don't. The CIA does."

CIA Headquarters, Langley, Virginia

"So you were right, boss, Renner's phone logs were interesting."

Marc Therrien handed a tablet to Leroux who looked at the calls, several of them highlighted. "What am I looking at?"

"That first highlighted call was one Renner made last night to a Voice over IP phone, so pretty much completely untraceable."

"You tried?"

"Yup, no success, but we're still working on it." He nodded toward the tablet. "That second highlighted call is an incoming one from another Internet phone number, received this morning, about twenty minutes before he was shot. The final highlighted call is an incoming that he received we think *as* he was shot."

"Probably telling him why he was about to die," surmised Sonya Tong. "I think I'd rather not know."

Therrien nodded. "Me neither." He reached over and swiped his finger across the display, another set of numbers appearing. "So, we weren't able to trace where this first VoIP phone was located, but we were able to determine the calls made to it. There haven't been many and they were all from other VoIP numbers. We think they're call-forwarding the VoIP numbers to burner phones so nothing can be traced. All that is, except one call."

Leroux's eyebrows rose slightly. "One?"

Therrien smiled. "Yup. And it was received not even five minutes before the attack in Paris."

"And you were able to trace the origin?"

Therrien's head bobbed excitedly. "Somebody screwed up, boss. They used a regular cellphone, not redirected. It's a burner so we can't trace the owner, but we were able to locate the cellphone tower the call was connected through."

Leroux leaned forward, staring at the tablet then at Therrien. "Where?"

"Just outside Paris, not twenty miles from where the helicopter landed."

Leroux felt a smile start to spread across his face as he leaned back in his chair. They finally had a lead, though it was thin. He had no doubt none of the highly trained mercenaries would screw up like this, and the fact the call was received so close to the Paris robbery suggested either someone who had no idea it was about to happen, or someone with information so vital to its success that they had to use an unsecured form of communication.

Or, like Therrien had suggested, someone had just screwed up.

"The location might mean nothing," said Tong as she spun her laptop toward Leroux, a map of Paris and the surrounding countryside displayed, the cellphone tower highlighted with an arrow. "They could have just been in the vicinity of this tower when making the call and be in another country now for all we know."

Leroux shook his head, tapping his desk. "I don't think so. We know Professor Palmer is alive, and according to the medical experts, she would have died if she didn't receive prompt medical attention, which means she had to have received it within about a thirty to forty-five minute drive of where the helicopter was found. The French police have scoured the country and there have been no reports of any woman matching her description, or any description, having been brought in with a gunshot wound to the abdomen. That means she was treated somewhere private. Also, we know from the conversation that Professor Acton had with her that she was being treated by a doctor named Heinrich—"

"Thousands of hits, we're trying to narrow it down," interjected Therrien.

"—and that she was in some sort of well-equipped lab. I'm betting that lab is within forty-five minutes of that helicopter landing zone, and that cellphone tower is also within that same radius."

"I've learned to never bet against you, boss."

Leroux looked at Therrien but said nothing, he still not used to having staff that kissed his ass, or being called 'boss'. Especially when half his staff were older than he was. He pursed his lips. "What's the range on that tower?"

"At most forty-five miles," replied Tong, spinning her laptop back toward her. "But terrain can impact that dramatically."

"Find out. I want to be able to get an overlay to our people in France."

"Yes, sir."

Therrien and Tong rose, leaving the office as Leroux began to type an email to the inner circle of this operation. They had a lead, finally, but it wasn't much. And even if the range of the cellphone tower proved to only be twenty miles, that left an area of over 1250 square miles to search.

Needle in a haystack?

Approaching Basilica of Sant'Agostino, Rome, Italy

Mario Giasson stifled a yawn, hoping no one had noticed, he raised better than to do such a thing in the middle of the day while on the job. But he couldn't help it. He hadn't slept more than two hours in the past two days and was quickly reaching burnout.

And there was no end in sight.

He turned in his seat, Francesco Greco driving, to look at their passengers, and his charge, Terrence and Jenny Mitchell.

"I spoke with the prosecutor and he said there won't be any charges against either of you."

Jenny nodded, it clear she was still troubled by what she had done. Killing a man at point blank range had to be psychologically scarring and with their schedule she hadn't had time to process what she had done, and what had almost happened to her.

It's going to take time.

Terrence jumped in his seat then fished out his phone, reading a text message, his face losing several shades of its usual ruddy color. He showed it to Jenny, her hands instinctively covering her stomach before she looked out the window.

"Something wrong?" asked Giasson, it clear they were both upset.

"No, it-it's nothing."

Giasson frowned. "It's clearly not nothing."

"I…I can't talk about it. Like I said, it's nothing."

"Show me your phone."

Terrence's jaw dropped, his eyes opening wide as Jenny's head spun toward Giasson. It was clear from both their reactions that the very idea horrified them, and it had nothing to do with an invasion of their privacy.

They were terrified.

"Now."

He held out his hand and Terrence reluctantly brought up the message, handing him the phone. Giasson cursed as he read the text received only moments before.

You failed to report your discovery. Next time she dies.

"Explain this."

"We can't."

"Why not?"

"If we say anything, they'll kill her."

"There's no one here but us, tell me now, it's perfectly safe."

Terrence and Jenny both shook their heads emphatically.

"They can hear everything. I don't know how, but they can." Terrence's lip trembled. "They probably heard everything you just said." He looked at his wife's stomach as Jenny continued to cover her baby.

"They're going to kill my baby," she whispered.

Kruger Residence, Outside Paris, France

"Your father is getting worse."

His mother's whispered words caused Dietrich's chest to tighten like a vise on his heart. He looked over her shoulder at the family patriarch, the man who had taught him how to be a father, a husband and a business leader. A man who was supposed to be around for at least another decade to continue to teach him.

"I'm not ready," he mumbled, a tear rolling down his cheek, self-pity gripping him.

His mother placed a comforting hand on his chest, his heart slamming so hard he was sure she could feel it. "Yes, you are. He said so himself earlier today that he is extremely proud of the man you've become, and that he will die knowing we are all in capable hands." She took his hand in hers, clasping it to her chest. "You are ready, my son. Don't forget, your father took over from your grandfather when he was only five years older than you are now."

"Yes, but Grandfather lived for another fifteen."

His mother frowned. "He did, but I'm afraid it wasn't much of a life. For most of it he was in pain, and when he wasn't, it was because the drugs had him barely awake. He didn't carry on a real conversation for the final five years." She sucked in a deep breath, covering her mouth as if ashamed of what she was about to say. "When I picture him, his final years, I sometimes think that this is the best thing for your father. If he dies now, he'll avoid all that suff—" The word caught in her throat, replaced with sobs as she collapsed in his arms, her entire body shaking with grief.

It overwhelmed him as he fought for control, fought to remain strong for her, but it was no use. The tears flowed. His chest heaved.

His mother pushed back gently, a lace handkerchief appearing from somewhere as she dabbed her eyes dry. "Look at me, I'm your mother, I should be strong."

Dietrich smiled, shaking his head. "I'm the one who's supposed to be strong."

She sighed. "We both must be strong for him." She looked over at her husband. "Is there any hope of finding this Spear of Destiny?"

Dietrich nodded. "Yes. In fact I'm leaving shortly. The professor has apparently found a document that proves they once thought the body was there."

"I don't understand. 'Once thought'?"

"I don't have time to explain, but it's the closest anyone has ever been to finding it. I'm leaving for Rome now." He strode over to his father, placing a hand on the man's forehead, brushing away some stray hairs. "I love you," he whispered, there no response other than a moan, his father's dreams tormented.

He hugged his mother then left without saying anything else, afraid he'd once again lose control. Quickly covering the distance from his father's chambers to Dr. Heinrich's lab, he took a moment to compose himself before entering. Heinrich was changing the woman's bandage when he entered.

"One moment," said Heinrich, the woman nodding, staring at him for a moment then turning away.

"How is she?"

"Her wound is infected. She needs more care than I can give."

"That isn't an option."

"Your father wouldn't want her to die."

Dietrich glared at Heinrich. "My father is almost dead. I'm in charge now."

Heinrich took half a step backward, bowing slightly. "I understand."

"The authorities might be closing in on this location. Can my father be moved?"

"I wouldn't recommend it."

"It may become necessary. In fact, it *will* become necessary."

"I'll make the arrangements."

"I want him and my mother moved as soon as you're ready."

"And what of her?"

Dietrich looked over at Laura Palmer, the wound on her stomach exposed and inflamed.

"If my father dies, she dies."

Basilica of Sant'Agostino, Rome, Italy

James Acton was almost giddy with excitement. The Vatican had arranged to have several large, battery powered lights brought into the catacombs, and once they had arrived, his slow progress had become rapid. With a notepad and pencil he had mapped out the catacombs, his practiced diagramming skills put to work as he sketched each section, indicating where the bodies were and which ones were labelled.

Some were, but many weren't.

But that hadn't been his concern. He was more interested in discovering the organization of the catacombs, if there even was one, and with many of the caskets engraved with dates, especially the more "recent" ones, he was able to find the section that appeared to have bodies from the fourteenth through sixteenth centuries, the rest of the catacombs appearing to be much older, very little newer.

And that had led rather quickly to his shocking discovery.

"Hello, Professor."

Acton jumped, spinning toward the voice to find Terrence and Jenny coming down the stairs, Terrence in the lead with a hand held out behind him to help Jenny. He was torn between continuing with what he had just discovered, and his curiosity in how things had gone.

He chose to be polite.

"Did everything go well?"

They both nodded. "I won't be charged with anything."

Acton breathed a sigh of relief at Jenny's words. "Thank God! That must be a huge weight off your shoulders."

She nodded, though she still seemed uneasy.

"Something wrong?"

She shook her head, a little too quickly. Terrence pointed at the wall where several lights were focused. "Did you find something?"

"Yes!" He beckoned them toward his find, only minutes old. "Look at this." In one of the alcoves dug out of the wall there was a casket, many centuries upon centuries old, but still intact. "There's a nameplate here that identifies the occupant."

"It's been scratched out," said Jenny, leaning closer, the awe in her voice suggesting whatever had troubled her a moment ago had been forgotten. "As if by a nail or something."

Acton nodded vigorously. "And look. That's an L, isn't it? And a G?"

Terrence got up close, squinting. "I think so. That's definitely an L. The rest of it I can't tell."

"None of the rest of them have had their nameplates tampered with like this. Now mind you I haven't looked at them all, but I've looked at probably a hundred, and this is the only one I found so far." He pointed at a box of tools he had brought down earlier. "Grab me the chisel and hammer."

Terrence complied, handing the tools over to Acton who quickly went to work, sticking the chisel between the top of the coffin and the side, gently tapping until he was in about an inch. He lightly pushed up on the handle, the top of the coffin rising slightly. As he worked around the edge, the work painstakingly slow, he had to resist the urge to simply rip the top off and get at what was inside, the repetitive, deliberate task leaving him with far too much time on his hands to think about Laura and the race against time he was in.

Please God, take care of her!

"Give me a hand here."

Terrence grabbed one end of the top, Acton the other, and they both gently rocked it back and forth until it came loose, thankfully in one piece, Acton a desperate husband but also a trained archeologist with a duty to preserve the past.

Unlike those barbarians in Mosul.

He felt a spark of anger ignite at the thought of anyone arrogant enough to believe they had the right to destroy artifacts thousands of years old because they felt they insulted their religion. How insecure in your beliefs did you have to be to feel a sculpture, handcrafted five thousand years ago, was an affront to your God?

He shook his head.

I don't have time for this.

He crouched down, squeezing himself into the alcove barely big enough to hold the casket, looking inside. A breath caught in his throat at the sight. The body inside was intact, at least from all outward appearances, it carefully wrapped in bandages from head to toe, the skeletal structure plain, any tissues long having decayed.

"Flashlight."

Somebody slapped one in his outstretched hands, his eyes not leaving the body, something having caught his attention. He flicked the light on and shone it near where the hands appeared to have been clasped over the person's chest.

"These bandages have been opened."

"What?" Terrence poked his head in, trying to get a look.

Acton pointed. "Look, see the discoloration here? These wraps are newer around the chest." Acton reached over and gently ran his fingers along the bandages, tracing a rib then pausing when he felt something else, something on top of the ribcage. Running his finger along the straight, hard

275

line, he came to a corner and continued to trace out what felt like a stone rectangle.

A stone rectangle gripped in the person's hands.

"I think it might be some sort of tablet."

"Underneath the wrappings? Why would they do that?" asked Jenny, she having replaced Terrence.

"They might have been trying to hide something, or it might have been some sort of private message, meant for God, not to be seen by man." Acton shrugged, stepping back from the alcove and stretching the kinks out. "Whatever the reason, we need to see what it says, if anything. Clearly somebody discovered it, probably when transferring the body to this newer casket, cut through the wrappings, read it, then rewrapped the body. I'm guessing that's when they discovered this wasn't Saint Longinus."

"Then let's do it!" Terrence began to root through the toolbox, triumphantly holding up a set of scissors.

Acton held up his hand. "I promised Father Albano I wouldn't disturb anything without talking to him first." Acton turned and rushed up the stairs, the excitement of imminent discovery fueling his tired frame, his worries over Laura almost pushed to the background as he sought out the elderly priest.

"Father, I think I've found him!"

Father Albano looked up from some papers he was reading, momentarily startled. "Found who?"

"Longinus. Rather, Tiberius."

Father Albano rose, a smile on his face. "Congratulations, my son. But all you have done is find the body of a man you weren't looking for, if I'm not mistaken."

Acton smiled. "True, but it may contain a clue as to where the real body is."

"How so?"

"We think there's a stone tablet concealed underneath the bandages used to wrap his body. It may contain information that could lead us to him."

"How can you be certain?"

"Without examining it, I can't."

"What are you asking me, my son?"

"I need your permission to cut open the bandages so we can see the tablet." As soon as the word 'cut' was spoken Father Albano's jaw dropped and Acton knew he was going to have a problem. He pressed forward, reminding the priest of why they were here. "My wife's life is depending on my finding Saint Longinus. I *need* to see that tablet."

Father Albano shook his head slowly, his eyes dropping to the floor for a moment before returning to Acton's. "I'm sorry, but I can't allow it. To desecrate the dead, it's…" He seemed at a loss for words, instead shaking his head. "I…don't…know."

"Perhaps if we consulted a higher authority?"

Father Albano looked up. "God?"

Acton smiled. "I was thinking someone a little closer to Earth."

Hotel Astor Saint Honore, Paris, France

"It's still a huge area."

Reading nodded as he, Dawson and Niner looked at the overlay provided by the CIA showing the cellphone tower's range based upon topographical and meteorological data at the time of the call. "Over three thousand square kilometers."

"That's insane." Niner stepped away from the screen, grabbing a bottle of water from the kitchenette. "There's no way we can cover that area, it's like looking for a needle in a haystack."

"True," said Dawson, "but this waiting is driving me nuts."

"I don't know how we're going to narrow this down any further." Reading leaned back and stretched. "But I'm going crazy as well. Jim is counting on us to find his wife before it's too late."

Niner sat back down. "He seems to be making progress."

"Yes, but in his own words he's simply found out why they once thought this soldier was buried there. He hasn't actually found him."

"And may never," mumbled Dawson who was bent over, his head hanging low between his knees, apparently deep in thought. He suddenly sat upright. "We have the phone number that made the call, right?"

Reading nodded.

"Let's call it."

"Wouldn't that just tip them off?"

Dawson shook his head. "No, we have equipment that can ping the phone just like the cellphone companies do. It will force the phone to send a signal back. We can then try to trace that signal."

"Won't it just lead to the same cellphone tower?"

Niner leaned forward, excited. "No, he's right. We wouldn't be tracing the cellphone tower signal, we'll be tracing the phone's signal. If we can pick up that signal we'll be able to narrow the area significantly, and maybe even pinpoint the damned thing."

Reading smiled. "I'm not even going to ask if we'd need a warrant to do this officially."

Dawson shrugged. "No warrants in our business unless we're operating on US soil." He looked at the Eiffel Tower through the window. "We're not in Vegas, are we?"

"Nope," replied Niner.

"Then that must be the real one."

Niner grinned. "No warrants."

Reading's phone vibrated on the table. "It's Mario Giasson." He swiped his finger, putting the call on speaker. "Hi Mario, it's Hugh. You're on speaker with our *friends*."

"Understood. We may have a problem. In fact, we *do* have a problem that our friends may be able to help with."

"This is White. What's the problem?" asked Dawson.

"Terrence Mitchell received a text message from our suspects. It says 'You failed to report your discovery. Next time she dies.' They refuse to talk about it, essentially claiming they've been told Jenny Mitchell will be killed if they do. They also claim that the suspects seem to know everything they're saying."

"Could they have a transmitter on them?" asked Niner.

"I don't think so. I had one of my men bring a scanner and they were clean. The only transmitting devices on them are their cellphones."

"That's probably it," said Dawson. "These guys knew they were coming; they had a driver there waiting to pick them up at the airport. All they had to do was lift one of their phones for a few minutes, install a special app or

279

insert a modified SIM card then return it. If I'm not mistaken Mr. Mitchell is fairly, shall we say, awkward? It would have been easy to bump into him once or twice to pull the phone then plant it again."

"What could they do if they modified the phone?" asked Giasson.

"They could set it to transmit everything the speaker picked up. They'd know everything being said within earshot of the phone."

"Then that's probably it. I'll confiscate their phones immediately."

"I wouldn't do that," said Reading. "If you do, they'll know we're onto them and we can't risk them panicking and killing Laura. It's best to just let things go on as they are, but making sure nothing is said about our progress in front of them."

"Do you think they could have compromised the Professor's phone?"

Dawson shrugged. "Anything's possible. You'll need to let them all know what's going on somehow without tipping off our suspects."

Reading leaned closer to the phone. "Be discrete, Mario. Laura's life just might depend upon it."

Basilica of Sant'Agostino, Rome, Italy

Mario Giasson reentered the Basilica, scribbling a note on his pad. He spotted Acton coming out of Father Albano's rectory, his eyes widening as if he had been looking for him. Acton opened his mouth to speak when Giasson held a finger to his lips.

Acton stopped, his eyes narrowing as he followed the mimed instructions. Giasson approached, holding up the pad.

Don't talk. You may be bugged. Give me your cellphone.

Acton nodded, fishing his phone out of his pocket.

"So, Professor, hungry yet?" he asked, scribbling another note and holding up the pad.

Terrence? Jenny?

"Getting a little peckish now that you mention it." He pointed toward the entrance to the catacombs.

"Maybe we should get the others and find out what they want for lunch. I'll have it brought in."

Acton nodded as they approached the entrance. He descended a few steps then called out. "Jenny, Terrence, can you join us up here please?"

"Yes, Professor!"

It took a couple of minutes for the two to climb the steps leaving Giasson and Acton to continue their forced small talk about lunch. "Well, since we're in Italy, I'm guessing you know a place with a good lasagna?"

"Isn't that a little heavy for lunch?"

Giasson held the pad up to the arriving couple, their shocked expressions thankfully not accompanied by any outbursts. They handed over their phones. "What do you two feel like for lunch?" asked Acton as

Giasson handed the three phones to one of his men, indicating he should be quiet.

"Perhaps a salad?" Jenny didn't sound certain, her mind clearly not on food as her eyes followed her cellphone's handoff.

Terrence almost seemed oblivious to the situation, his stomach taking over. "I'm starved. I'm thinking fettuccini alfredo with grilled chicken and some garlic bread."

"I'll have someone order it," replied Giasson, handing off a scribbled note to another one of his men with their lunch orders. He then pointed to the rectory, leading the way to Father Albano's office. Glancing back, he shook his head as Terrence tiptoed, Pink Panther style, Acton rolling his eyes with a smile. The door was open and before Father Albano could say anything, he held his finger to his lips, ushering the others inside then closing the door.

"Okay, we don't have much time," said Giasson. "We believe one or more of your phones may have been bugged, for lack of a better word."

"How?" asked Terrence. "They've never been out of our sight."

"Are you sure? Nobody bumped into you at some point, the airport perhaps?"

Terrence turned beet red, Jenny taking his arm. "In fact, there were quite a few such…umm…encounters?"

"Then it's possible. This means that since then they've heard every single word said."

"Which means they know what we've found!" Acton shook his head. "But why should we care? We have to tell them when we find it anyway."

Giasson nodded toward Terrence and Jenny. "Why don't you tell us what's been going on?"

Acton looked surprised at the question, his head swiveling between Giasson and the students, then locking on Terrence when he began to speak.

"They told us we had to report back to them if you found anything, or if you tried to trick them. If we didn't, they'd kill Jenny."

Acton's jaw dropped as he looked at Jenny's stomach then her scared face. "Oh, Jenny. Are you okay?"

She shook her head. "I'm terrified. I've been on pins and needles ever since we arrived. I'm sorry we lied to you, Professor, but…" She cradled her stomach, looking down at it.

Acton placed a hand on her shoulder. "There's nothing to be sorry for. You did the right thing. Your baby comes first." He turned to Giasson. "What do we do?"

"I've spoken to Hugh and the others and their recommendation is we do nothing. If they suspect something, it might put your wife or Mrs. Mitchell in danger. But we need to be very careful about what we say around the phones. There can be no references to what is happening in Paris. If they get wind of any progress there…well, we just can't risk it."

Acton nodded, his face grim. Giasson knew Acton was a good man, and though he was clearly worried about his wife, he seemed to be equally concerned for Jenny.

"Okay, here's what we do," said Acton, turning to Terrence and Jenny. "You two get your phones and go back into the catacombs. Keep doing whatever you were doing. Talk about lunch, talk about the baby, whatever. If you can't keep it natural, say nothing at all." He turned to Giasson. "I'm pretty sure my phone is okay, but we'll assume it's not. They didn't know I was involved until they took Laura, and since then I've had no contact with the public. I went from the hotel to the limo, to the private flight here, into your car then here."

"We did go to the scene of the shooting to pick them up."

Acton frowned. "I forgot about that. You're right, anything's possible. But we don't have time to worry about that."

Giasson nodded. "You're right. The longer those phones aren't on your persons, the more chance there is for them to get suspicious."

"Okay, let's go."

Giasson turned to Father Albano, who had sat at his desk, saying nothing the entire time. "Sorry for the intrusion, Father."

The old man simply raised his hands and shrugged, still saying nothing as they left his office, closing the door behind them. Jenny and Terrence took their phones, heading down the stairs to the catacombs, Terrence talking about his soon to arrive pasta, the talk of food seeming to set him at ease.

Acton pocketed his phone. "Listen, we found the body but we need to cut some wrappings."

"So do it."

"Father Albano won't give his permission. He says he doesn't have the authority."

Giasson smiled. "I'll make a call."

"I'll be downstairs."

Acton had all of the necessary tools prepared, the lights positioned properly, and the order of his cuts already planned when Giasson descended the steps. "You have permission."

Acton grinned, Jenny and Terrence as giddy as he was. He took the small scissors, gently slipping the bottom blade under his choice for the first bandage to cut.

He snipped.

The cloth was dry, almost brittle, and cut easily, little flecks of fibers bursting in all directions, mini-eruptions of time giving way to his necessary curiosity. It didn't take long to cut through the several dozen strands, the bony hands of whom he presumed would be Tiberius revealed, clasped around a small stone tablet about the size of an iPad though about an inch thick. Reaching for the top corners, he gently wiggled it free, careful not to shift any of the bones unnecessarily.

"Got it!" he hissed as he stepped back, placing the tablet on the surface of the alcove, replacing the scissors with a brush. Clearing away the dust, he shone his flashlight on the surface, the words causing him to grab Terrence by the shoulder and shake him in excitement. "We were right!"

"*You* were right, Professor," said Terrence, hugging Jenny.

"What does it say?" asked Giasson, looking over their shoulders.

"It's in Latin. Translated, it says, 'Here lies my father, Tiberius of Mantua, a Christian and friend to the great Longinus. May God forgive our deception.' This is it! This is the proof we've been looking for!"

Giasson's eyes narrowed. "Proof of what? Where's Longinus?"

Acton grabbed him by the shoulder, waving the tablet. "Isn't it obvious?"

"Apparently not."

"He's in Mantua!"

Mantua, Italia

62 AD, Fifteen years later

Tiberius looked up at his son, the grief on the young man's face heartbreaking. He wasn't supposed to be dying, not yet, not so young, but no one could have predicted what had happened that night. Roman soldiers had arrived in the city and attacked their small church, killing or maiming anyone who resisted and hauling several away for crucifixion, he was certain. He himself had been sliced open badly, the village doctor having already given his verdict.

No hope.

"My son, you must do something for me."

"Anything, father, anything."

He reached up and took his son's hand in his, squeezing it. "You heard the edict from the Emperor. All Christians are to be killed, all their icons and graves destroyed."

His son nodded, his eyes darting toward the ichthys over his bed, the symbol of a fish used among fellow Christians as a secret sign of their faith. "I saw the edict."

"My body is unimportant."

"Yes it is!"

Tiberius smiled, patting his son's hand. "I know, I know. But the body of Longinus is far more important. His body must be preserved until such a time as the followers of Jesus' teachings no longer have to cower in fear."

"But how?"

"Nobody knows I'm a Christian. Move Longinus' body to my grave where he may rest in peace, then treat mine as his, moving it should it become necessary. Should it be found and burned, then so be it; Longinus will have been saved. And should it be preserved until a day in which Christianity thrives, the truth shall be revealed should it be God's will."

A shooting pain shot up his side causing him to gasp and wince. He felt his son's grip tighten. "Father!"

He took several slow, tentative breaths, then when he was confident the pain had gone, tried to forget the jolt of reality, his body rapidly weakening as he continued to bleed. He pulled his son closer. "Did I ever tell you of how I first met Longinus?"

His son smiled, sitting on the side of his bed. "Many times, Father, but I'd love to hear it again."

Tiberius brought his son's hand to his mouth and kissed it.

"One last time then."

Kaufman rarely felt fear, but he had to admit there was a slight tightness in his chest that some might interpret as such, but he thought it was more likely disappointment.

Disappointment in himself.

He had screwed up, there was no other way to put it, and now his employer, a man he only knew as Dietrich, had called for an update.

"Something's wrong, sir. The phone went quiet for almost five minutes, absolutely no sounds. The Vatican Inspector General, Giasson, read our last text message and knows something is going—"

"You mean *your* last text message," replied Dietrich. "You were foolish to send it."

"Yes, sir." There was no point in denying it. He shouldn't have sent it, but hindsight was always twenty-twenty and he had weighed the risks in sending it when he did, siding with the dramatic chilling effect the text would have on his targets. He hadn't anticipated the text being read by the man sitting in the front seat of the car. "They refused to answer any questions, and at the time I was confident they weren't aware of the software we planted on his phone, but now with this unexplained silence, I think they just might."

"So we've lost our best source of intel thanks to your screw up."

"They don't seem to be shy about talking, sir. In fact, they've just discovered where they think the body is."

"Why didn't you inform me?"

"They just made the discovery moments before you called. I was prepping an email."

"Where, dammit, where?"

"Some place called Mantua. I Googled it and it's in northern Italy, about four to five hours from here by car."

The front doors of the basilica opened and Giasson exited along with several of his men followed by the professor and the students. Two cars pulled up and the entourage climbed inside, Giasson scanning the area, his eyes coming to rest on him.

"Oh shit!"

Kaufman shoved in the brake, pressing the button on the dash to start the car as Giasson began to shout, pointing at the car and waving at his men to advance. He slammed his car in gear, cranking the wheel as he checked his side mirror for traffic. Removing his foot from the brake he shoved down on the gas pedal, sending the car surging into the light traffic as he reached for the Uzi 9mm on his passenger seat. Grabbing it, he pointed it out the window and squeezed the trigger, spraying several dozen rounds within a few seconds at the pavement, sending his pursuers scattering for cover.

Tossing the weapon back on the seat, he made a hard left and lost himself in the traffic.

Oh shit!

He grabbed his phone from between his legs and put it to his ear.

"—is going on?"

"Sorry, sir, they made me and I had to make a quick exit."

"Did I hear gunfire?"

"Yes, sir. Don't worry, no injuries."

"I don't give a damn about that. You've been made and they know about our eavesdropping."

"Not to worry, sir."

"Don't tell me not to worry! It's my father's life that's on the line here!"

"I'm sorry, sir, I didn't mean that the way it sounded. What I meant was that they made *me*. My partner is still in position. They're not going anywhere without us knowing exactly where."

Kruger Residence, Outside Paris, France

"I have to talk to you."

Laura opened her eyes, Dr. Heinrich's whispered tone suggesting urgency. She felt around the bed for the control, finally finding it and pushing the button to put her in a more raised position as the doctor stepped back outside of the curtains, as if checking to make sure they were alone. "What is it?"

"I think we're leaving soon," he said, checking her bandage. "I don't know what they intend to do with you, but…"

He didn't finish his sentence, but she was pretty sure what he wanted to say.

He feared the worst.

He had already expressed his fears that Dietrich was unstable and it was clear he had no trouble with killing.

And if they're leaving…

Was she a loose end that needed to be tied up?

Heinrich reached into the pocket of his lab coat. "Here's your phone. I'm going to put it under your pillow." He held up a set of car keys. "This is the key to my car. It's parked at the back of the house. A green Fiat. You can't miss it, it's the cheapest thing there. If things look bad, go out the door into the hallway. Go to your right to the end of the hall, down the stairs to the ground floor, then turn right. Follow the hall about half way, there's a door there."

Laura shifted her body as a test of her wound and winced. "I don't know if I can make it that far."

"You might have to. I've programmed the GPS in my car for the nearest hospital. It's not far, maybe fifteen minutes. If you can get yourself there, even if you tear open your wound, they'll be able to save you."

Laura's heart was pounding hard now, his fear infectious. It was clear he truly felt this was her only option, but she didn't understand why he would be going to such risks to help her. "What will they do to you if they find out you've helped me?"

He shook his head. "I've been ordered to move Herr Kruger and I'm not sure he'll survive much longer. If he dies, I'm probably dead." He sighed. "This has all come on too suddenly for poor Dietrich. He wasn't ready." He pushed the phone and the key under her pillow. "Be ready to leave at a moment's notice. Stay awake if you can."

Laura nodded, reaching out to grab his arm as he turned away. "Why are you doing this?"

Heinrich patted her hand then squeezed it. "Because I took an oath to save lives, not take them."

Church of Santa Maria del Gradaro, Mantua, Italy

"I'm afraid you've come a long way for nothing."

Acton frowned, the attitude of the priest frustrating, he having made them wait almost half an hour before 'gracing' them with his presence.

He was the complete opposite of Father Albano who had been a joy to work with.

This one gives priests a bad name.

"As I tried to explain—"

Once again Father Ricardo cut him off. "Yes, yes, you're looking for the body of Saint Longinus. And as I have told you, he is not here. Yes, this church was built on the very ground where he is thought to have been buried two thousand years ago, but I can assure you, *if* he is here, his body has been long lost. The church was built *on top* of where it was thought he was buried. On. Top. Even if it were true that he *was* actually buried here, you'd never be able to get to the body."

Acton sucked in a long, slow breath, calming himself. "As I've tried to—"

"I'm sorry, but I really don't have—"

"His Holiness sends his regards, and would appreciate your cooperation in this matter."

Giasson's words took the arrogant wind out of Father Ricardo's sails. "His Holiness?"

Giasson nodded. "Yes. He has personally approved this research expedition. I'm certain he would expect your full cooperation."

"Oh of course, of course, absolutely. I meant no disrespect, it's just that I deal with this a dozen times a week, pilgrims finding out on the Internet

293

that Longinus is buried here, when he is *not*, and it just gets, well, frustrating."

"I can understand that," replied Acton. "What if I told you we're not looking for the body of Longinus?"

"But you said—"

"If you'd let me finish, I'd have told you we were looking for the body of Tiberius."

Father Ricardo's eyebrows rose up his forehead as his jaw dropped. "Tiberius," he muttered, repeating it several times before spinning on his heel and rushing deeper into the church.

"Should we follow him?" asked Terrence.

Acton held out his hand. "I'm thinking 'yes'."

They quickly followed the spry priest through the chapel and out a side door, lush green greeting them, the late afternoon sun still warm on the skin despite the cool temperatures. They found the priest standing in front of a stone marker on the ground, the writing on it almost worn away from years of weather. It was one of about a dozen in a row along the outer wall.

The priest turned to Acton, all signs of arrogance and impatience wiped clean. "Why do you seek the grave of Tiberius?"

Acton pulled the rubbing he had taken of the tablet buried with the body in Rome from his satchel. "We found this in the Basilica of Sant'Agostino."

The priest eagerly read it, the significance not lost on him as his curled finger tapped against his lips. "Oh my, oh my." He paused, looking at the marker. "Oh my." He looked up at Acton. "Basilica of Sant'Agostino, where he was rumored to have been buried?"

Acton nodded, smiling. "Yes. We found a record that they had the body, but later discovered it wasn't Longinus, instead it was a man named

Tiberius. We found the body in the catacombs. This tablet was in with the body."

"And you came here." His words were whispered, he clearly in awe at the significance of what this discovery might mean. He looked down at the marker. "You're suggesting that rather than the body of Tiberius being buried here, it is actually Saint Longinus himself?"

Acton looked down at the marker, the name Tiberius barely visible. He felt his pulse quicken in excitement as he realized he might actually be standing on Longinus' grave. He looked at the priest and smiled, nodding. "We think so. With your permission—"

"Of course! Of course! We dig!"

CIA Headquarters, Langley, Virginia

"I've got that guest list, boss!" Marc Therrien waved his tablet as he stepped into Leroux's office. "I just emailed it to you." He dropped into a chair, his fingers flying over the screen as Leroux checked his email.

"Have you begun running them?"

"Yup. It's quite the list though. Hundreds."

Leroux nodded, scanning the list quickly. "We should eliminate the women."

"Never!"

Leroux looked at Therrien, puzzled for a second at his outburst, then chuckled, turning back to his screen.

"And he had a German accent, so let's just see if we can find…" His eyes flew down the list, coming to rest on one of the names. "Here's one. Dietrich Kruger, Vice President of Kruger Pharmaceuticals."

Therrien's fingers tapped away and moments later he was holding up his tablet. "Kruger Pharmaceuticals, based in Paris, France, moved almost twenty years ago from Germany."

"Odd."

"According to their Wikipedia entry, tax incentives."

Leroux's fingers were also busy searching for images related to the company. "There!" He pointed at his screen, a photo of some ribbon cutting dated almost twenty years ago showing the President of the company with a large group of dignitaries opening the new plant in France.

And standing beside the man were his wife and young son.

"Could that be young Dietrich?"

"Must be." Leroux isolated the boy's face, sending it over to an aging program that quickly began its work. As the image slowly morphed in front of them, Therrien rose from his seat, leaning in closer and closer.

"My God, it's got to be him."

The machine beeped, the final image displayed.

And if it weren't for the different hairstyle, it would be a near spitting image of the man in the photo provided by Mai Trinh, and the surveillance footage from Vienna.

"We've got him."

Church of Santa Maria del Gradaro, Mantua, Italy

Acton's back was breaking, sweat soaking through his shirt, the chill in the late afternoon air making its presence felt every time he paused to take a break. As they dug deeper and deeper Father Ricardo revealed that according to legend the graves and their markers had been discovered when the original church had been built centuries before, and placed on the surface in the exact spots they had been found.

We might be just digging a hole to China.

Acton kept his thoughts to himself, not wanting to dampen the spirits of Terrence and half a dozen volunteers, mostly altar boys, who were eagerly shoveling away at the dirt, the excitement of possible discovery fueling them.

The distinctive sound of a shovel hitting stone caused everyone to stop.

"Did you find something?" asked Jenny, frustrated at not being allowed to dig, her husband wisely putting his foot down, the risk of the hole, now almost ten feet deep, collapsing in on itself genuine.

Acton looked up at her. "Give us a minute." He looked at the two altar boys who were in the hole with them. "Let's take it easy now. Hands and buckets only." They began scooping handfuls of dirt into buckets that were then pulled out of the hole, it too deep to throw it out with the shovel. Within minutes they had revealed the outer edge of a stone sarcophagus, Terrence and Acton exchanging excited grins as the brushes appeared, every speck of soil quickly cleared off the top.

Revealing nothing.

"Odd," observed Acton. "No engravings, nothing."

"Maybe on the sides?" suggested Terrence.

298

"Could be, but that's going to take a lot more digging. Let's get this top off first and see what's inside."

Crowbars were handed down along with several two-by-fours. Acton and Terrence each jammed their crowbar into the seam as all six altar boys lifted the one edge with all their might.

Acton's bar slid in. "Got it! Now let's get that board wedged in there." He pushed down on the bar, the top lifting slightly, two of the boys pushing the board into the opening. "Not too far! Watch your hands!"

They quickly let go of the board and Acton let up on the crowbar, the heavy lid biting into the wood, a musty smell of more than a millennia of rot escaping.

He loved that smell.

It meant untouched ancient wonders, unplundered by thieves, unspoiled by mother nature.

It meant hope.

They made quick work of propping up the other end, then the other side, heavy ropes slid through either side, the ends tied off and handed to those standing above.

"Okay, everyone out except for Terrence. I don't want to risk this thing slipping on anyone. Terrence, stay at the far end, watch your feet. We're going to let those on the ropes do the heavy lifting, then when they've got the one side up, we'll push it over so that it rests against the dirt. Be careful, it might come sliding back at us and this thing is heavy enough to do some serious damage."

"Be careful, Terrence!"

"I will, love, I will." He lowered his voice. "If *I* get hurt, I'll never hear the end of it. 'You should have let me do it, you're the clumsy one!'."

Acton chuckled, the Jenny impression spot on.

"I heard that!"

"Of course you did, love!"

Acton looked up at those on the ropes. "Okay, we need to do this together, evenly. On the count of three, I want you all to heave. If anyone thinks they're going to lose their grip, speak up right away, and everyone gently ease off and let the lid lower again. We don't want any sudden drops. Understood?"

Giasson was translating and a chorus of si's responded.

"Okay, one, two, three, heave!"

The ropes became taught as a chorus of grunts erupted from above, the heavy stone slab not moving at first, then finally, ever so slightly, it rose an inch, then another, Acton shoving several more boards in the gap just in case it had to come back down.

But it didn't.

The long edge closest him rose in a jerking motion, tilting toward the opposite side, and in less than a minute was past the 45 degree mark. "Okay, now," he said to Terrence, both of them taking a hold of the lid and shoving toward the other side. It tipped quickly now, the extra bit of manpower sending it sliding over the lip and falling against the earthen wall of the hole with a thud. "Okay, that's enough!" He surveyed the walls towering above them, making sure nothing was going to cave in on them, when Terrence cried out.

"Professor!"

Acton looked down at the now open casket, his mouth agape, his heart slamming in his chest with excitement at the sight before them. A man, wrapped from head to toe just like Tiberius had been, was laid out in the sarcophagus, his left hand clasped over his chest with the distinctive outline of a stone tablet underneath.

And tucked into the sarcophagus on his left side was an earthenware jar, a wax seal on the top, the legends suggesting that if this were indeed

Longinus, then this container may very well hold the sponge he helped clean the body of Christ with.

And on the other side, gripped tightly in his wrapped right hand was the shaft of a spear, and near the head of the former soldier, the metal spearhead, still intact.

The Spear of Destiny!

He grabbed Terrence by the shoulder, shaking him several times, saying nothing. He pulled a pair of scissors from his pocket and carefully cut the wrappings as everyone above lay down on the ground, their heads hanging over the edge as they watched history unfold, the lights set up earlier supplemented now by the flashes from cellphones as the young boys documented the experience.

The tablet revealed, he gently removed it from the two thousand year old grip, brushing the dust from it, making sure his eyes didn't focus on the writing, he wanting to preserve the moment of discovery for when it could be completely read.

He held it up so Terrence could see it as well and translated the Latin loudly so all above could hear.

"Here lies Longinus, Christian martyr, witness to the crucifixion of our Lord, healed by the blood of our savior, and friend to my father Tiberius. May God forgive our deception."

Cheers erupted from above, hands clapped and Acton put his arm around Terrence, squeezing him sideways, it the best hug he could give. He placed the tablet in a bucket and it was gently pulled up, then the jar which he left unopened.

Leaning over, he carefully cut through the bandages holding the spear in the right hand, then with a silent prayer of forgiveness, opened the fingers, one by one, until the spear could be slid free. He felt an electricity flowing through him, an overwhelming rush of faith renewed as he held in his hands what had until moments ago been mere myth, legend, a single-line reference in a text written almost two millennia ago, an oral tradition not written down for centuries now proven true.

He was overwhelmed, and for a moment forgot why he was here, what had driven him to this discovery.

Instead, he was lost in the excitement, and it wasn't until he turned to Terrence and realized it wasn't Laura, that the excitement was pushed aside and the resignation set in that this incredible discovery was about to be handed over to a madman in exchange for the life of his wife.

But did he have that right?

As he handed the spear up to Giasson, who handled it with equal reverence, he realized that this was a piece of history, a piece of history important to billions of people around the world, something that might be a direct link to the Son of God. He had little doubt this was the Longinus of legend. Carbon dating would help resolve some of the questions, at least confirming he was from the right era, and mineral testing of his bones might be able to show he was in Judea for an extended period of time, and when the wrappings were removed, it would definitely reveal whether or not he had been beheaded.

The question that would remain was whether or not Longinus was actually there on that fateful day, though at this moment Acton had little doubt. If the carbon dating confirmed he was from the first century AD, then the tablet would predate any written reference to him, meaning it couldn't be based upon any lore created centuries later.

And it would be one of the earliest references referring to the crucifixion.

But now wasn't the time to debate what this discovery meant. He climbed up the ladder and into the fading sunlight, hands clapping him on the back as the celebrations continued, a group of people having already dropped to their knees, their hands clasped in prayer at the miraculous proof of their faith. Acton desperately wished Laura was here to take part, this something she would have loved, and the fact she wasn't cast a pall over the entire proceedings as his internal debate raged on whether or not he had the right to give this spear to a madman who might destroy it.

"We found it!" cried Terrence, hugging Jenny as he climbed out of the hole.

"Yes you have."

Acton spun toward the voice, the German accent immediately recognizable. Two men stood not ten feet away, weapons raised, the man from the security footage in Vienna standing between them with a smile on his face.

"Congratulation, Professor Acton. I have to admit, I never thought you would succeed, but it would appear that with the proper motivation, anything is possible."

"What is this?" asked Father Ricardo. "Who are you?"

"Who I am is unimportant. What you have there, is." He held out his hand, beckoning. "Hand it over."

Giasson looked at the spear then Acton, it clear he too was torn. Acton nodded slightly, there no choice now, his self-doubt at his right to decide the destiny of this spear solved for him at the point of a gun.

Giasson stepped forward with the spear when Father Ricardo jumped in front of him. "No! You can't do this! This belongs to the church, to Christians everywhere! It is a direct link to our Lord Jesus Christ, proof that He existed! It has the power to unite all those who have ever doubted His existence and bring peace to this world divided by competing beliefs." He pointed at the spear. "*This* has the power to unite the divided, to save thousands of lives. Imagine what tomorrow will be like when the world learns of our discovery here today. If you give this sacred relic, this Blood

Relic, to these men, nobody will believe what we found here, all that could be gained will be lost and evil will have triumphed once again."

The German began to clap, slowly, deliberately, an amused smile on his face. "I've never been described as 'evil' before. And though I admire your faith, I doubt this one spear will change the world." His smile disappeared. "But it just might change mine." He pulled his own weapon, aiming it at the priest, looking at Giasson. "If you want him to live, hand it over, now."

"I'm sorry, Father." Giasson put a hand on the man's shoulder, looking him in the eyes for a moment, Father Ricardo's shoulders slumping in defeat as he stepped aside. Giasson held the spear out in front of him and the man stepped forward, taking it carefully then handing it to one of his men who immediately placed it into a case, sealing it inside.

At least they seem to be treating it with care.

"What about my wife?" he asked, stepping forward. "You promised me you'd free her if I found the spear."

"I will, once we've confirmed that this is indeed the genuine spear."

"But how will you do that?" asked Acton, exasperation entering his voice. "How can you possibly know?"

The man smiled. "If it's genuine, then it will have the blood of Christ on it. And if it has the blood of Christ on it, then it will heal my father."

His father!

Now he finally knew what this was all about. This man's father was the reason behind everything, a motivation he could understand, though not condone—the deaths of so many inexcusable.

"But what if it doesn't work?"

"Then, Professor, I'm afraid your wife's time will have run out."

Outside Paris, France

Dawson looked at the laptop and shook his head. They had been roaming the countryside surrounding the cellphone tower for about an hour with no luck. They had successfully pinged the phone when they first arrived, but that had been the limit of their success.

"Still nothing."

"Maybe it's been turned off?" suggested Reading from behind the wheel.

"Could be. If they have any inkling we're getting close they might have implemented additional security protocols and shut down their unsecured communications."

Reading frowned as he made a turn. "Then this whole effort will be in vain."

Niner shoved his head between the seats, looking at the laptop. "Yeah, but at least we're out of that damned hotel room."

Dawson's phone vibrated in his pocket. He fished it out and took the call.

"Speak."

"Mr. White, this is Leroux. We've identified the suspect!"

Dawson smiled. "I'm going to put you on speaker." He tapped the button. "You're on with Mr. Reading and Mr. Green. Repeat what you just told me."

"We've identified the suspect. His name is Dietrich Kruger. Details on him are sketchy, but we've got an address for the family home, I'm sending it to your phone now."

Dawson read the text message and entered it into the car's GPS.

"Christ, that's not even two minutes from here!" exclaimed Reading, checking his mirror before pulling a U-turn.

"Excellent work," said Dawson. "Notify the locals and have backup sent to that location immediately."

"Already done. They should be arriving on site within forty minutes."

Niner cursed. "Forty minutes? Even Dominos delivers faster than that."

"Best they could do, sorry."

Dawson grunted. "Forty minutes it is. White, out."

He ended the call as Reading drove past a large estate set a good distance back from the road, it well lit in the early evening light. "That must be it."

"Don't slow down, we don't want to draw any attention." Dawson pointed to a thick grove of trees about a mile down the road. "Let's park up there, toss the hood up and recon the area."

Reading nodded, keeping his speed steady then pulling over to the side of the road once they were safely out of the direct line of sight of the house. He pulled the hood release as they climbed out, Dawson grabbing a set of binoculars from a duffel bag in the backseat and heading to the trees. Taking a knee behind a thick oak, he peered across the manicured lawn at the house. "We've got a good angle on the front and left side."

Niner took a knee on the opposite side as Dawson heard Reading cursing at the hood, unable to find the latch for a moment. "Some activity near the two-three corner. Is that an ambulance?"

Dawson adjusted his binoculars, nodding. "Yup. Looks private. They're loading somebody in the back."

"Looks pretty sick. Definitely not our guy."

Reading crept up behind them. "Anything?"

"We might have found the guy they're trying to cure." Dawson handed the binoculars to Reading who looked through them then nodded, handing them back.

"Any sign of Laura?"

"Negative. But it looks like they're bugging out."

Niner rose, looking at his watch. "Our backup is still thirty-five minutes away. These guys are going to be long gone by then."

Reading nodded. "Either with or without Laura."

"If they take her with them, we may never find her again," said Dawson.

Niner turned, placing his back against the tree as he inspected his weapon. "And if they're not taking her, they're probably not leaving her alive."

Reading stood, concealed by the oak. "We have to go in, now."

Dawson looked at Reading. "Agreed. But covertly. We don't know how many hostiles we're dealing with and we can't risk them killing Professor Palmer. We have to reach her before we're discovered."

"And a big police operation is probably *not* the way to do that," said Niner. He pointed to some hedges, about five feet tall, surrounding much of the house. "It's almost dark. We can probably get to those trees without being noticed."

"Agreed. Let's gear up."

They retreated to their SUV and quickly donned body armor, weapons and ammo. Within minutes they were performing a comm check.

Dawson looked around, the sun almost set behind them. "Hugh, you and I will head in fast, low, single file. Niner, you'll watch the upper windows, warn us if there's any activity. If Niner spots anything, we drop and freeze until we've got the all clear, understood?"

Reading nodded. "Let's go before the police arrive and blow this whole thing."

Dawson immediately set out across the grass at a quick crouch. Reading was close behind, his breathing quickly getting labored as the older man struggled to keep up. Dawson had read his file and had tremendous respect for him, a decorated soldier from the Falklands War and a highly respected detective at Scotland Yard for years.

But he was a little out of shape.

A desk job and nearly sixty years on the old body will do that to you.

He glanced slightly behind him but didn't slow down. Reading could catch his breath once they reached the cover of the hedge, slowing down now only increasing the risk of being spotted.

"Hold."

Dawson dropped to the ground at Niner's warning, Reading grunting as he hit a moment later.

"I've got activity, second floor, one-two corner."

Dawson looked and could see the window, lit, somebody crossing in front of it, then back again several times.

Packing?

"They won't see you with that light on. Proceed."

Dawson jumped to his feet, sprinting the final twenty yards, still bent over, then dropped to a knee behind the hedge, turning back to find Reading still another ten yards out but closing fast.

He dropped onto all fours, his chest heaving as he caught his breath. "I've got to get back in shape. Interpol is killing me."

Dawson smiled. "You're doing fine. I do this all day every day and you kept up. Take a moment to catch your breath then we'll go around to the back, see if we can find a way in there." He activated his comm as he pulled out his binoculars. "We're in position. I'll cover you."

"Roger that."

Dawson glanced over his shoulder and could barely pick out Niner in the dusk. Raising his binoculars he scanned the windows, watching for any onlookers, finding none. Moments later Niner slid in beside them, barely breathing heavy.

Dawson looked at Reading. "Good to go?"

Reading nodded. "What I'd give to be twenty years younger."

"And as handsome as me," added Niner.

Reading shook his head. "No, I couldn't stand to be so short."

Dawson punched Niner on the shoulder, hard. "Owned."

Niner dropped his head. "I need a hug."

"Well, you're not getting one from me," replied Dawson as he rose and hurried along the hedge toward the back of the house, the loading of the ambulance and several cars continuing only yards away.

Dawson stifled a laugh as Reading rebuffed Niner as well. "Don't look at me with love in your eyes."

When Dawson reached the far corner of the hedge he had a clear view of the rear of the house, no one in sight and several doors appearing unguarded. Reading and Niner reached his position and he pointed to several gaps in the hedge that allowed access to the backyard featuring a large pool and tennis court.

"Keep low and fast. We need to clear those gaps without being seen. We'll go side-by-side so there's only one thing to see at a time, not three, understood?"

Nods.

"Then let's go."

Reading took up position to his left, Niner to his, and Dawson motioned for them to advance. The three men quickly passed the first gap, almost ten feet wide, Dawson keeping an eye on the activity to their right, his heart pounding a little harder until the hedge blocked his view once

309

again. The next gap was at the rear of the house, out of view of those in the parking area, meaning the only risk now was anyone inside the house that might be looking.

"There's a door," whispered Reading. "It's not much farther than the next cover."

Dawson nodded, Reading right. He turned to Niner. "See if you can open it, watch out for alarms."

Niner nodded and sprinted toward the door.

And was immediately lit up by several security lights on motion detectors.

Shots rang out moments later.

Laura bolted upright in her bed, immediately regretting it as excruciating pain raced through her body. She grabbed at her stomach, resisting the urge to lie back down, her movement then only needing repeating. Another burst of gunfire eliminated any doubt as to what she had just heard and she realized her time had come.

Either they're eliminating witnesses, or someone's here to rescue me.

Either way she knew she wasn't safe just lying in this bed.

Swinging her legs over the edge, her bare feet touched the cold ceramic floor sending shivers up and down her body. Reaching under the pillow she retrieved her phone and Heinrich's car keys then tentatively pushed the curtain aside revealing an empty lab.

Out the doors and to the right.

She took a step toward the doors when she felt something tug at her arm. She looked and cursed, the IV needle still inserted, connected to a stand with a dextrose drip. Stepping back toward the stand she nearly collapsed with the pain, reaching forward and grabbing the metal contraption, steadying herself.

She looked at the base of it, on wheels, and rather than free herself, instead grabbed it with both hands, using it as a support as she slowly made her way to the doors that should lead to the hallway Dr. Heinrich had described.

Another stab of pain radiated through her entire body causing her to gasp aloud as she slowly slid down the IV stand toward the floor.

I can't make it!

Dr. Heinrich looked toward the rear of the house as the security team raced toward the blazing lights, somebody shouting about intruders. Gunfire erupted, several short bursts, causing him to jump into the back of the ambulance, Herr Kruger sedated on a stretcher, his wife holding his hand. The doors slammed shut behind him and within seconds the ambulance pulled away, every single bump in the gravel driveway being felt, shocks apparently an afterthought in the design.

His phone rang and he answered it after grabbing onto the side of the stretcher for balance.

"Hello?"

"It's Dietrich. I've got it!"

Heinrich's eyes popped wide as he looked over at Mrs. Kruger. "The spear? Are you sure?"

"Absolutely. And I've got a sealed jar that's supposed to have a sponge used to clean his body."

Heinrich shook his head as he looked at the failing man's vital signs. They were weak and thready. If he had any hope he would have to be exposed to the blood without delay. "When can you get the relics to me?"

"We're in the air now, should be landing in less than two hours. How long will it take for you to do your part?"

"More time than I think we have. We're evacuating to the backup location now; there's intruders on the property."

"The police?"

"I don't know, I didn't see them, but there's gunfire."

Dietrich cursed. "If it were police you'd know. It's that damned Professor Acton and his friends. Where's Professor Palmer?"

"We had to leave her behind."

There was a pause then a chilling reply. "I want her dead."

Heinrich's chest tightened as he turned away from Mrs. Kruger who was now listening intently. "You don't need to do that. You have what you were looking for. Let her be."

The phone went dead.

Niner hit the deck as two shots cracked behind him, the lone guard who had rounded the corner first dropped by one of his team. He didn't bother looking to see who, instead jumping to his feet and sprinting toward the door, their hoped for element of surprise shot. Time was of the essence, Professor Palmer now in serious danger. Reaching the double doors that led to the side of the large stone patio, he kicked hard at the center, his entire body left ringing as what were obviously reinforced doors didn't budge.

He tried the handle.

The door opened as Dawson and Reading arrived, their weapons covering both directions, Dawson squeezing the trigger twice before all three were inside the house. Niner pointed at the door. "Lock it, it's reinforced."

Reading turned the lock, Niner rushing through the large living area toward what looked like a hallway.

A startled woman in a maid's uniform came around the corner and screamed, begging in German not to be hurt. He grabbed her by the arm and yanked her into the room. "Do you speak English?"

She nodded, saying nothing to prove it.

"Where's Professor Palmer?"

She shook her head, her eyes narrowing in confusion.

"The woman that was shot, they would have brought her here two days ago."

"Ahh, the Fräulein! She upstairs in lab."

Niner didn't bother telling the woman that Professor Palmer was definitely a Frau. "What room?"

The woman's eyes lost focus for a moment as she thought, suddenly pointing toward the stairs to the right. "Upstairs, third door on left."

Niner pointed to a bar on one side of the room. "Get behind there and stay down until the police arrive."

She nodded but didn't move. He pushed her toward the bar, it enough to get her in motion as Dawson and Reading covered the door leading to the hall.

"Ready?"

Dawson nodded. "Let's go!"

Niner took point, rushing up the stairs two at a time, all the while his Glock 22 extended in front of him, covering the angles, making sure they didn't walk into a bullet. As they reached the second floor he turned to see two men rush into a room about half way down the hall, guns drawn.

He counted the doors and cursed.

Third door on the left.

At least a dozen gunshots rang out as he charged forward.

Laura had no choice but to tear the IV from her arm, the stand now a hindrance on the steps. She took a glance back down the long hall to see two men enter the lab and open fire, another man rushing to join them, the fog of pain she was in separating him into three blurred forms then a single cohesive one repeatedly.

I have to keep going.

She grabbed the railing with one hand, her wound with the other, ignoring the fact it was now soaking wet, her stiches torn. She knew if she continued she would most likely die.

But she had no choice.

Those men had just entered her room and fired, probably through the curtains her bed lay behind.

Dietrich Kruger had obviously ordered her death.

Leaning heavily on the railing she stumbled toward the ground floor, rounding the first landing as another burst of gunfire was heard above.

Her knees gave out and she fell forward, her hand on the railing breaking her fall slightly, but the force too great for her to hold on. She lost her grip and tumbled down the remaining dozen steps, her cellphone and the keys sliding across the marble floor she came to rest on.

"Help me."

But her voice was barely a whisper.

Reading burst into the room to find Niner standing over the bodies of two men. They were in some sort of lab, well-equipped but deserted, with no sign of Professor Palmer.

"Laura!" he cried as he spotted a set of rollaway curtains, a large number of bullet holes leaving him to think the worst. A pit formed in his stomach as he tossed the nearest one aside, resisting the urge to close his eyes and protect himself from the sight of another dead friend.

But all he found was an empty bed.

Thank God!

"She's not here," he said, quickly searching the entire lab for any place she may have hidden herself, finding nothing.

"There's some blood here," said Niner, pointing at the floor near the door. "It looks like someone was dragged."

Reading looked at the smudges and nodded. "Or someone dragged herself."

Dawson cursed. "We're going to have to search the entire place, room by room."

Niner looked at the blood on the floor. "If she's bleeding, she might not have much time."

Reading felt himself tense up.

"Then let's stop wasting it."

Laura looked up as footsteps rapidly approached. She didn't care who it was anymore, the pain too great, her strength quickly waning. If they wanted to kill her, she didn't care, her spirit having been crushed already today with the news the doctor had given her only hours before.

"Fräulein! Are you okay?"

Laura looked up to see the German hausfrau that had been bringing her meals since her arrival, even helping her go to the bathroom. The woman had been a godsend and if there was anyone in this house besides Dr. Heinrich she'd want to see right now, it was her.

"Helena," she whispered, the woman dropping to her knees, helping Laura to a seated position. "I need you to get me out of here."

The woman nodded, helping Laura to her feet then throwing her arm over her shoulder. They began to walk when Laura stopped and pointed.

"Keys, phone."

Helena steadied Laura against a wall then retrieved the two items, stuffing them in the pockets of her apron and resuming their walk toward a side door just beyond the stairs.

"Dr. Heinrich's car," gasped Laura, Helena nodding her understanding as they stepped into the night, several cars racing from the parking area filled with panicked staff. Gunfire behind them spurred them toward the modest green Fiat parked near several BMW's and a Mercedes.

They stumbled toward the car, the progress slow and painful, but they finally made it, Helena unlocking the car and helping Laura into the passenger seat. Once inside, Helena rounded the car as Laura gasped in pain, both hands now pressing against her wound, her hands soaked with blood. Helena started the car and pulled out of the parking spot, putting it in gear and hammering on the gas, apparently as eager to get away as she was.

"GPS. Hospital."

Helena looked at Laura then at the dash mounted GPS, tapping the display, unsure of what to do. She cranked the wheel to the right and accelerated as they reached the road, the house now behind them. Helena returned her attention to the GPS, one hand on the wheel, the other trying to operate the unfamiliar GPS.

Laura began to black out, the pain simply too great, when she looked up at the road and cried out as the car drifted across the lanes, Helena not paying attention.

The car rolled into the ditch, tossing Laura's body toward Helena then onto the roof as the car slid to a halt. She looked over at Helena, lying on the roof beside her, her neck twisted, eyes wide as they stared into nothing.

"No!" moaned Laura as her world turned to black.

BLOOD RELICS

Church of Santa Maria del Gradaro, Mantua, Italy

James Acton grabbed his phone, answering it immediately, praying it was Dietrich with word that his wife had been released. They had been waiting for almost two hours now while the police questioned everyone involved, Giasson smoothing things over when it had been discovered their intention all along had been to hand over the relics. He was exhausted and running purely on adrenaline, unsure of how much more he could take.

"Hello?"

"Hi Jim, it's Hugh."

Acton's shoulders slumped. "I thought maybe you were Dietrich."

"Sorry to disappoint. We've secured the Kruger household but there's no sign of Laura."

Acton felt his stomach leap, the last of his hope cleaved from him.

He said nothing.

"She was definitely here. We found her hospital bed and some of her clothes but she's gone. They must have taken her with them. An ambulance left earlier with a sick man, we assume Herr Kruger, but we're pretty sure she wasn't in it."

"But you can't be sure."

"No, we can't. But I don't think they'd put her in an ambulance with him. The police are beginning to block off all roads in the area. If we're lucky, they'll catch them in their net."

Lucky.

What a horrible word.

Lucky. Lucky if they'll find my wife. Lucky if she'll still be alive. Lucky.

317

He didn't blame Reading for the choice of words, it was after all just a word, but for some reason it struck home as the situation seemed more dire than ever. The police were at the Kruger residence and the occupants had been forced to flee. Would the move cause the death of Dietrich's father? If it did, would Dietrich blame him? If he did blame him, would he take it out on Laura?

"You have to find her, Hugh. She's all I have."

Two miles from the Kruger residence, Outside Paris, France

Laura woke, her entire body aching, the pain in her stomach a dull throb. She looked about, disoriented, it taking a few moments before she realized where she was.

On the roof of an upside down car.

She looked out the window but all she could see were the sides of the ditch they had flipped in, the walls high, but there was something else. Turning her head slightly she gave a little cry of dismay when she saw the entire front of the car had slid into a culvert, the chances of them being seen from the road near impossible.

"James, help me!" she whispered as she laid herself back down, staring at the body of the woman who had tried to help save her. She reached out for her hand, to try to provide some comfort to the newly departed soul, but didn't have the strength for it, her arm instead collapsing, her fingers catching on the pocket of the woman's apron.

Causing her cellphone to spill out.

A spark of hope gave her a momentary surge of energy as her fingers crawled toward the phone. Holding her thumb against the sensor, the phone activated and she tapped the screen several times, speed dialing James and putting it on speaker.

The phone only rang once.

"Laura!"

"Help. Me."

She passed out before she could hear the reply.

319

Reading sat on the rear bumper of their 4x4, Dawson and Niner standing nearby as they awaited any word on Laura or the Krugers. His phone vibrated on his belt and he unclipped it, looking at the call display.

"It's Giasson." He swiped his thumb. "Hello, Mario, any news."

"Laura called Jim, he's on the phone right now with her but she's not speaking. We need you to trace the call!"

Reading snapped his fingers, getting Dawson and Niner's attention. "We need to trace a call being made to Jim's phone, now!" Dawson got his phone out, quickly dialing as Reading gave Niner Acton's number. "It's Laura, she called him but isn't saying anything."

"They're still connected?" asked Niner as Dawson began to talk to someone.

"Yes."

Niner's eyes narrowed. "Whose phone?"

"Huh?"

"Whose phone did she use?"

Reading stared at him for a moment then jumped up as he realized why Niner was asking. "Mario, did she use her own phone?"

Muffled words were exchanged on the other end. "Yes."

Reading smiled at Niner, nodding.

"Then let's use the equipment in the back!"

"Mario, I'll call you back. We're going to track the cellphone signal from here."

"Okay, keep me posted."

Reading clipped his phone on his belt as he climbed into the driver's seat, Dawson in the passenger seat still on the phone, Niner in the back with the equipment. The best Dawson's contact was probably going to provide would be a cellphone tower, but with the equipment Niner was now activating, they might be able to pinpoint her exact position.

If they had enough time.

He started up the engine and turned the truck around, heading down the driveway, several police officers shouting at them to stop.

We'll sort it out later.

"I've got it!" exclaimed Niner. "Hang a right at the road."

Reading cranked the wheel, the tires chirping as they gained traction on the pavement, spitting loose gravel at the officers stationed at the foot of the drive, several jumping into their cars to give chase.

"Keep going straight, the signal is getting stronger."

Reading looked in his rearview mirror and cursed, the flashing blue lights behind him starting to close in. He pressed a little harder on the accelerator as the dark countryside flew by. He didn't want to miss anything but in a moment of clarity he realized he shouldn't be worried, it was Niner doing the looking, and that was purely at radio waves.

He pressed harder, at least now maintaining the distance.

"Stop!"

Reading slammed on the brakes, the vehicle shuddering to a halt as Niner jumped out, Dawson, still on the phone in a whispered conversation, joining him. Reading put the vehicle in park and stepped down, the police cars in pursuit rapidly closing the distance.

"She's here somewhere, the signal's really strong."

Reading surveyed the area. It was an intersection, a smaller road intersecting the one they were on, reflective stop signs about the only thing he could see beyond his headlights.

Except a strange glow coming from the ditch.

Laura!

He sprinted forward as the police cars screeched to a halt, the officers jumping out, barking orders. Reading ignored them, instead jumping into the ditch as he spotted a small overturned car half inside a culvert running under the intersection, one of its headlights shining dimly.

He looked in the rear window and saw two bodies lying on the roof of the car, a cellphone between them, still glowing.

"I found her!"

He pulled his weapon and smashed out the rear window as Dawson and Niner jumped in after him, the police lining the ditch. Reaching inside, he grabbed Laura by the wrist but she didn't react.

"Laura, can you hear me? Laura!"

He pressed his fingers along her radial artery and tried to calm himself, gently adjusting his fingers, looking for a pulse but finding nothing.

But she was still warm.

He moved his fingers again and cried out as he felt the beat, weak but still there.

"She's alive!"

Assistance Publique Hôpitaux de Paris, Paris, France

Laura opened her eyes, everything a blur. She could feel the warmth of sunlight on her face and the comfort of soft sheets surrounding her. The gentle beeps of several machines nearby were quickly replaced by hushed voices. She blinked a few times, allowing her eyes to focus on the ceiling tiles then turned toward the voices.

And smiled.

"She's awake!" James jumped from his chair, rushing to her side as he took her hand in his. "How do you feel?"

She smiled. "Better."

"You had us scared there for a while."

"What happened?" she asked, reaching down to feel her wound. She found a clean dressing and very little pain when she pressed on it.

"You were in a car crash. Hugh and the others found you just in time."

She looked at the window, the sun blazing in. "How long has it been?"

"Three days."

Her jaw dropped. "Three days? But—"

"You nearly died, hon. You lost a lot of blood and an infection had set in. They've got you on antibiotics and you're responding very well. They think you wouldn't have survived another half hour." He sighed. "We were lucky."

Lucky.

She looked past her husband to see Reading standing in the doorway, a smile on his face. "Hi Hugh."

Reading stepped inside, resting his hands on the rail at the foot of her bed. "Feeling better?"

She nodded. "Almost normal, actually. I'm sure I don't, but compared to how I *was* feeling, it's a miracle." She smiled. "A miracle I understand I have you to thank for."

"Hey, I knew he'd take all the credit if we let him in there alone."

Laura turned toward the door and her smile broadened as she spotted a grinning Niner, Dawson right behind him. She motioned with her head for them to come in, Giasson following them into the rather small room.

She didn't care.

She was just happy to be alive.

And free.

"What happened? Did they catch him?"

Reading shook his head. "No, not yet. Dietrich Kruger, the man who kidnapped you, and his father haven't been found. We eliminated four of his men and we think there are at least two more, but we're pretty sure it's over."

"Why?"

"Because we found him."

Laura felt a rush flow through her body as she looked at her husband. "Longinus?"

He nodded, grinning. "We found him in Mantua, along with the spear and the sponge used to cleanse the body."

She squeezed her husband's hand. "I'm so proud of you, I knew you could do it."

"Terrence and Jenny helped, and so did Mario."

Mario leaned into view. "I just provided security and translators."

"Translators?"

"It's a long story," said James, patting her hand. "I'll tell you all about it when you're stronger."

"Where's the spear?"

"He took it."

"Dietrich?"

James nodded. "Yes. We recovered all of the stolen artifacts at the house and they're being returned, but the spear and the jar holding the sponge are still missing. I'm afraid we'll never see them again."

Laura felt a deep sadness fill her to the core, the very thought of such an incredible discovery being lost to the ages because of a madman's insane quest disgusting her. And as the emotion overwhelmed her it reminded her of the news she had received from Dr. Heinrich, all joy at her reunion wiped from her being.

"Terrence and Jenny are outside, they'd like to say hi for a moment."

Laura looked at her husband, shaking her head. "I need to talk to you first, alone."

He looked at the others who said quick goodbyes, the room soon empty. She took her husband's hand in both of hers and held it to her chest. "I have some bad news."

She watched as concern etched itself across his face.

"What is it?"

"There were complications."

"What do you mean?" He looked at her stomach. "You mean with your wound?"

She nodded. "Dr. Heinrich scanned me and confirmed it." She burst into tears, sobs racking her body. "Oh James, I'm so sorry!" She could see his own face cloud over, his love for her so deep she knew he could never stand to see her upset.

"What is it?" he asked gently, leaning toward her, clutching her hands. "You can tell me."

"I-I.." She looked away, squeezing her eyes shut, trying to fight off the tears that refused to stop. "I can't have children anymore."

James gasped, the grip on her hands loosening for a moment, that momentary reflex crushing her inside as she felt the bond between them break, all their future plans destroyed, their marriage torn asunder by a madman's quest to save his father.

His grip tightened again and she turned back toward him, a thin thread of hope tugging at her. She looked at her husband through tear filled eyes and saw the anguish on his face, his own tears pouring down his cheeks, he too devastated at the news.

"I'm so sorry, James, I'm so sorry."

He reached up with one of his hands and caressed her cheeks, wiping away some of the tears. "It's not your fault."

"Do-do you still love me?"

A cry erupted from him as he collapsed on her and hugged her, his chest heaving with sobs. "Of course I do," he said as he held her, "of course I do. Never doubt that I love you, no matter what."

"But our children—"

"Are nothing if you aren't in my life." He let go of her and sat up slightly, looking down at her as he ran his fingers through her hair. "I love *you*. My life is incredible because of *you*. Am I disappointed we can't have children of our own? Of course, but do I blame you? Of course not. I could never blame you for that, and I could never love you any less because of it. *You* are my life. *You* are the one I want to spend the rest of my life with, to grow old and die with, and whether or not we have children of our own to share that with is unimportant, as long as I have you."

She reached up and rested her hand against his cheek, wiping away the still flowing tears.

"I love you so much."

He smiled and turned his head slightly, kissing her palm.

"And I love you."

Somewhere in South-East Asia
Six months later

The roar of the ocean was something Dietrich would never tire of. The weather was idyllic, the sand was perfect, and the company even better. He had put an exit plan in place the moment he had decided to break the law in order to save his father, a plan that had meant liquidating a significant portion of their assets and transferring them to secret accounts around the world. Even if the authorities found an account, they'd be hard pressed to find them all.

And so far they'd found none.

He sipped his piña colada, savoring the rich, cold drink as he watched his son play near the water, his wife keeping a watchful eye nearby, his own mother at her side. Smiling at the bartender, he took the tall glass of imported German beer, brought in just for them, and returned to the reserved area of the beach, separated by several cloth windbreaks.

He handed the beer over.

"Thank you."

"You're welcome, Father."

THE END

ACKNOWLEDGEMENTS

Sometimes decisions made in prior novels of a series pose challenges to the author later on. I try to keep my characters as timeless and "ageless" as possible so that you the reader can continue to enjoy their exploits in the years to come, and I can continue to write them as well. Unlike actors, characters on the written page don't have to age.

Just think if they had decided to have the Simpsons age with each new season. Bart would be heading into middle age soon, Homer staring in Expendables 4.

It works with some series, Agatha Christie's Hercule Poirot (one of my favorites!) comes to mind, but Poirot wasn't exactly fighting terrorists and scurrying around ancient ruins.

And if I sell over one billion Acton thrillers, I just might look at retiring the character.

But since I need to feed my family, I keep soldiering on, keeping my characters enmeshed with current events, but essentially leaving them at their original ages, "magically" allowing the world to age around their own timelessness.

I think it works, especially when you consider most of these books take place over an extremely compressed timeframe with little gap between them.

But where it doesn't work is when you want characters to evolve outside of the physical. One of those quandaries was the relationship between James and Laura. They fell in love, got engaged, got married, moved into a single home, and so on. The next logical step in my mind was children.

Which would probably kill the series, since Acton telling Laura to "go long" while he tossed the baby over as some ancient cult opened fire on them just wasn't believable—though I'm sure I've seen that on cable somewhere.

As I wrote this novel the idea of how to address this permanently came to me, and the result is the heart wrenching revelation that Laura can no longer have children. When I wrote the opening scene, shooting her in the abdomen, it had never occurred to me what I would eventually do with that. I wonder if I had shot her in the shoulder, would this turn of events have followed.

But now that the deed is done, my mental torture of my beloved heroes (for I do love these people, they're very real to me after so many years together) will allow me to continue with their adventures without having to worry about how to keep getting them into trouble with little feet under foot.

I hope as a result we'll enjoy many more years of the professors getting into trouble.

As usual there are many people to thank. Big shout out as usual to my dad who did most of the research, another big one to Richard Jenner for helping make my British characters more British, Brent Richards for some weapons info, Ian Davidson for some info on motorcycles, Fred Newton for car racing info, Marc Quesnel for letting me know the history of a certain fashion designer, and of course my wife, daughter, mother and friends for their continued support.

One special note to Ian Kennedy: Yes, Ian, you win, your scar is bigger than mine.

And on one final note, yes, years ago I actually did ask if the new battery for my car had been blessed by the Queen.

It hadn't.

They weren't amused.

And it still didn't solve the problems.

To those who have not already done so, please visit my website at www.jrobertkennedy.com then sign up for the Insider's Club to be notified of new book releases. Your email address will never be shared or sold and you'll only receive an email or two a month as I don't have time to spam you!

Thank you once again for reading.

ABOUT THE AUTHOR

USA Today bestselling author J. Robert Kennedy has written over one dozen international bestsellers including the smash hit James Acton Thrillers series, the first installment of which, The Protocol, has been on the bestsellers list since its release, including a three month run at number one. In addition to the other novels from this series including The Templar's Relic, a USA Today and Barnes & Noble #1 overall bestseller, he writes the bestselling Special Agent Dylan Kane Thrillers, Delta Force Unleashed Thrillers and Detective Shakespeare Mysteries. Robert lives with his wife and daughter and writes full-time.

Visit Robert's website at www.jrobertkennedy.com for the latest news and contact information.

331

Available James Acton Thrillers

The Protocol (Book #1)

For two thousand years the Triarii have protected us, influencing history from the crusades to the discovery of America. Descendent from the Roman Empire, they pervade every level of society, and are now in a race with our own government to retrieve an ancient artifact thought to have been lost forever.

Brass Monkey (Book #2)

A nuclear missile, lost during the Cold War, is now in play--the most public spy swap in history, with a gorgeous agent the center of international attention, triggers the end-game of a corrupt Soviet Colonel's twenty five year plan. Pursued across the globe by the Russian authorities, including a brutal Spetsnaz unit, those involved will stop at nothing to deliver their weapon, and ensure their pay day, regardless of the terrifying consequences.

Broken Dove (Book #3)

With the Triarii in control of the Roman Catholic Church, an organization founded by Saint Peter himself takes action, murdering one of the new Pope's operatives. Detective Chaney, called in by the Pope to investigate, disappears, and, to the horror of the Papal staff sent to inform His Holiness, they find him missing too, the only clue a secret chest, presented to each new pope on the eve of their election, since the beginning of the Church.

The Templar's Relic (Book #4)

The Vault must be sealed, but a construction accident leads to a miraculous discovery--an ancient tomb containing four Templar Knights, long forgotten, on the grounds of the Vatican. Not knowing who they can trust, the Vatican requests Professors James Acton and Laura Palmer examine the find, but what they discover, a precious Islamic relic, lost during the Crusades, triggers a set of events that shake the entire world, pitting the two greatest religions against each other. At risk is nothing less than the Vatican itself, and the rock upon which it was built.

Flags of Sin (Book #5)

Archaeology Professor James Acton simply wants to get away from everything, and relax. A trip to China seems just the answer, and he and his fiancée, Professor Laura Palmer, are soon on a flight to Beijing. But while boarding, they bump into an old friend, Delta Force Command Sergeant Major Burt Dawson, who surreptitiously delivers a message that they must meet the next day, for Dawson knows something they don't. China is about to erupt into chaos.

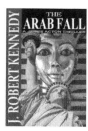

The Arab Fall (Book #6)

An accidental find by a friend of Professor James Acton may lead to the greatest archaeological discovery since the tomb of King Tutankhamen, perhaps even greater. And when news of it spreads, it reaches the ears of a group hell-bent on the destruction of all idols and icons, their mere existence considered blasphemous to Islam.

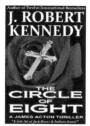

The Circle of Eight (Book #7)

The Bravo Team is targeted by a madman after one of their own intervenes in a rape. Little do they know this internationally well-respected banker is also a senior member of an organization long thought extinct, whose stated goals for a reshaped world are not only terrifying, but with today's globalization, totally achievable.

The Venice Code (Book #8)

A former President's son is kidnapped in a brazen attack on the streets of Potomac by the very ancient organization that murdered his father, convinced he knows the location of an item stolen from them by the late president.

A close friend awakes from a coma with a message for archeology Professor James Acton from the same organization, sending him along with his fiancée Professor Laura Palmer on a quest to find an object only rumored to exist, while trying desperately to keep one step ahead of a foe hell-bent on possessing it.

J. ROBERT KENNEDY

Pompeii's Ghosts (Book #9)

Two thousand years ago Roman Emperor Vespasian tries to preserve an empire by hiding a massive treasure in the quiet town of Pompeii should someone challenge his throne. Unbeknownst to him nature is about to unleash its wrath upon the Empire during which the best and worst of Rome's citizens will be revealed during a time when duty and honor were more than words, they were ideals worth dying for.

Amazon Burning (Book #10)

Days from any form of modern civilization, archeology Professor James Acton awakes to gunshots. Finding his wife missing, taken by a member of one of the uncontacted tribes, he and his friend INTERPOL Special Agent Hugh Reading try desperately to find her in the dark of the jungle, but quickly realize there is no hope without help. And with help three days away, he knows the longer they wait, the farther away she'll be.

The Riddle (Book #11)

Russia accuses the United States of assassinating their Prime Minister in Hanoi, naming Delta Force member Sergeant Carl "Niner" Sung as the assassin. Professors James Acton and Laura Palmer, witnesses to the murder, know the truth, and as the Russians and Vietnamese attempt to use the situation to their advantage on the international stage, the husband and wife duo attempt to find proof that their friend is innocent.

Blood Relics (Book #12)

A DYING MAN. A DESPERATE SON.
ONLY A MIRACLE CAN SAVE THEM BOTH.

Professor Laura Palmer is shot and kidnapped in front of her husband, archeology Professor James Acton, as they try to prevent the theft of the world's Blood Relics, ancient artifacts thought to contain the blood of Christ, a madman determined to possess them all at any cost.

Available Special Agent Dylan Kane Thrillers

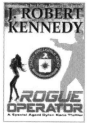

Rogue Operator (Book #1)

Three top secret research scientists are presumed dead in a boating accident, but the kidnapping of their families the same day raises questions the FBI and local police can't answer, leaving them waiting for a ransom demand that will never come. Central Intelligence Agency Analyst Chris Leroux stumbles upon the story, and finds a phone conversation that was never supposed to happen but is told to leave it to the FBI. But he can't let it go. For he knows something the FBI doesn't. One of the scientists is alive.

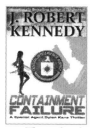

Containment Failure (Book #2)

New Orleans has been quarantined, an unknown virus sweeping the city, killing one hundred percent of those infected. The Centers for Disease Control, desperate to find a cure, is approached by BioDyne Pharma who reveal a former employee has turned a cutting edge medical treatment capable of targeting specific genetic sequences into a weapon, and released it.

The stakes have never been higher as Kane battles to save not only his friends and the country he loves, but all of mankind.

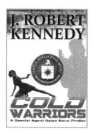

Cold Warriors (Book #3)

While in Chechnya CIA Special Agent Dylan Kane stumbles upon a meeting between a known Chechen drug lord and a retired General once responsible for the entire Soviet nuclear arsenal. Money is exchanged for a data stick and the resulting transmission begins a race across the globe to discover just what was sold, the only clue a reference to a top secret Soviet weapon called Crimson Rush.

Death to America (Book #4)

America is in crisis. Dozens of terrorist attacks have killed or injured thousands, and worse, every single attack appears to have been committed by an American citizen in the name of Islam.

A stolen experimental F-35 Lightning II is discovered by CIA Special Agent Dylan Kane in China, delivered by an American soldier reported dead years ago in exchange for a chilling promise.

And Chris Leroux is forced to watch as his girlfriend, Sherrie White, is tortured on camera, under orders to not interfere, her continued suffering providing intel too valuable to sacrifice.

Available Detective Shakespeare Mysteries

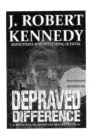

Depraved Difference (Book #1)
SOMETIMES JUST WATCHING IS FATAL

When a young woman is brutally assaulted by two men on the subway, her cries for help fall on the deaf ears of onlookers too terrified to get involved, her misery ended with the crushing stomp of a steel-toed boot. A cellphone video of her vicious murder, callously released on the Internet, its popularity a testament to today's depraved society, serves as a trigger, pulled a year later, for a killer.

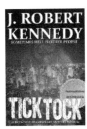

Tick Tock (Book #2)
SOMETIMES HELL IS OTHER PEOPLE

Crime Scene tech Frank Brata digs deep and finds the courage to ask his colleague, Sarah, out for coffee after work. Their good time turns into a nightmare when Frank wakes up the next morning covered in blood, with no recollection of what happened, and Sarah's body floating in the tub.

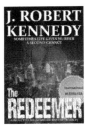

The Redeemer (Book #3)
SOMETIMES LIFE GIVES MURDER A SECOND CHANCE

It was the case that destroyed Detective Justin Shakespeare's career, beginning a downward spiral of self-loathing and self-destruction lasting half a decade. And today things are only going to get worse. The Widow Rapist is free on a technicality, and it is up to Detective Shakespeare and his partner Amber Trace to find the evidence, five years cold, to put him back in prison before he strikes again.

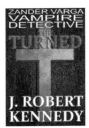

The Turned: Zander Varga, Vampire Detective, Book #1

Zander has relived his wife's death at the hands of vampires every day for almost three hundred years, his perfect memory a curse of becoming one of The Turned—infecting him their final heinous act after her murder.

Nineteen year-old Sydney Winter knows Zander's secret, a secret preserved by the women in her family for four generations. But with her mother in a coma, she's thrust into the front lines, ahead of her time, to fight side-by-side with Zander.

Made in United States
Orlando, FL
31 March 2023

31600886R00209